Fame and Fortune

TINA-MARIE MILLER

Fame and Fortune

www.tinamariemiller.co.uk

Cover Design by

The Book Khaleesi

www.thebookkhaleesi.com

Edited by

Jessica Grace Coleman

www.colemanediting.co.uk

'Emily's Child'

From the Album

'Precious Times'

Included with kind permission from singer/songwriter

Daz Rice

www.dazrice.co.uk

Other books by

Tina-Marie Miller

Millie's Boots

Everything Happens For A Reason

The Curious Miss Fortune

Alexandra Antigone

My love. My life.

xoxox

.

CHAPTER ONE

As Barnaby Rose checked his watch for the umpteenth time, he absentmindedly ran his hand along the length of his tie. He was unusually nervous for two reasons, the first being that he was about to show a potential buyer around the lucrative Swinford St. George Golf & Country Club, and the second being that he was about to come face-to-face with the person behind the voice that had so intrigued him these past few weeks. He was keen to make the most of this fortuitous engagement, given that the commission from the sale would enable him to comfortably invest in a new business venture he wanted to get in on.

Spotting a white car approaching in the distance, Barnaby straightened up and smoothed down his short, brown hair as the vehicle descended down the long driveway, the crunching of the gravel beneath the tyres distracting him momentarily before the car pulled up alongside him.

Smile readied in position, he almost gawped as the driver stepped out of the vehicle.

'You must be Barnaby?' She held out a perfectly manicured hand whilst he soaked up the image of beauty before him – but not inappropriately, of course. Fifteen years' experience of running his own independent estate agency had taught him plenty about how to deal with clients.

They shook hands, her grip firm but not overbearing as she greeted him warmly, 'Delighted to meet you.'

Barnaby nodded in response before asking, 'Did you receive the brochures I sent you? I do hope they were useful, particularly as you mentioned your concern about the land at the back of the property.' He smiled politely. His mild manner always put the most difficult of clients at ease, not that she was one of them.

'Yes I did, and I have to say it's better than I'd anticipated; I'm super keen to have a look around.' In turn, her own returned smile and easy-going manner quickly settled any nerves on his part.

'Let's make a start then, shall we?' he asked, gesturing towards the reception area. 'I arrived a little earlier and have already unlocked most of the areas to enable a smooth tour.'

She smiled again, clearly impressed. 'That's brilliant, thank you,' she beamed as she followed him towards the main reception doors, being sure to scrutinise every inch of the magnificent building along the way.

'Considering it's been empty for the past year I'm sure you'll agree it's in great condition,' Barnaby said as they walked, 'although – as you know – there's still much room for improvement.' He raised his eyebrows knowingly.

She nodded in agreement; after her extensive and thorough research, she was well aware of the commitment that lay before her. This was a major investment, after all. Finally – after many years of hard work – it was now beginning to pay off and, if all went to plan, this would be the icing on top of a *very* large cake.

She continued allowing Barnaby to lead the tour, enjoying the sound of his soft, well-spoken voice as he guided her from room to room in the vast 102-bedroomed property. Along the way her mind quickly filled with ideas and potential building alterations, and every now and then she would pause to jot down a few notes in a blue leather-bound A4 notebook she was carrying.

As they approached a set of huge oak doors Barnaby paused, turning to face her. 'Ready?' he asked, his eyes twinkling in anticipation of her reaction.

He wasn't disappointed; when he carefully eased the doors apart, she gasped in awe. 'Goodness me!'

They had entered the Lady Blythe ballroom. It was named after the wife of the original owner, Lord Edgar Westbrooke, and was one of the few remaining functioning ballrooms in the local area.

Gazing at the twelve-foot high ceilings and four impressive handcrafted chandeliers, her mind went into overdrive. 'I seemed to have overlooked this in my research!' she exclaimed.

Barnaby smiled. 'Rumour has it that when Lord Westbrooke's son, Lyndon, took over the reins in 1976 he wanted to preserve it as much as possible –

given its history – and therefore refused to hire it out. I believe it was occasionally used for private parties, though, and it has been very well maintained, as you can see.'

She nodded absentmindedly as she drank in the magnificent setting. 'Do you know how many people this can cater for?'

'About four hundred comfortably,' Barnaby replied instantly, 'and the private bar and reception area makes it ideal for a whole range of functions in addition to the main hotel.'

'Yes, I get that,' she whispered, almost to herself.

He could see that she was impressed, and whilst he couldn't quite read her expression due to the sunglasses she'd yet to remove, he revelled as he watched her slowly make her way around the ballroom and adjourning areas. She was certainly more than easy on the eye, radiating an elegance he hadn't come across for a long time. Well, perhaps not since Tiggy Lawrence's return to the Hamptons, anyhow.

Thinking of Tiggy reminded Barnaby that he was supposed to be meeting up with her, Harry, and his parents later that day, and he checked his watch discreetly; he didn't want his client to think he was trying to rush the viewing – far from it. *But if this goes well, then...*

'Shall we move on?' he asked politely.

They continued the rest of the tour at an easy pace, and from the many different questions she asked, it was quite clear that she'd done her homework – and that she was serious. Barnaby couldn't think of anything more irritating than a client whose only intentions were to have a good old nose around somewhere, just to satisfy their own curiosity.

They now had just two areas to view – the spa and the golf course – the spa being in dire need of attention. It was nothing more than a kidney-shaped swimming pool, and in the far corner there was situated a wooden shed, which apparently served as a sauna.

This was the part of the tour that Barnaby had been most concerned with, given that it required a lot of investment. However, she took it all in her stride as she slowly yet confidently examined each area, continuing to make notes as they went along.

When they were done, Barnaby led the way out of the spa and through the back patio doors, which led onto the 18-hole golf course.

'In its day,' he explained, 'this was a popular course with an undulating 6,000 yards. The present owner has kept on a skeleton staff to ensure it's kept well maintained but it's not been open to the public for some time. With a bit more TLC it could certainly regain its popularity again.'

'Absolutely,' she nodded, 'that's why I questioned the land further along. I've actually come up with some great ideas for this area.'

Her words took him by surprise. 'Oh? So you're definitely interested, then?'

She looked up from her notebook and smiled broadly. 'I've had my eye on this place for quite some time, and today's visit has just confirmed my desire to buy it.'

Given that most of his clients preferred to play the long game, Barnaby could barely contain his pleasure at her forthrightness.

'I'm super keen to get moving on this as quickly as possible too,' she enthused, while still maintaining her professional eloquence, 'therefore it's safe to say you have yourself a deal, Mr. Rose, and barring the paperwork, you could say you're now looking at the new owner of the Swinford St. George Golf and Country Club.'

Beaming, he went over to shake her hand and *seal the deal*, so to speak. 'Congratulations,' he said happily, 'you've certainly landed yourself a fantastic property with a wealth of opportunity. I wish you much success!'

'Thank you,' she replied, returning his fervour, 'and I fully intend to make the most of it too. It's time to breathe some new life into this place!' She removed her glasses as she spoke and for the first time he recognised who she was.

'You're...' he gasped.

'Yes I am, and you've just gained!' she quipped.

Barnaby laughed out loud, shaking his head at her pun. After all, she was renowned throughout the health and fitness industry. *Who'd have thought it?*

And, if things went as intended at his meeting later, they would both have gained that day – in more ways than one.

CHAPTER TWO

H olding a tray full of delicious breakfast foods, Anthony Sullivan scooped up the morning post from the front doormat before carefully making his way upstairs. He loved spoiling his wife Ianthe as much as possible, and now that they were both retired, the opportunity presented itself more often than not – and their love life was certainly benefitting too!

'Oooh coffee,' Ianthe cooed as she sat upright, feasting her eyes on the heavily laden tray that Anthony set before her. 'Anything of interest?' she mused, referring to the post in his hand as she poured them both a cup of the welcomed beverage.

'Just the usual drivel, no doubt,' he joked, raising his eyebrows, which made Ianthe chuckle.

When he'd taken over as Chair of the Hamptons Parish Council, Anthony hadn't bargained for the inordinate amount of mail that would arrive on a daily basis, most of which was completely pointless and a waste of taxpayer's money. However, this morning's offering appeared more fruitful.

'We have an invitation, my darling,' he said, pausing to accept a piece of toast that Ianthe had spread generously with his favourite lime marmalade.

'Oh yes?' she replied, in between mouthfuls of the succulent melon Anthony had sliced for her earlier.

'To participate in the annual Cotswolds County Majorette of the Year competition.'

Ianthe paused, dabbing at the corners of her mouth with a pristine white linen napkin before replying, 'But we don't have a Majorette team, Anthony.'

'Not *yet* we don't, my darling – but wouldn't it be an amazing event for the Hamptons to get involved in, especially if we win?' he answered, grinning. 'It could secure the parish council more funding for next year, which would enable us to finally refurbish the cricket pavilion and children's play area at Hampton Ash – and much sooner than planned. And that means, of course, that we'd then be able to participate in the County fixtures too.'

Ianthe nodded enthusiastically; cricket was a love they both shared. 'But how do we go about forming a team of Majorettes?' she asked after a moment of thought.

'Ah!' Anthony exclaimed. 'I've just had an idea for that. Now that we've got Diana Fortune's drama club up and running, why don't we ask her to gather a team together? As I understand it, most of the children from the Hamptons have enrolled there anyway and I'm sure they'd be delighted to get involved.' He paused, staring into the distance as he had another thought. 'Remember, too, that Lily took part in the school's talent contest last year and she learnt baton twirling all by herself!'

Ianthe smiled knowingly. She loved how Anthony took every chance he could to involve their grandchildren in village life.

'Yes, well that hardly makes for Majorette of the Year,' Ianthe pointed out, 'and whilst Lily can twirl a baton – quite expertly too, I have to say – you can't expect the others to pick it up so quickly.' She smiled. 'Perhaps you should discuss it with Diana? Test the waters? It can certainly do no harm, after all.'

'Good idea. I'll swing by The Orchard once I'm dressed and run it by Alexander first – then he and I can go and approach Diana together.'

Filled with renewed enthusiasm, Anthony finished his toast and kissed Ianthe before jumping into the shower, eager to get going for the day so he could put the ideas into place that were now whirling through his mind.

Although he was concerned not to overload Diana, he felt sure she'd welcome a further distraction following the disastrous events of last year. The whole village were still gossiping about her son, Aster Maxwell, and his attempt to murder his ex-lover, Tiggy Lawrence. It was all becoming quite tiresome now and it was definitely a constant reminder that both Diana and Tiggy could well do without. Thankfully, Aster was currently incarcerated far away in a high security psychiatric unit.

Anthony shuddered at the thought of what might have been if it weren't for Harry and Patrick's unexpected intervention that day.

Whilst it made a grisly tale fit for a romantic tragedy, there *was* an upside – if you could see past the abhorrence of it all – in so much as Diana's true identity finally being revealed. Whilst Aster's victim, Tiggy, was still to overcome the horrific ordeal she'd endured that day, Diana being ousted as *the* Diana Fortune – a former Hollywood icon known for her role in the ultra successful hit US drama *Out of Control* – had thankfully presented a welcome diversion.

The papers had had a field day at the time, of course, so much so that re-runs were still being shown on both UK and US screens, and even the music of Diana's late mother – the popular US jazz singer Deanna Beaumont – had been resurrected too.

This had led Anthony, along with Alexander Harvey and Charlotte Palmer-Reid, to come up with the idea of opening a drama club, something Diana had jumped at. Ever since, the former star had been thoroughly enjoying herself.

Recalling her enthusiasm fuelled Anthony's determination further. One way or another he'd get the Hamptons Cricket Club into the County fixtures – he just hoped Diana's cooperation would be forthcoming, enabling that to happen sooner rather than later.

CHAPTER THREE

'Richard – stop it, *stop!*' Poppy giggled. She'd been trying to finish scrambling the eggs for breakfast when he'd sneaked up behind her, slipped his arms around her waist, and started nuzzling her neck.

He continued unperturbed whilst she wriggled beneath his grasp, squealing, until she pulled away and began waving the wooden spatula at him, still laughing. 'You'll get egg on your face if you don't stop!' she teased as he began trying to wrestle it from her, causing them to laugh even more. Monty, their young chocolate brown Labrador, bounced around them as he barked excitedly, desperate to join in with the fun.

'Oh, for goodness' sake,' Lily mock chided as she entered the kitchen, 'you two are worse than a couple of kids.'

Richard turned his attention to his daughter, giving Lily a morning hug whilst Poppy opened the back door, allowing Monty to race off into the garden to work off some of his energy.

'Oh, you love us really,' he teased Lily, and soon he had her giggling along with the both of them.

Poppy served her family plates of scrambled egg with hot buttered toast, calling out to their son Roderick as she did so.

When he came rushing in he was grasping a replica toy Puma helicopter, which he was swishing this way and that. Ever since Poppy and Richard had taken him to visit the RAF base at Chipping Melbury he'd been obsessed with being a helicopter pilot, and the toy had become a regular fixation.

'Prepare to land, Lieutenant!' Poppy exclaimed, playing along whilst Roderick placed the Puma safely next to his morning glass of milk, much to the amusement of them all.

'Are you going to drama club after school, Lily?' Poppy asked, surprised when the girl screwed up her face in response.

'Nah, I don't think so.'

Poppy frowned. 'It's no, and why not?'

'I thought you loved the drama club, Lily,' Richard intercepted. 'Miss Fortune's had nothing but praise for you; she says you have a real flair for acting.'

Richard and Poppy exchanged concerned looks before glancing back at their downcast daughter.

'It's not much fun now there are so many other children there,' Lily said quietly.

This time they exchanged knowing looks.

'Ooh, a bit of competition, eh?' Richard teased. 'Well, that's not necessarily a bad thing. Come on, eat up – I'm doing the school run today.'

'Oh yes,' Poppy replied, smiling eagerly, 'doesn't your new buyer start today?'

'That's right! Which reminds me, actually, are you still okay with us renting out our cottage to her until she gets settled?'

Poppy nodded. 'Of course, I'll just fetch the keys. I had Billy go over there yesterday to tidy the garden and fix the fence panel that had blown down in the bad weather last week. Just hang on a sec.'

'Right, you two,' Richard addressed Lily and Roderick, 'go and clean your teeth and get your bags ready – we'll be leaving in five minutes.'

The children rushed out just as Poppy returned with the keys.

'There you are, darling,' she said, handing them over. 'It's a good thing we held onto your old home after getting married; it's certainly come in useful on more than one occasion. I hope she finds it comfortable.'

'Oh, I'm certain she will,' Richard replied. 'I've arranged to meet her there actually as I thought she could offload her luggage before joining me at the office later on.'

'Will you be home on time tonight then?' Poppy asked as Richard sidled up for a goodbye kiss.

'I will indeed, my darling, and if this new buyer is every bit as good as I've been led to believe, I'll soon be spending a lot more time here too.' With that he swooped Poppy up into his arms for a long, lingering kiss, much to her delight.

As she waved them off, Poppy thought over Richard's words again, smiling. She liked the idea of them spending more time together. *And who knows what else we might find time for?* she thought, affording herself a cheeky wink.

* * *

Francine Dubois checked her appearance one last time before departing her hotel room and heading down to reception; she wanted everything to be perfect today, including herself.

As she proudly handed over her Hambly-Jones department store credit card to settle her account, she enjoyed the feeling of satisfaction it gave her. As of today, she was officially the Senior Buyer for the exclusive *Magnifique Madame* range of opulent lingerie, as well as the right-hand woman to Richard Hambly-Jones – or so she believed.

Richard. The mere thought of him sent shivers down her spine and released a flutter of lustful butterflies that immediately began twirling around in her stomach.

Giving thanks to the receptionist, she held her head high as she walked elegantly and confidently out of the hotel and towards the brand new Audi A5 Richard had organised for her.

She stopped for a moment to appreciate its beauty, running her hand along the sleek silver bodywork and allowing herself another satisfied smile. *If I play my cards right I'll be enjoying much more than this beauty.*

After packing her belongings into the back and settling herself in the driving seat, Francine set off towards Orchard Cottage, smiling as she went.

A new job, a new home, and hopefully a new life!

CHAPTER FOUR

Lucy Whittaker brushed a weary arm across her brow before sinking down onto the steps of 34 King's Oak Road, her new home.

Our new home!

She was so thankful that she'd decided to arrange for the removal company to deliver her belongings a day earlier – *I'd never have managed to get it all done in one day.*

Having just taken in the last of the personal belongings she hadn't wanted the removal company to transport, she was now taking a bit of a breather and using the time to survey her new and exciting surroundings.

Lucy had heard great things about the Hamptons, and from what she'd experienced so far it seemed to support such claims. It was beautiful, and clean, and immaculately well kept. To top it off, everyone she'd met so far had been really friendly and welcoming.

Earlier, she'd stopped by the Hampton Stores to buy some milk and had soon got into quite a conversation with James Turvey, who'd told her he was the shop owner. *Not bad looking, either.* She smiled to herself and then rolled her eyes. *Though I'm not sure I want to go there again!*

As she sat on her new steps Lucy's thoughts drifted back over the past twenty-one years, making her shake her head; she'd certainly come a long way since then.

Twenty-one years ago, Lucy had been working for a leading publisher right in the heart of the City of London. It had been fascinating, fast-paced, and more than a little stressful. As a senior literary agent, Lucy had the opportunity to meet a number of well-known celebrities, which was how she'd first met the leading celebrity hypnotist and motivational speaker, Raoul De'ath. He was every bit as intriguing as his name – and he was her client! Lucy had been delighted. Raoul had written a series of non-fiction self-help books that he wanted to publish and he couldn't have picked a better time for it.

Following the success of his recently launched TV show, his office had been inundated with calls, emails, and letters from a wealth of people all desperate to seek his help. From addictions to depression, fears to phobias… you name it; there were plenty of people who wanted help with it all. Almost overnight his website had gone into overdrive, so much so that his team were struggling to keep up. Of course, this was a lucrative account for Lucy, and when his books hit the top spot, selling over six million copies, they'd celebrated in style – in more ways than one. As Raoul's career skyrocketed, the US was soon calling and he was long gone before Lucy realised their one-night stand had ended with a pregnancy.

After she'd welcomed their beautiful son Ian into the world, Lucy was able to continue working from home, offering professional proofreading and editing services alongside being a full-time mother. Then, when Ian had started nursery, Lucy employed the services of an au pair – who was additionally able to help out around the house – leaving her free to take on even more work.

She'd made a lovely family home for them in Holland Park, just off Kensington High Street, which afforded her the opportunity to travel in and out of the city as required. She worked hard, toiling for long hours and often working late into the night but relishing every moment – given that at one point she never imagined she'd ever get to experience the joys of motherhood.

Her son Ian had developed into a polite and well-spoken young man, and while he could be a bit of a handful at times, on the whole they enjoyed a good relationship, sharing many similar interests.

Lucy had often thought of Raoul over the years as she'd witnessed his career soar to greater and greater heights, especially across the pond. Having written to him with details and photographs about Ian shortly after his birth, however, she'd made it clear that she expected no more from Raoul than he was prepared to give – if anything. She was more than secure and could easily afford to give Ian the good life he deserved. She'd left the door open for Raoul but she'd never heard from him again. She was fine with the way things had worked out, though, and she certainly had no regrets in that respect.

Sometimes, when she got frustrated with Ian, she would have welcomed the opportunity to have found out a bit more about Raoul and his own background, but given that he was such an eccentric who was well known for his demanding behaviour, she felt sure that Ian was merely mirroring his father's personality traits.

And here we are.

After Ian had secured a place at University last year, Lucy had decided to move too; she'd long harboured a yearning to move back to the country – having been born and bred there – and this was the perfect opportunity to do so. The city life had served its purpose, but now she wanted to take things a bit easier. *And, if James Turvey is anything to go by, I can't wait to meet the rest of my neighbours.*

Smiling, Lucy stood up, suddenly reinvigorated; she was ready to complete the unpacking and was starting to feel right at home in the Hamptons.

* * *

Evie Coombes threw back her head, laughing hysterically as she allowed her husband Rupert to carry her over the threshold. It wasn't that they'd just got married – far from it; they'd tied the knot a little over eight years ago – it was that today they were celebrating moving into their new home in the Hamptons, and Evie was incredibly excited.

Rupert's' company – Coombes Analytics, a pharmaceutical company based in Chipping Melbury – had enjoyed great success in recent years, affording them a lifestyle envied by many and also giving them the ability to purchase their dream home. This also presented Evie with the ideal opportunity to indulge her artistic talents.

She'd fallen in love with Hazel Lodge at first sight; when they'd met up with local estate agent Barnaby Rose for their first viewing, the building's whitewashed Georgian facade and generous-sized windows had beckoned them inside immediately. Then, as they'd stepped through the entrance and onto the parquet flooring they'd been greeted by a magnificent central staircase leading to a large gallery of bedrooms and bathrooms. Although in need of a complete revamp – given that the decor hadn't changed since it had been built in the 1970s – they'd both seen the vast potential in the building, and when Evie had discovered the spacious outbuilding at the back and realised it would make the perfect studio, her mind had been made up. Having spent the last ten months project managing the refurbishment, it was now a real delight for them to finally move in.

'To us!' Rupert toasted as they clinked glasses, grateful for the bottle of *Veuve Clicquot* Barnaby had thoughtfully laid on, together with a basket of fresh strawberries and a huge bouquet of white lilies – the delicious fragrance from the flowers was already permeating through the downstairs hallway.

'You've done a sterling job with the renovations, darling,' Rupert complimented as they made their way up the staircase to the first floor, the smell of fresh paint and newly papered walls pleasantly filtering into their nostrils as they walked. 'I love what you've done with the master bedroom – very *objet d'art.*' He turned and winked at her, making her laugh.

'I wish I could take all the credit given that I'm an artist,' Evie replied, smiling, 'but the renovations are really down to Will and Able Cohen – and, of course, we have Tawfique to thank for the interior design.'

Rupert returned her smile as he took another swig of champagne from his glass. He *loved* it whenever Evie name-dropped. 'Isn't that the chap our solicitor told you about?'

'Yes, that's right; Tawfique Fortnum-Phipps is the same guy who did the renovations for Riverside Hall,' she replied. 'In fact, I was considering organising a little soiree to get to know some of our neighbours and thought of inviting Tawfique along too. What do you think?'

'A most excellent idea, darling,' Rupert enthused before taking another drink. 'We should invite as many people as possible. I believe there's quite a few influential individuals around here; it would be good to get to know them.'

'Of course.' She weaved past her husband then, eager to show him the guest suite adjacent to their room. 'Tell me, what do you think of this?' She eyed him carefully as she swept the door open, keen for him to share in her enthusiasm.

He arched an inquisitive eyebrow. 'Bit small for a guest room, isn't it?' he said eventually.

'But that's the point, silly,' she giggled. 'It would make the perfect nursery, don't you think?'

'I think,' Rupert began, taking the glass from her hand and placing it alongside his on a nearby dresser, 'that we'd better get in a bit of practice before we make any plans in that area, Mrs Coombes.'

Evie shrieked with laughter again as he scooped her up into his arms and carried her, laughing, into the master bedroom. With a swift movement, he kicked the door shut behind them.

Sometime later when Evie woke up, she took a brief moment to remember where she was – such were the unfamiliar surroundings of their new home. Slowly, she reached out and stroked the side of the tall headboard – which was covered in a deep, rich, grey-coloured velvet – that formed part of the queen-sized bed Tawfique had commissioned on their behalf.

Rupert snored gently beside her, a combination of their love-making and several glasses of champagne clearly having taken their toll.

She smiled to herself, admiring Tawfique's handiwork as she glanced around their wonderful, sophisticated bedroom. The burnt orange flock wallpaper he'd designed perfectly complemented their bed, which was adorned by two bevelled mirror chests, both of them supporting impressive black marble table lamps. A *Palazzo* mirror had been placed above each chest and a cream deep pile carpet covered the floor from wall to wall.

Smiling even more, Evie looked over to the far right, where the door leading to the nursery was situated. Suddenly, it seemed to become the main focal point of the house as she was reminded of their previous conversation. *If earlier events are anything to go by, practice does indeed make perfect!*

She snuggled back up to her husband, eager to make more progress once he woke up.

* * *

'It looks like we're not the only ones moving in today,' Pradeep said, nodding across the Church

Green as a removal truck pulled up onto the drive of Hazel Lodge. He helped his wife Esha out of the car before retrieving their daughter, Salena, from the back. At just two months old she was sleeping soundly, completely unaware of the chaos that was about to unfold as their own removal vehicle began to arrive.

Pradeep ushered Esha inside with Salena and left the removal guys to it. 'Take Salena through to the playroom and I'll make us all a cup of tea,' he told her kindly.

Esha smiled with relief as she left him to it; she was tired and she wanted to keep her focus on their new daughter.

Pradeep busied himself unpacking cups and saucers whilst he waited for the kettle to boil, thankful that they'd listened to his mother's advice and had packed a few essentials themselves instead of leaving it all to the removal guys.

He leaned against the kitchen worktop and took a deep breath, relishing the fact that they were in their own surroundings at long last. It had been six years since Esha had agreed to be his bride, and recalling how beautiful she looked on their wedding day brought a smile to his face – as she did every day.

Directly after their marriage they had moved in with his parents, who were delighted to be sharing their three-bedroomed terraced house, along with Pradeep's two younger brothers and their dog, Mitzi. Although it was a bit of a squeeze and a bit chaotic at times, Pradeep and Esha were most grateful to have a place to stay whilst enabling them to save for their own home.

Despite both of them having good jobs – Pradeep was a qualified General Practitioner specialising in Psychotherapy while Esha worked as a clinical research assistant for a local hospital – house prices were escalating fast and they were beginning to think they'd never get on the property ladder. Then, when Esha had discovered she was pregnant, their goal of buying their own home seemed even further away. Impossible, even.

It wasn't long, however, before – much to their delight – things unexpectedly took a turn for the better.

A few months before Salena was born, Pradeep attended a conference held by the Royal College of Practitioners where he was introduced to Dr Jon Anderson by a mutual friend, who was aware that Pradeep wanted to further his interest in Psychotherapy whilst still working as a GP – something his current practice wasn't at all interested in. He and Jon hit if off immediately and were soon chatting away like old friends. When Jon divulged that his practice was actively seeking a partner with this very specialisation, Pradeep couldn't believe his luck. A formal interview was arranged and Pradeep was invited to spend time at the Hamptons Medical Practice before being offered the position. This partnership afforded him a higher salary, enabling the two of them to finally secure their dream home – with the added bonus of being right in the heart of the countryside.

They had deliberately delayed their move-in date, believing that by planning ahead it would allow for Esha to deliver their baby safely and also afford them time to settle as a family unit. However, when Esha went into labour they hadn't anticipated that she'd have to endure such a prolonged and difficult birth.

And that was just the start of it. For the first few weeks afterwards, Esha had found it difficult to bond with her new daughter and Pradeep had been absolutely beside himself with worry. His parents had been an enormous support, though; when they'd welcomed Esha into their family they'd welcomed her into their hearts too, and they were anxious to help in any way possible. Even his younger brothers were keen to show their support – always fetching Esha little treats they thought she'd like or fussing over the new baby.

As the time drew nearer for Pradeep to take up his new position, regret began to sink in, and although he considered leaving Esha and Salena in the safe haven his family had created for them while he went ahead with the move alone, Esha wouldn't hear of it.

Now, Pradeep was pleased he'd listened to her. Over the past few weeks – since they'd decided to move – Pradeep had seen a significant improvement in his wife's wellbeing, and her recent interactions with Salena were as you would expect from any new mother. However, it was still early days and Pradeep knew there was a long way to go yet.

The most important thing was that he was determined to do everything in his power to help nurse his wife back to full health, and he truly believed that beginning a new life in the Hamptons was going to be for the great benefit of them all.

He only hoped he was right.

CHAPTER FIVE

'Sara? *Sara!*' Charlotte Palmer-Reid raced down the staircase and immediately began weaving in and out of the downstairs rooms, searching for her errant daughter. 'Sara!' she called out again as she went, her cheeks flushed and her heart beating overtime.

'Where's the fire?' complained her son, Sebastian, as she frantically pushed past him and out of the front door.

'I'm looking for Sara; where *is* she?' Charlotte exclaimed.

Sebastian just shrugged his shoulders and went off in search of breakfast. He'd only got up early because he had to attend a revision session first thing; being in the final year of Sixth form, he wanted to ensure that he got the best grades possible, enabling him to secure a good place at University. *Anything to get away from this mad house.*

'Jonathan!' Charlotte snapped as she approached her husband, who was dithering in and out of the back of his car doing who knows what, 'I can't find Sara; can't find her anywhere!' She was beginning to panic now.

Jonathan immediately stopped what he was doing and rushed over to her, placing his hands gently on her shoulders and trying to hide his frown. *This was becoming a bit too regular.*

'It's okay, Charlotte,' he reassured her, 'Sara's just popped across to Meadow View. I sorted out the pantry today and found a bag of carrots that were on the turn. She's taken them for Louisa's pony – she'll be back in a minute.' He waited for the now familiar relief to sweep through Charlotte's body as she absorbed his words and started calming down. A second later, it happened.

'Oh... I, I was just worried... you know,' she stammered, shrugging helplessly.

Jonathan sighed. Seeing her so forlorn like this made his heart ache. Ever since the dreadful incident with Aster Maxwell and Tiggy Lawrence last year, Charlotte had become obsessed with their daughter's wellbeing; if she so much as sneezed the wrong way Charlotte was on hand with tissues, paracetamol, and all manner of lotions and potions. And, if Sara was so much as a minute later than she should be, Charlotte would be on tenterhooks, imagining all sorts of horrific things.

At 14, Sara was understandably less than impressed by this sudden change in her mother's behaviour. Just when she should be starting to go out more and hang out with her friends, Charlotte had become overly possessive, wanting to know Sara's every move ahead of time – which was beginning to have an effect not just on Sara, but on the whole family.

Jonathan opened his mouth, desperate to release the words that had been sitting on his tongue for several months now, but after seeing Charlotte brush a stray tear away from her eye his words remained unspoken, yet again creating another barrier between them. *We'll soon have built a dam at this rate.*

Slowly, he guided her back inside and into the kitchen, where he set about making a fresh pot of coffee, trying to keep her – and himself – calm.

It wasn't long before Sara returned, the scenario before her immediately speaking a thousand words. Before Charlotte could get a word out, Sara rolled her eyes and went to get ready for school.

Jonathan sighed. *This was all becoming a bit too much for everyone.*

* * *

'Hello Ian, how are you?'

'Morning,' came the reply.

Lucy Whittaker smiled, delighted to hear the sound of her son's voice on the telephone. It had been well over a week since they'd last spoken and, although at 20 he was more than capable of looking after himself, he was still at University and she liked to keep an eye on him.

'Mother,' he continued, 'I've got some exciting news.'

'Oh yes?' Lucy asked, still smiling. 'What's all that about then?'

'Well, I went to a career convention yesterday and there was a group of guys from France who gave us a lecture on internship opportunities, and...'

Lucy frowned, the smile dropping off her face instantly. 'What? What guys, Ian? What are you talking about?' She wasn't sure she liked the sound of this.

'If you'd let me finish, Mother,' Ian responded tartly, 'I'll tell you.' There was a pause, and Lucy could imagine him rolling his eyes. 'As I was saying,' he carried on, 'these guys are from one of the top technology corporations who have offices all throughout Europe and the US, and they're looking to offer summer internship programmes to people on my course! It will help boost our overall grades at the end.'

'Boost your grades?' Lucy repeated. 'But that's ridiculous, Ian; you're on schedule for a First, why do you need to boost your grades any further?'

Ian sighed heavily. *Here we go.*

'You're not listening to me, are you, Mother?' he asked, his voice full of frustration. 'It's not just that; it's an opportunity to gain real experience in the workplace, which will not only bolster my chances of gaining employment once I graduate, but will also mean there's every chance I'll be offered a permanent position after that too. Between you and me,' he added, lowering his voice to avoid being overheard, 'I had a chat with their IT Director afterwards and he said they'd be chomping at the bit to have someone with my skills and qualifications on board right now.'

'Oh seriously, Ian, that's ridiculous,' Lucy sighed. 'What skills? You haven't even ventured out into the workplace yet.'

'Excuse me?' he shot back. 'What do *you* know? It's all you can do to switch a computer on, Mother. I'm programming in at least three languages right now and my personal tutor said my database development skills are the best she's seen in a long time.'

Lucy paused for a moment, trying to decide how to word her reply without annoying her son any further. 'I've no doubt about that, Ian, therefore surely it's better to finish your degree before heading off on an internship? You could always do that afterwards. After all, it seems from what you're saying that your skills are well sought after anyway.'

'You're not listening, are you?' Ian replied, his voice getting louder now. 'Honestly, I don't know why I bother. Anyway, I've already signed up for it so I'll be off at the end of May.'

'You've done what?' Lucy asked, her voice coming out far shriller than she'd intended. Slowly, she dragged a chair from the kitchen table and sat down. She was shaking, her mind whirring with Ian's latest fad.

'I'm off to the south of France,' Ian explained. 'I've got approval from the University so it's all go. I can't wait!'

Lucy's throat went dry. She knew better than to challenge the situation further but she just couldn't stop herself. 'I can't believe you've gone ahead with this, Ian!' she exclaimed. 'Without speaking to me first! And as for receiving approval from the University – don't parents have a say in these matters anymore?' She was getting frustrated now, and she didn't care if Ian knew it.

'I'm 20, not 13,' he mocked, laughingly. 'Anyway, it's all in place now so there's nothing more to be said.'

Lucy's bottom lip trembled as a wave of fear washed through her; something didn't feel right but she couldn't quite put a finger on why. She took a deep breath. 'Well, if that's what you want, Ian, then I really hope it all works out for you.' She just about managed to keep the tremble from her voice – not that Ian would have noticed at that point as he continued to rave on excitedly about his trip.

After they'd said their goodbyes Lucy put the phone down pensively. Although it was a few months off yet, she'd been looking forward to spending the summer with him, knowing it would be his last before finishing his final year. It wasn't that she minded him going away – far from it. If this was as good as he professed it to be then it was an excellent opportunity not to be missed. However, previous experience had taught her than Ian was always going off on one whim or another, and it usually didn't end well.

She just hoped that this time, his actions would prove her wrong.

* * *

CRASH!

Tiggy Lawrence froze on the spot as a loud smashing sound resounded throughout the whole of the downstairs.

She had just begun building a fire in the drawing room for later that evening, and her hands shook as she dropped the kindling into the fireplace before running her hands nervously down the front of her jeans. Her right hand instinctively went to her throat, the vivid memories of the last time she'd been in this very scenario coming back to haunt her. Whilst the physical scars may have healed, her mental and emotional wellbeing were still very much a work in progress.

BANG!

She jumped as yet another crash rang out. Then, standing up, she swallowed hard, telling herself there was bound to be a perfectly reasonable explanation for all the noise. After all, Harry had arranged for locks to be fitted on all the windows and for extra security for the front and back entrances, including a state-of-the-art video door entry system. *Everything's secure – I'm perfectly safe.* Or was she?

Taking a deep breath she slowly ventured towards the source of the disturbance, which appeared to be coming from the kitchen. As she approached the door she tentatively pushed it gently open, fearful of what she might have to confront on the other side but determined to face it nevertheless.

At first she couldn't see anything obviously out of place, but as she pushed the door open just a bit further, there it was.

'Mulbers!' She laughed, a huge surge of relief sweeping through her as she went over to scoop up the bewildered ball of ginger fluff that was surveying the mess scattered all around the sink. 'How did you get there, mister?' She hugged him close to her and rubbed her face into his soft, silky fur, relieved it had been nothing more sinister.

Taking a look around Tiggy realised that she'd left the window open after cooking breakfast earlier. The cat must have jumped through it, knocking off a few pot plants along the way.

'I bet you're hungry,' she chatted lovingly as she carried him over towards the cupboard where his food was kept. Knowing what was to come, he wriggled himself free, desperate to perform his usual dance routine for her. As Tiggy ripped open the foil packet and mixed the chicken and gravy contents up with the biscuits she'd prepared earlier, Mulbers didn't know how to contain himself. The aroma soon filtered through the room and by the time she placed the bowl of food before him, the cat was beside himself. She sat down at the table and watched him carefully take each mouthful, his eyes closed tight as he munched his way through the feast, clearly enjoying every morsel.

To say that the past year had been traumatic was an understatement. Tiggy was still to come to terms with her father's death, no matter that it had been expected; after returning to the family home following a nine year absence, Tiggy's time with her father was to be sadly short-lived. She still held deep regrets that on the night her father passed away, she was deep in the throes of passion with Aster Maxwell. Of course, little did she know then that he'd go on to make an attempt on her life.

She shuddered, rubbing her arms as a distraction – something she found herself doing often these days, at least when the most distressing of thoughts entered her mind. *If it weren't for Harry and Patrick...* She closed her eyes for a brief moment as the recollection of that fateful day set in.

She'd had a lot to face up to after such a long time away: her father Charles' terminal illness, her stepmonster Bobbie and her ex-fiancé Patrick Montague... not to mention the dismay she'd felt at discovering her beloved family home had practically descended into rack and ruin.

The idea of refurbishing Riverside Hall had breathed new life into her desperately ill father, and had also given them a basis on which to rebuild their fragile relationship. Resolving the past with Patrick had not been so easy, at least not at first; Tiggy was still reeling from discovering him in a compromising position with her stepmother years before – something she later realised was far from what it had seemed at the time.

Therefore, when Aster Maxwell had set his sights on her, she could have been easily forgiven for falling for his infallible charm. This tall, dark, handsome stranger with impeccable style and exquisite good looks became irresistible to her... until that night; that one night. The one time when she should have been with her father, she wasn't –instead she was coveting just metres away next door.

Tiggy shuddered again, shaking her head. She'd had no idea that this had all just been part of Aster's plan. As a highly skilled surgeon and medical professional, he'd been well aware of Charles' impending fate before they ventured out that night, but he'd had more on the menu than lust – he'd wanted to get his hands on Tiggy's inheritance. Fortunately, it had all backfired on him, with dire consequences.

Thankfully, by this time, not only had Tiggy rekindled her childhood friendship with Harry Martin – the family solicitor – but also with Patrick, who owned and managed the Home Counties Equestrian

Centre. Knowing that Tiggy wanted to start a riding school of her own, following the refurbishment of Riverside Hall and the adjourning stables, it was pure luck that he'd decided to visit Tiggy that fateful day with the latest equestrian brochure that he'd thought she'd be interested to see. Then there was Harry, who had unexpectedly cut short his conference, desperate to spend time with Tiggy since their relationship had moved on to another level.

Thanks to their quick thinking, Tiggy was still here today to relive the harrowing events of the past.

Having finished his meal, Mulbers was now giving himself a good wash, and Tiggy reached down and scooped him up, desperate for some comfort. Harry had wanted to get them a couple of guard dogs – his work meant that he wasn't able to be with Tiggy as much as he liked – but she hadn't been keen on the idea, so they'd settled for a cat. Harry had agreed and had driven them over to Midford County Cattery, which was like showing Tiggy a box of chocolates and telling her she could only take one; she wanted all of them!

Mulbers – or Mulberry, his official name – had taken it upon himself to wander over to her straight away and weave his huge, furry body in, out, and around Tiggy's legs. She'd gathered him up and was taken in instantly by his huge, amber-coloured eyes. She held tightly onto him as they were shown around the various little wooden huts housing what seemed to be an inordinate and diverse amount of felines – and there was plenty of choice – but it was clear that Mulbers was the one. He had been a welcome and loving addition to the family ever since.

Tiggy brushed away a few tears that had fallen silently down her cheek; she wasn't one to cry, but then, she hadn't expected to have ever found herself in such a macabre scenario as she had that night.

Desperate to shake off her gloomy thoughts, she carefully placed Mulbers onto his favourite chair and started cleaning up the broken plant pots from his earlier adventure, ensuring to secure the window she'd forgotten about leaving open earlier.

As she worked she remembered that they were expecting guests that evening, which helped lift her mood somewhat. Sheldon, Mary, and Barnaby Rose were coming for dinner. It had been ages since she'd felt like socialising but had been easily persuaded by Sheldon's excitement over a project he wanted to discuss with her and Harry.

'We'd better get that fire built, Mulbers, we've got guests coming.' Her furry friend perked up and followed her into the drawing room, both never more grateful than at that moment to have each other's companionship.

* * *

Lily Hambly-Jones' bottom lip trembled, but she was determined not to cry.

'Leave her alone!' Lily's best friend Anna-Maria shrieked, but she was scared too and could only watch in despair as Kerry Madison – having grabbed Lily's wrist – twisted her arm around and pushed it hard up against her back.

'Think you're such a smarty pants, don't you!' she growled, pushing harder against Lily's arm and causing her to wince.

Anna-Maria could see that her friend's eyes were starting to fill with tears and she immediately began to fret. 'I'll tell!' she shrieked, causing Kerry to push Lily aside and grab her instead, shaking Anna-Maria by the lapels of her jacket.

'Do it and you'll be next, Miss Goody Two-shoes,' Kerry snarled, pushing her face closer. 'Just because your mum's a teacher, it doesn't make you invincible.'

Lily quickly forced herself in between the two of them. 'It's me you've got the problem with, Kerry, so leave her alone – she hasn't done anything wrong.'

Kerry moved her face menacingly towards Lily's then, her hands clasping and unclasping into fists.

The truth was, Lily wasn't even sure what she'd done to upset Kerry so much in the first place. Ever since they'd returned to school following the February half-term, Kerry had been going out of her way to be as mean to her as possible. She'd begun by pushing Lily about whenever she got the opportunity, kicking her hard on the shins when they were on the sports field or knocking her books and pens off the desk whenever she just *happened* to pass by. She was also tired of all the hurtful comments Kerry kept saying to her and the spiteful names she called her. And then, today, when Lily and Anna-Maria had made the mistake of going to play at the far end of the field where they couldn't easily be seen, Kerry had followed them.

Thankfully, at that moment the school bell rang, signalling the end of lunchtime play.

'See you at drama club,' Kerry sneered as she walked away, leaving Lily and Anna-Maria to recover. Lily rubbed her arm; it hurt.

'You've got to tell, Lily, else she'll keep on doing it!' pleaded her friend.

'No!' Lily shot back. 'It'll just make things worse, trust me.' She thought for a moment, staring into space. 'I think it's best that I keep away from drama club for a while; I wasn't enjoying it anyway.'

Anna-Maria knew that was a complete lie; she'd seen how her friend's face lit up whenever they entered the Ashton Abbey hall together where the drama club was held. Lily loved being in the thick of it and Miss Fortune was always complimenting and encouraging her.

'Oh, don't be like that – I'll be there and I won't go if you're not going.'

Lily sighed, rolling her eyes. She knew full well that if that happened, Anna-Maria's mum, Mrs Davies, would get suspicious and would hold a full inquisition – of that Lily had no doubt – which would involve her mother and father and goodness knows who else.

'Fine!' She threw her hands up in the air in frustration. 'Let's just get back to class, shall we? Otherwise we'll get in trouble there as well.'

Anna-Maria linked her arm through Lily's; she wanted to hug her but thought that might make her cross.

Thankfully, they had art and crafts for the rest of the day, which meant they were allowed to either paint, glue, or sew. Either way, they worked alone, and Lily was grateful to have the time to think. *Kerry Madison was beginning to prove a bit of a problem – in more ways than one.*

Lily remembered the conversation she'd overheard the previous evening. Her grandfather had been telling her parents about a competition he wanted the drama club to get involved with. If Lily wanted to be part of it, which she really did, she'd have to be on her best behaviour, so whatever it was she'd done to upset Kerry needed to be resolved – and fast.

I just hope no one else gets hurt in the meantime.

CHAPTER SIX

*S*adie Alcock placed her hands over her ears, pushing them harder in an attempt to drown out the argument raging in the kitchen below.

When something caught her eye underneath the dresser by the huge bay window of her bedroom, she quickly crawled on all fours to retrieve the pink fluffy earmuffs her grandmother had bought her just this past weekend. After fixing them in place, she heaved open the bottom drawer of the huge oak dresser and retrieved the packet of custard creams she'd hidden there a few days ago.

She jumped as a loud BANG resounded throughout the house, which usually signalled her father's departure as he slammed the outhouse door in frustration. It was a scenario that was becoming all too familiar these days and Sadie didn't like it one bit.

She crept carefully across the threadbare Persian rug that covered the floorboards beneath – the still vibrant blues and reds giving it an air of comfort despite it having seen better days – and carefully peeped out the corner of the window. She saw *her father marching angrily towards the cowsheds – well, the sheds that used to house the cows, anyhow.*

Although she was now eight years old, Sadie didn't fully understand what had happened in the past six months, except that her parents seemed to be constantly screaming at each other. She did know, however, that some of the cows had got sick; something to do with BSE. Her mother Jen had tried to explain it all to Sadie, also delivering the additional horrific news that because the ones that were ill couldn't be cured, the whole herd had to be culled. Upon hearing this, Sadie had burst into tears.

She'd been sent away to her grandmother's then – for almost a week – and when she returned to Upper Pethewick Farm, the family home she knew and loved so well, she was sad to see it had lost some of its charm; the once thriving and endlessly busy environment had been replaced with an atmosphere full of gloom and despondency.

Her father now spent most of the day drinking whiskey whilst her mother's perpetual attempts to get the farm moving again fell on deaf ears or escalated into a row – as was the case today.

Sadie sighed despairingly as she sat on the floor, her back against the door. She liked the firmness of the wood; it made her feel grounded. 'Why do things have to change?' she asked herself, thumping her legs angrily. When it didn't hurt enough, she thumped them again and again until the pain brought tears to her eyes, making her sob. She sobbed for the loss of the beloved cows that she used to help feed and milk every day; she sobbed for the loss of love that had disappeared from the house since the sickness began; but most of all she sobbed because she felt so alone and scared and didn't know what the future held for them anymore. She was only eight, after all.

Pulling the sleeves of her grey cardigan over her hands, she wiped away her tears. Then, spotting the half-eaten packet of biscuits, she reached out for another one. 'Well, at least I've got you,' she said, smiling to herself as she enjoyed the satisfying crunch of the shortcake biscuit followed by the sweet sugary cream inside. 'I wonder what Mum's got for dinner...'

CHAPTER SEVEN

Diana Fortune put the phone down and rubbed her hands together with glee.

After Anthony Sullivan and Alexander Harvey's unexpected visit last week to discuss the Hampton's invitation to participate in the Cotswolds County Majorette of the Year competition, Diana had been in touch with some of her old contacts who had recommended a choreographer to assist her – and she'd just accepted the offer!

Delighted, Diana shrugged into her large, cosy black cashmere coat before collecting her handbag, gloves, and walking stick, eager to go and share the news with Anthony. Channing House – the home he and Ianthe shared – was just a short walk from the Rectory, which would enable her to kill two birds with one stone given that she wanted to discuss a few things with Reverend Fisher too.

A crisp, clear, but nonetheless cold day – as usual for early March – greeted her as she stepped outside

The Boathouse and made her way towards the church green. As she went she spotted a couple of removal vans, idly wondering if someone was finally moving into Hazel Lodge; ever since Lionel and Vera had sold up, that area of the village had seemed so lifeless, especially with both The Haven and Springfield lying empty for the past year or so too.

I just hope the neighbours aren't putting people off.

'Morning Diana!' greeted Rita Denby as she rushed out of The Firs.

'Hello Rita,' Diana reciprocated, albeit a little hurriedly. Rita was renowned for being a committed village gossip who was forever interfering in everyone else's business. She also wouldn't hesitate, however, to give you the shirt off her back if you needed it, and it was this generous nature that caused most people to at least *try* to tolerate her.

'Off to the Abbey?' Rita enquired, knowing full well that wasn't the case; it was common knowledge that Diana used the main hall at Ashton Abbey after school every Monday, Wednesday, and Friday for drama club, and as it was Tuesday and just a little after 11 a.m., this was clearly stating the obvious. However, Diana was reticent to reveal the true purpose of her journey, especially given how Rita liked to have a finger in as many pies as possible.

Diana recalled how she'd given Alexander Harvey a hell of a time when he'd directed the Hampton Players the previous year; even though he'd created a new, special role as Stage Supervisor specifically for Rita in an attempt to keep her in hand, the power had gone straight to her head and he'd had to get quite firm with her in the end.

Diana didn't need, or want, that sort of hassle in her life. *The Fortunettes* – as they were to be called – was her gig, and it was going to stay that way too.

'Just sharing morning coffee with Anthony and Ianthe, Rita,' she replied as she rushed past. 'You know, our usual Tuesday get-together.'

Rita nodded knowingly, clearly happy that she wasn't missing out. 'Well, enjoy, and do give everyone my best!' She waved at her before heading back inside The Firs, leaving Diana to wonder if she kept a permanent watch out through the front windows of her house, seeing as no one ever seemed to pass by without being accosted.

'Diana!' greeted Anthony warmly as he held open the front door of Channing House and ushered her in. 'It's so lovely to see you. Do go on through; Ianthe's just made some fresh coffee.'

Discarding her coat and gloves along the way – which Anthony took care of – Diana greeted Ianthe and sat down in her usual armchair next to the fireplace, relishing the warmth from the fire that Anthony had stoked up just moments earlier. She smiled contentedly; the three of them had become firm friends and she felt right at home there.

'I have exciting news!' she exclaimed, her blue eyes glittering like two shiny sapphires as a wide smile spread across her face, causing Ianthe and Anthony to laugh with excitement – both of them enjoying seeing their friend look so happy.

'Oh, do tell!' encouraged Anthony eagerly whilst Ianthe handed them each a cup of coffee.

Diana's smile widened. 'Remember I told you about my friend Frank Bannister, the award winning director and producer?' They nodded their heads in recognition. 'Well, he's been directing that UK drama on satellite, *Northern Rights* – you know, the one everyone complained about when it was first launched due to all the hard-hitting storylines?'

'You mean the one that won a BAFTA for best drama last year?' Anthony interjected.

'And the year before that too, apparently,' added Diana. 'In fact, it's in its fifth series now, can you believe it?' She shook her head. 'Anyhow, one of the show's main character's – Lydia? Lydia Cooper I think the name is – is in a coma after receiving a beating from her husband Shane, who caught her *in flagrante delicto.*'

Anthony and Ianthe shook their heads, looking more than a little perplexed. 'Oh dear!' exclaimed Anthony after a moment. 'I have to say, it's not something we watch, I'm afraid.'

'No matter, I don't watch it either – for the record,' Diana replied, laughing, 'but the actress that plays Lydia – Camilla Barrington-Smythe – has been given a six-month break from filming whilst they develop her character; the season five finale is due to air at the end of April, I believe, and in the meantime the writers are deciding where to take the character next.'

'She had a part in that costume drama shown at Christmas, didn't she?' Ianthe mused.

'Yes, that's right, and apparently she's also been in a few of those afternoon dramas shown on the *BBC*… or so Frank told me, anyway.'

'So, how does this affect us?' Anthony asked, eyebrows raised. He really wasn't sure where the conversation was going, and by the looks of things, neither was Ianthe.

'Well,' said Diana, pausing a moment to add some dramatic tension to her announcement, 'Camilla's agreed to come and choreograph *The Fortunettes* – for the majorette competition!'

Now they all had big smiles on their faces.

'Really?' Ianthe asked. 'That's fantastic, Diana! How on earth did you manage that?' She sat a little more upright in her chair, thrilled at having secured such a prestigious appointment.

'To be honest, I think she's a little lost at finding herself being written out in the interim – especially as her contract's not actually up for renewal just yet – so she was looking for something to bridge the gap. She's incredibly keen to get involved, though, and is relishing the opportunity to do something different for a while.'

'Is she experienced, though – in choreography, I mean?' Anthony questioned.

'Of course; it's all part of an actor's training, Anthony.' Diana sighed. 'It's just that at my age, I'm not as nimble as I used to be, which is why I wanted to bring someone else in – and besides, a fresh perspective always goes a long way.'

'Absolutely, I completely agree with you,' said Anthony before adding, 'but just one more thing.' He paused awkwardly for a moment. 'Has she asked for a fee?' While Diana had been talking he'd been mentally running the Parish Council bank balance and financial commitments quickly through his mind.

'Oh, don't you worry about that,' Diana said, putting up her hand. 'It's all taken care of.'

'But, if she's...' Anthony started, though it was clear that his protest was pointless.

'Put it this way,' said Diana. 'Think of the good it'll do for the village – having her here in general, but more so if we win.'

Anthony and Ianthe exchanged excited glances at this new and interesting prospect, anticipating the potential benefit. It could really put the Hamptons on the map.

'In that case,' said Anthony, 'let's organise a celebratory dinner for her. It'll be a great way to welcome her to the village.'

'That's an excellent idea, darling,' enthused Ianthe. Diana nodded her head in agreement whilst Anthony reached for the telephone.

'I'll give Poppy a call,' he said. 'We all know she and Richard host the best parties and I've no doubt they'll be thrilled to be involved in this too.'

Ianthe and Diana exchanged further looks of excitement as Anthony chatted away on the telephone.

The residents of the Hamptons loved a good party, and if the previous year's Autumn Ball was anything to go by, they were no doubt going to be in for a memorable evening.

* * *

'Ah, Richard, you're here at last!' Francine Dubois swanned into Richard Hambly-Jones' office and sat herself down in one of the plush tan leather seats facing the huge mahogany executive desk he was currently working at.

He glanced up from his computer, quite unable to hide his irritation at her forthrightness. 'Good morning, Francine,' he said, before adding, 'do you usually just walk into people's offices without knocking?'

Taken aback, she flushed slightly and straightened up. 'Oh, I'm sorry I...'

'Was Margaret not in her office?' he interrupted. 'I presume you checked my availability with her first?'

'Well, y-yes,' she stammered, 'but I... I mean, as your Senior Buyer for the exclusive *Magnifique Madame* range I assumed it was acceptable to just come in. I've...'

'Well, it isn't,' Richard interrupted her again as he stood up, indicating that he wanted her to leave. 'As we discussed on your induction day, you need to liaise with Margaret if you'd like to discuss something with me. I have a tight and busy schedule; that's why I employ a PA. For that matter, that's why I employed you too – to free up more of my time, not to *take* up more of my time.'

Seemingly unperturbed, Francine stood up. 'Of course, my apologies. It's just... a new ship and all that,' she quipped with a wink, to which Richard did not respond. 'It's certainly not urgent,' she continued, 'so I'll speak to Margaret and let you get on.'

Shutting the door behind her, Richard began to wonder if she really was the right person for the job after all. She seemed to be forever at his door, which he wouldn't have minded one bit if she'd had good reason to be there – and not simply use it as a poor excuse for inane chit-chat, as had often been the case of late.

Sighing, he went back to his desk and called Margaret. 'Has she gone?'

'Yes,' came the reply. 'Sorry about that, Richard. She just barged straight in; I didn't get a chance to stop her.'

Hearing the exasperation in his PA's voice made Richard even more frustrated. Margaret had been in the family business for years and was his right-hand woman. He didn't want anything – or any*one* – to upset her.

'It's not your fault,' he sighed. 'She's just a tad overzealous. You know what these newbie's can be like.' Although he wasn't certain that quite applied in this case. 'What does she want, anyway?' Whilst Francine's approach wasn't the best, he still wanted to make certain it was nothing that required his immediate attention.

'An invitation.'

'Invitation?'

'Yes, an invitation to a private viewing of a new line Francine wants to introduce you to.'

Richard sighed again. 'Well, I'm not going – that's what I employ *her* for. Tell her, will you, Margaret, that if she wants me to approve a new line she needs to get samples sent here.'

Richard put the phone down, still somewhat disgruntled. This wasn't quite what he'd been expecting from a high-flying purchasing executive with extensive experience working for some of the top department stores in London, New York, and Paris that her very detailed CV was littered with. He couldn't imagine this sort of behaviour being acceptable in such environments whatsoever.

He frowned. Perhaps Francine Dubois wasn't quite what she purported to be after all. And, if that was the case, he was going to have to keep a very careful eye on her.

* * *

'That was delicious, Tiggy. My compliments to the chef!' remarked Sheldon as he mopped up the residue of the delicious Lobster Thermidor from his huge, bushy grey moustache.

'I couldn't agree more,' Mary – Sheldon's wife – enthused. 'The rice pilaf works perfectly as a side dish. You know, I don't think I've ever had this before.'

Tiggy smiled across at Harry. 'Thank you, but I'm afraid I can't take the credit for this,' she said as she gestured at the near-empty plates, 'it's all courtesy of Piers and Marcus.'

This brought forth nods of approval. Piers and Marcus were the landlords of the Maide of Honour public house situated next to the Rectory. A much-loved couple, they were firm favourites with the locals. They had introduced a takeout service a few years ago – which had quickly escalated into fine dining catering – and Tiggy and Harry called upon them regularly.

Now that everyone seemed to have finished their food, Tiggy stood up and began collecting their dinner plates. 'Can I interest anyone in dessert?' she asked as she worked. 'It's lemon cheesecake with a raspberry coulis.'

'Oh, goodness! Not for me, thanks,' Sheldon said, patting his large, protruding stomach with satisfaction.

Mary nodded in agreement with her husband. 'It sounds quite delicious, darling, but I'm full too; I'd love a cup of coffee, however, if there's one going.'

'Of course,' Tiggy replied, smiling. 'Harry, why don't you take everyone through to the drawing room and I'll bring through a fresh pot in a moment?'

Once they'd left she busied herself clearing the table in the dining room and rinsing off the dishes in the kitchen before placing them into the dishwasher, smiling as she did so. She was appreciative of the efforts Harry had made arranging tonight's dinner for them and their guests. It had been ages since they'd hosted visitors and so far the evening had been really enjoyable. Barnaby was on good form too, she was pleased to note, given the success stories he'd shared during dinner.

This thought reminded Tiggy of the reason for their guests' visit in the first place and she quickly set about preparing coffee, adding the box of *petit fours* Piers had provided for good measure.

The coffee served, Tiggy sank down onto the sofa next to Harry as all eyes focused on Sheldon.

'Thank you for hosting us this evening; we're all well aware that the past year or so hasn't been easy for you – for either of you,' he said softly. Tiggy cast her gaze downwards while Harry reached out and clasped her hand comfortingly.

Sheldon, Mary, and Barnaby had all been an amazing support to them during this time. They'd been long-term friends of Tiggy's parents, Charles and Lydia Lawrence, and Sheldon had been Charles' right-hand man at Lawrence Homes. He and Mary had known Tiggy ever since she'd been born, with their son Barnaby coming into the world a short time after. They were part of the family and a staple in her life, which right now – along with Harry – was just what she needed.

She looked up into Harry's eyes and smiled, returning his squeeze before refocussing on Sheldon, intrigued as to what he had to say.

'A few months ago,' he continued, 'I approached Harry and Barnaby with an idea.' Tiggy raised an eyebrow, uncertain as to where the conversation was heading, considering this was all news to her. 'It's okay,' Sheldon reassured, sensing her unease, 'I promise you, just hear us out.' Tiggy smiled, nodding at him to carry on. 'We heard there was a possibility that a property was going to become vacant here in the Hamptons. Harry and Barnaby have been working together to check it out and have also been investigating the viability of our idea.' Reaching behind him he pulled out a long, white roll of paper – which Tiggy immediately recognised as an architect's drawing – and proceeded to lay it out on the coffee table. 'This is the layout of The Swan pub on the Hampton Ash Road. The current proprietors, Jamie and Chris Bonner, have had enough and are selling up.'

'Really? I'm sorry to hear that,' Tiggy replied, though she was still very much confused as to what Sheldon was alluding to.

'Well, to be fair, since Piers and Marcus started offering food to go, the Bonners have struggled to get any decent custom.' They all acknowledged this, knowing full well that not one of them had frequented The Swan in the past year or so. 'So, I thought why don't we buy it and run it ourselves?'

Tiggy sat upright, stunned at first, before bursting into laughter at the foolishness of his suggestion. 'But… didn't you just say that they aren't getting any custom?'

'Ah, but what if it became something other than just a pub?' Barnaby teased.

'Exactly,' continued Sheldon. 'What if we introduced a bit of glamour into the Hamptons and created our very own bistro and wine bar?'

All eyes swivelled towards Tiggy, eager to gauge her reaction.

She spent a few moments processing Sheldon's words before responding. 'But what do any of us know about running a wine bar, let alone a bistro?' she pointed out. 'I can't even cook, for God's sake!' she joked.

'Well,' replied Harry, 'the idea is that we'd employ a chef – a decent one at that, of course – and we'd hire staff to run the bar.'

'Whilst we sit back and enjoy the profits,' chipped in Barnaby.

'Hang on a minute, though, what about Piers and Marcus? They've been so good to us, Harry.' Tiggy turned towards her fiancé, who gathered her hands together and kissed them reassuringly.

'We'll be upfront and honest with them from the start, of course, and we have no intention of stealing their business. We hired a market research company to garner public opinion and the results speak for themselves.' He looked over towards Sheldon, who was rifling through some paperwork. After a moment he handed her a copy of the report from the research they'd commissioned. 'We're thinking of introducing a particular cuisine – French or maybe Spanish, it's still up for discussion – and this is more of a wine bar than a pub, darling. It's very much *in vogue* these days, and completely different to what Piers and Marcus offer.' Tiggy knew that to be true and began to nod in approval as she read through the report.

'There's one more thing,' Sheldon said, scanning the faces of his audience before clearing his throat, 'we'd thought we could call it LC's Bar.' He waited for her reaction, thankful for the pause as the lump in his throat was making it somewhat difficult to say any more at that point.

'LC's?'

'Lydia and Charles, after your parents,' he explained. 'We thought it only fitting given the huge contribution they gave – not just to the Hamptons but to so many – both through their charity work and the magnificent homes Charles designed and built.'

Tiggy had stopped listening; she was overcome with emotion at his suggested tribute and Harry comforted her whilst the others looked on. It was a touching moment for them all.

'Mary and I aren't getting any younger, Tiggy – I'll be 78 this year – and it'd be a great adventure for us both.' Sheldon smiled. 'For all of us.'

Sheldon's words hung in the air as Tiggy took a few minutes to compose herself. Then, taking a deep breath, she announced, 'I'm in!'

She smiled as a resounding cheer echoed around the room.

CHAPTER EIGHT

Pradeep Chandola collected his medical bag from the downstairs study, then, placing it back down on the floor, went through to the kitchen again.

'I forgot to mention,' he called out, 'my contact numbers are on the pad next to the telephone in my office.' He was anxious, and not just because he was about to start his new job – today was also the first day that their new nanny, Bronwyn Saddleback, would be left in charge.

Pradeep looked Bronwyn up and down again, wondering if she really was the right person for the job after all. Although fully qualified, she was only 21 and had just a year's previous work experience.

'You still here?' Bronwyn asked. 'I thought you'd left already.' She was busy in the utility room, sorting through the washing, her sing-song welsh accent floating across to him. 'You need to get on, lovely, else you'll be late.' She expertly poured powder and fabric conditioner into the relevant compartments of the washing machine then switched it on before heading back to the table and clearing away the breakfast dishes.

Baby Salena was sleeping soundly following her earlier feed – after Bronwyn had bathed and changed her – and Pradeep's wife Esha was enjoying a well-deserved lie-in upstairs.

Satisfied that she was in control, Pradeep went to collect his medical bag and, this time, actually set off for the surgery.

I'm a GP and a trained psychotherapist yet I seem to have more problems than most of my patients.

Knowing he mustn't be distracted on his first day – or any day – he tried to push his family concerns aside as he headed into work.

* * *

'Morning, Matt!' greeted James Turvey on his way back to the Hamptons Stores. He'd just dropped off a grocery delivery at Lucy Whittaker's house and, as she'd invited him in for morning coffee, was feeling quite buoyant.

'Good morning, James, you look like you've lost a penny and found a fiver!' Matt quipped, noting the bounce in James' step as he walked along the King's Oak Road and approached Honeycomb Lodge, where Matt lived.

James smiled coyly, though he clearly wasn't going to give anything away. 'Enjoy a nice lie-in today, did you?' he teased. It was well known that Midford County Police changed shifts at 7 a.m., 3 p.m. or 11 p.m., and as it was just after 10 a.m. and Matt was in uniform it seemed quite out of character for the well-loved Sergeant and Hamptons resident to be just leaving for work.

Matt laughed. 'You don't miss a trick, do you, James? Ever thought of joining the force?' he joked back. 'Actually, I took a few hours out to revise – it's impossible to concentrate down at the station.'

'Revise? I didn't know you were studying; anything interesting?'

'I've got my Inspector's exam this afternoon,' Matt confided proudly. 'Bill's due to retire in a few months and I'm hoping to step into his shoes.'

Everyone in the Hamptons knew Inspector Bill Wilson who, like Matt, had begun his career as a young PC – only he'd first joined over 40 years ago and had worked his way through the ranks. He'd earned great respect from the residents of the Hamptons and the surrounding villages for his no-nonsense approach.

'So, old Bill's retiring, is he? Well, I'd better not keep you – good luck for the exam, Matt, I'm sure you'll pass with flying colours!' James encouraged.

'Thanks, I'll...'

At that moment they were both distracted by a loud flapping noise, and as they looked towards the source they saw a red *Fiat 500* trundling along the road before coming to a halt just before them.

'Look's like a damsel in distress,' winked James, indicating the female driver. 'I'll leave you to it – customers waiting and all that!' And he was off before Matt could even respond.

Checking his watch, Matt knew he had a few hours before his exam but he'd planned to spend that swotting up a bit more as opposed to dealing with the scenario in front of him now. However, it wasn't in his DNA to turn his back on someone who needed help and he went to offer his assistance just as the driver was getting out.

'Can you believe this?' The tall, slim, attractive driver raked her fingers through her well-groomed ash blonde hair before kicking at the flat tyre in frustration.

'Don't worry,' Matt reassured her, 'I'll have this changed for you in a jiffy.' He began undoing the bright, shiny buttons of his police jacket; he didn't want to arrive for the Inspector's exam covered in dirt and oil. 'Matt Hudson,' he introduced himself. 'I'm the local Sergeant here.'

'...and my knight in shining armour,' the lady added as Matt retrieved the jack from underneath the front passenger seat. 'My god, how did you find that? I wouldn't have had a clue where it was.'

Matt smiled. 'You get to learn a lot about cars in my job. Are you just passing through?'

'I'm here I think,' she responded scattily, which made them both laugh. 'Sorry, I'm Camilla and I'm guessing this is the Hamptons, right?'

Matt nodded in acknowledgement. He'd loosened the wheel nuts and was now jacking up the car. 'Yes, it certainly is. Are you moving in then?'

'Well, yes and no,' she began, causing Matt to smile again. 'I've just accepted a short-term placement here so I guess I'm moving in, but not for very long.'

Matt eyed her discreetly as he worked. He guessed she was late 20s to early 30s, and judging by her well-groomed appearance she was affluent too. *No doubt heading towards Hampton Waters.*

'That sounds intriguing,' he commented as he secured the spare tyre into place.

'I'm staying with Diana Fortune, actually,' she chatted cheerily, 'helping her work on a project with the local children. I'm really excited about it too; it's such a change from my normal day-to-day job.' Matt didn't pick up on the reference, and finishing up, he checked his watch again. 'Oh, I'm sorry, am I keeping you?' she asked. Her concern seemed genuine but Matt didn't have time to stand around chatting.

'It's all part of the job,' he smiled. 'I do have to get off, though.' He indicated his hands. 'I'll nip inside and wash this off first. You just need to carry on along this road now and when you pass The Hamptons Health and Beauty salon on your right, continue for about half a mile and you'll come across The Boathouse on your left. It's set back off the main road, though, so you'll need to watch out for the sign beforehand. Okay?'

Camilla smiled and nodded, meeting his gaze. *What gorgeous green eyes.* 'Thanks so much, you're a life saver,' she gushed. 'Perhaps I could repay you with a drink sometime?' She handed him a card, which he placed distractedly into his trouser pocket. 'Give me a call when you're free and we'll arrange something.'

Matt waved her off and then headed back inside Honeycomb Lodge to get cleaned up, mimicking the bounce in his step he'd noted in James earlier.

Right now, however, he had to focus. *Inspector's exam first, potential date later.*

* * *

CRASH!

'What the fuck..?' Harry sat up, his eyes wide in concern as a loud smashing noise reverberated from downstairs, one that was quickly followed by the sound of breaking glass.

Tiggy sat up too and they both froze for a moment, listening hard and trying to make sense of the noises. They'd been enjoying a lazy morning lie-in – the air still heavy with their passionate morning encounter – and the disturbance caught them completely off-guard.

'Stay here,' Harry instructed as he hastily pulled on a pair of jogging pants and then slowly tiptoed down the stairs.

Tiggy slipped out of bed and pulled on a nearby dressing gown, all manner of thoughts whirling through her mind as she tied the silky material in place. She could hear Harry muttering in the kitchen beneath their bedroom and was momentarily alarmed until he began to ascend the stairs, bringing the intruder along with him.

'Mulbers!' she cried out, stepping forward to accept the huge bundle of ginger fur from a smiling Harry. 'Not again!'

'Oh? A repeat offender, eh?' Harry teased, rubbing Mulbers' ears as he purred loudly in response.

'Did you leave the window open again, Harry?' Harry dipped his head in mock shame at having been caught out and Tiggy laughed. 'It must be something he was used to doing at his previous owners' house; every time the window's left open he just jumps straight in.'

'Well, he's knocked a few crystal glasses onto the floor this time, I'm afraid. But don't worry, I've checked him over and he's completely fine – glass free. Let me go and clear it up before making us some brunch.'

Harry went back downstairs whilst Tiggy slipped back into bed, cuddling her furry companion. He was enjoying the fuss immensely.

A short while later, having showered and dressed, Tiggy went to join Harry in the kitchen, keen to continue the discussion about their latest adventure.

'It's all ready for you, darling,' he said, greeting her with a kiss and pulling out a chair from the kitchen table for her to sit down on. The heavy pine made a dragging noise as it moved across the stone tiled floor, a sound that was soon replaced by Mulbers' cries at the realisation that his food bowl was empty. 'Yes, yes, you too,' Harry comforted as he ripped open a fresh packet of cat food whilst Tiggy began tucking into the hot sausage and mustard Panini's he'd prepared for them.

'You did well to secure Tawfique,' she enthused in between mouthfuls, 'it'll be good to work with him again – especially as we know what he's capable of, given the renovations here.'

'Exactly, although to be honest he was just as keen to work with us again,' Harry explained. 'Apparently, after restoring Riverside Hall, he was flooded with more work than he could shake a stick at and has had to take on a couple more designers as a result.' Harry reached for the coffee pot and poured them both a fresh cup before seating himself opposite Tiggy. 'And, of course, the Cohen boys have come out of it well too.'

Tiggy recalled Will and Able Cohen, whose building skills were much sought after in the

Cotswolds, and both of whom had been a huge support during her father's last weeks.

'Will they be working on LC's bar too?' she asked and Harry nodded in confirmation. 'It'll be just like getting the family back together then,' Tiggy joked.

'That's a great way to look at it,' he said, agreeing with her, 'and just think of the legacy.' They exchanged a deep, knowing look and reached for each other's hands.

Sated for the time being, Mulbers sat and cleaned himself whilst they continued their discussion, jumping up onto Tiggy's lap after a minute or so.

'Awww, I've got no time to fuss you this morning,' she said as she stroked his back lovingly. 'Perhaps we need to install a cat flap for you, mister,' she cooed before snuggling her face into his soft fur.

'That's a great idea!' Harry jumped up and retrieved his laptop from the kitchen counter. 'Why don't you have a look at some whilst I get showered and dressed? I'm sure one of the builders would be happy to install it for us once the work on LC's bar is under way.'

Opening the laptop, Tiggy started scrolling through the deluge of offerings online with one hand whilst continuing to stroke Mulbers with the other. As she looked she could hear the rushing of the water from the shower in the background mingled with Harry's singing, and it made her stop for a moment.

I can't remember the last time I felt like this.

Tiggy stood up and, still holding her feline friend close, she went over to the kitchen windows, looking out towards the freshly renovated stable block that had lain empty for far too long.

Perhaps it's time I got things moving again.

Placing Mulbers carefully down on the floor, she retrieved the latest equestrian brochure from the pine dresser that Patrick delivered on his weekly visits.

'Is that the post?' Harry asked as he reappeared, his blond hair still wet from the shower, which always seemed to enhance the blueness of his eyes. Recognition set in and he stilled. Part of the purpose of renovating Riverside Hall and the adjoining stable block was to afford Tiggy the opportunity to run her own riding school, but Aster Maxwell had seemingly scuppered such plans.

'I was just thinking,' she mused, flicking through the pages detailing an array of beautiful, strong, and well-groomed horses, each seeking a new home, 'that it's about time we got that riding school idea off the ground.' She turned to look at him, knowing that he'd be filled with concern. 'If I begin looking at suitable horses now, I could aim to open up by next spring – by that time LC's bar would be up and running too.'

Smiling, Harry went over and gathered her into his arms, pausing for a moment to brush a strand of her long, golden hair away from her face. 'You know there's no rush – the wine bar's going to be full on and I don't want you to get overwhelmed by it all.'

She smiled at him reassuringly. 'I haven't felt this happy for such a long time, Harry; I really feel ready to get going again. And another thing...' Being somewhat shorter than Harry she tilted her head to look up at him as she asked, 'Haven't we got a wedding to organise too?'

Harry's eyes widened for the second time that day as a huge smile spread across his face. 'Are you sure? I mean, there's going to be a lot of arrangements to make besides the bar.' His eyes flickered from left to right as he tried to read hers, desperate to ensure her sincerity, knowing full well that too much pressure could halt her recovery, and even make it go backwards.

'Oh, Harry!' Tiggy exclaimed, tears filling her eyes. 'You're the best thing to ever come into my life and I can't wait to become your wife! Of *course* I'm sure – I never had any doubts. I've had enough of sitting around here, day after day, brooding; from now on it's onwards and upwards!'

As they embraced, Harry held onto her like he never wanted to ever let her go.

'Right you,' he said eventually as he reluctantly pulled away from her, 'we've got a designer to meet! Grab my keys, will you, darling, whilst I just take my phone off charge? Then we can get going.'

Harry disappeared into the study whilst Tiggy fetched the keys from the holder in the boot room, thankful he wasn't there to witness her hands shaking at the thought of going outside.

Taking a deep breath, she opened the back door and stepped out into the cool March air.

So far so good.

It was time to put the past behind them and finally move on. *Time to focus on the future – together.*

* * *

Dr Jon Anderson took a few moments before calling through his next appointment. Living and working amongst his patients was never going to be easy, and over the years he'd long since learnt to separate his personal feelings from his professional stance. He was only human, however, and this wasn't always as easy as it sounded.

'Good to see you,' greeted Jonathan Palmer-Reid, shaking the doctor's proffered hand before settling himself down in the comfy padded leather chair in front of Dr Anderson's desk.

'Thanks for coming in, Jonathan,' he began, smiling comfortingly. 'I wanted to discuss the recent tests you had following your annual medical.'

'Oh?' Jonathan asked, frowning. 'Should I be worried?'

'Well, yes and no,' Dr Anderson said softly, clasping his hands together as he met Jonathan's gaze. 'The blood tests you had last week have come back and I'm concerned to see that your liver result shows raised enzymes.' He paused whilst he looked back at the computer screen displaying Jonathan's records. 'And your cholesterol test has come back as being very high too. How did you get on with the home blood pressure monitor we lent you?'

Jonathan rifled through his pockets, eventually handing over a crumpled sheet of paper with a few numbers randomly jotted down on it.

'It wasn't easy,' he admitted, flushing with embarrassment. 'I didn't want to worry Charlotte so I've been trying to take readings in between cases.'

'Yes, I'd heard you'd been called to the bar – congratulations.'

'Thanks,' Jonathan replied. 'Having spent so many years as a city lawyer, I now wish I'd qualified sooner. I didn't expect to be quite this busy, though – not that I'm complaining!'

'I'm sure,' Dr Anderson murmured whilst reviewing the haphazard readings. 'However, you should be aware that if you don't start to make changes now, things will only get worse. These readings are far too high, particularly for someone who's only just 44.' He looked up at him again. 'And, to be honest, you really could do with losing a few pounds.'

Jonathan nodded; he knew that was putting it mildly. His city suits were straining under the pressure of his ever growing waistline – only just last week a button had flown off his jacket during the train journey to Paddington as he'd nonchalantly looked on.

'I can give you something for your blood pressure today but you need to start thinking about making some serious lifestyle changes,' the doctor continued. 'When was the last time you did any exercise?'

Jonathan shrugged his shoulders. 'Before I got married, maybe?' He sighed, shaking his head. 'I really don't know, to be honest.' He was beginning to feel quite uncomfortable now, something that didn't go unnoticed by Dr Anderson.

'Look, I'm not here to judge – believe me – and I can give you a plethora of advice to help you make the changes you need to make, but ultimately you have to be willing to make those changes yourself – and right now, before this escalates into something far more serious.'

'I get what you're saying,' Jonathan acknowledged. 'I know I've let things slip. It's just far too easy to come home after a long day and sink a few glasses before dinner… and then a few more after.' He was referring to his love of wine, which didn't surprise Dr Anderson. He was well aware that most of the residents of the Hamptons regularly enjoyed a glass or two – including himself. 'Of course, I've been so worried about Charlotte too.'

'Oh?' Now it was Dr Anderson's turn to show concern.

'Well, you know, all this business with Aster Maxwell's attempt on Tiggy's life; Charlotte's not felt safe ever since.' He leant forward, placing his head in his hands before rubbing his eyes and looking up again. Dr Anderson hadn't noticed until then just how tired and strained he looked.

'I'm sorry to hear that, I didn't realise,' the doctor replied. 'I can see it's obviously putting a strain on you; why don't you ask her to come along and see me?'

'I've tried,' Jonathan cut in, somewhat exasperated, 'but she won't hear of it. She won't even admit that there's a problem, but it's affecting all of us – especially Sara. She's constantly fretting over her.'

Dr Anderson pondered this before responding. 'It's been a while since Charlotte and Lizzie had a good catch up, hasn't it?' Lizzie Anderson was as much loved by the villagers as her husband. 'I'll ask her to invite Charlotte over – it's amazing what they discuss when they get together,' he joked. 'I'm sure it'll do them both good to spend some time with each other.'

Jonathan nodded enthusiastically, relieved. He knew full well that if anyone could get Charlotte talking, it would be Lizzie.

He stood up and the two men shook hands again before Dr Anderson handed over a prescription for the promised blood pressure medication. 'Take one every morning. Come and see me again in a month, and we'll check your blood pressure again in the meantime.'

Jonathan nodded. 'Thank you.'

Stepping out into the fresh air, Jonathan took a deep breath. Despite Dr Anderson's concerns over his health, the thought of Lizzie's impending invitation to Charlotte had lifted his spirits. He knew that most of the villagers thought his wife was nothing more than a spoilt bitch with their big house, lavish lifestyle, and affluent friends, but that wasn't the Charlotte he knew and deeply loved.

That Charlotte was the one he was desperate to get back again – at any cost.

* * *

'Hello Barnaby.' That voice got him every time and he straightened up in his seat in an attempt to quell the fluttering sensation currently surging through his stomach. 'I'm super pleased we managed to get things moving so quickly, so thank you for that.'

'It's my pleasure,' he enthused in response. In fact, Barnaby was *super* pleased too; not only had the sale of the lucrative Swinford St. George Golf & Country Club afforded him the opportunity to invest in LC's Bistro and Wine Bar, but he also had his eye on another property he hoped to invest in.

'I was calling to ask if you could furnish me with a few of the local trade contacts you mentioned? I'd like to get things moving as soon as possible.'

'No problem,' Barnaby replied. 'Actually, I thought you might ask so I've already put a list together for you, which should arrive in your inbox around about... now!'

She let out a throaty laugh. 'My, that was quick work – and there was me hoping I could entice you to join me for lunch and bring it with you.'

Barnaby silently cursed his overzealousness, his mind abuzz. 'Well,' he cut in, 'I had been meaning to call you. Lyndon Westbrook popped in yesterday and left several framed photographs of aerial shots he'd commissioned over the years. He thought you might like to display them as part of the club's history.' Barnaby wiped his brow, impressed at his quick thinking, knowing full well that the pictures had been sitting there gathering dust ever since he'd taken on the commission.

'Well, it's a date then,' she replied without hesitation. 'I look forward to seeing you later – shall we say about 1 p.m.?'

'Perfect,' Barnaby replied, smiling to himself. He certainly didn't need asking twice. That would give him just enough time to drive over to the Hamptons to meet up with the others before heading back to Swinford St. George.

Who'd have thought it – me, Barnaby Rose, having lunch with her!

* * *

'Aye, aye,' teased the desk sergeant as PC Laura Benjamin stepped out from the locker rooms and into the custody area that all staff had to walk through before leaving Midford County Police station, 'don't you scrub up well?' Sergeant Phil Harris was well known as being a bit of a lothario with the ladies, and he certainly had the good looks to match: short dark hair, huge brown eyes framed by long dark lashes, and a charming smile to boot.

Laura couldn't help but blush as she passed the desk.

'Where are you off to? I might swing by later!' He laughed and a couple of nearby colleagues joined in.

'I keep telling you, Serge – over fifties is on a Thursday.'

At that a host of guffaws rang out. Even Phil was chuckling.

'Well, you just be careful out there,' he winked, 'and if there's any trouble, give us a call.' He buzzed a smiling Laura out of the station and she made her way to her car.

She didn't usually enjoy getting ready for a date straight from work but her new boyfriend wanted to meet up earlier than they'd originally planned so she didn't have time to head home first.

Once in the car she checked her appearance in the rear-view mirror. She wasn't one to wear a great deal of make-up in general, and having been blessed with great skin she needed no more than a few sweeps of the blusher brush and a flick of eyeshadow to enhance her hazel eyes. Finally, she applied a coat of pink lipstick and smoothed her brown, shoulder-length hair into place.

Right, let's go!

As she drove towards Chipping Melbury she couldn't help thinking how dire her love life had been over the past few years. At 29, she'd hoped to have been heading towards marriage by now. *No such luck!* She'd dated a few guys off and on – mostly from the force – and more recently had enjoyed quite a few nights out with Matt Hudson, but he appeared to be stuck on an ex, which had stopped her from taking things any further.

Perhaps this one's different. He'd certainly wooed her so far – buying her chocolates, sending a single red rose encased in a jewelled box not to mention a bottle of expensive Champagne, and a couple of weeks ago they'd enjoyed a romantic weekend away in the Lake District. But Laura was no fool, and she was playing her cards close to her chest with this one; instead of rushing in as usual, she was going to allow the relationship to develop and play out in its own time.

✱ ✱ ✱

Lily Hambly-Jones hated walking home from school. She'd stayed behind for netball practice, and usually, Mrs Davies – her best friend Anna-Maria's mother and Year 1 teacher at the Hamptons Primary School – drove them home, with Lily's mum collecting her younger brother Roderick after school. But today Lily had forgotten that Anna-Maria had to leave early for the dentist, and not wanting to create a fuss, she decided she'd rather walk than have to go to the school office. Mrs Rhodes-Brown – the school secretary – was very nice and all, but she could be a bit nosey and Lily didn't like that.

She decided to walk along the Hampton Waters Road rather than take the quickest route along King's Oak Road, as if she went that way not only would she have to walk past Kerry Madison's house but also past the adventure playground where she knew Kerry and her cronies liked to hang out.

It'd been a tough day too. When Lily had asked to use the toilet during maths, she'd returned to find that Kerry had written swear words all over her pencil case and had also snapped her favourite ruler in half. It was one that her grandfather Percy had bought for her when he'd returned from his holiday to Torquay with his new wife, Rosie. Lily liked Rosie and she said they'd chosen it for her because it had a picture of a beautiful *Stargazer* lily on it, next to her name. She'd treasured it ever since. And now it was broken, beyond repair.

Lily walked with her head down, such was the weight of the trouble it felt like she was carrying, oblivious to the fact that Kerry had just spotted her and was now using a shortcut in order to trap her enemy.

Before she could even comprehend what was happening Lily stumbled as the full force of Kerry slammed against her back and knocked her flat onto the ground. She pushed herself upright, wincing in pain as she noted the blood running into her white socks from the grazes she'd got when her knees hit the rough ground.

'Oh look, it's Little Miss Perfect,' Kerry mocked spitefully. 'Lost your way home, have you?' Lily kept silent, knowing that however she responded it would only fuel Kerry's anger. 'What's the matter, cat got your tongue?' She pushed hard on Lily's shoulder, which unsettled her, but she just about managed to remain upright – though it was certainly a struggle considering how much heavier and taller Kerry was than her.

'Where are your little supporters then?' she continued. 'Not here to save you now, are they?' she asked, before spitting in Lily's face. 'What sort of friends do you call them!' She lunged forward then, grabbing Lily's ponytail hard and dragging her to the ground, all whilst screaming insults at her.

Kerry was shouting so loudly, and was so enraged, that she didn't notice when the Swinford St. George Grammar School bus arrived. She was completely dumbstruck, therefore, to find herself being dragged off Lily just moments later by her older brother, Sam, and his friend, Sara Palmer-Reid.

'What the hell are you doing, you crazy bitch?' shouted Sam. He had his arms around Kerry, pinning her own arms tightly to her sides whilst Sara went to Lily's aid.

'Oh Lily, what's she done to you?' she asked gently.

Despite trying to keep her emotions in with all her might, Lily found she couldn't hold back the tears a moment longer; she started sobbing into Sara's shoulder whilst Sam attempted to calm his sister down.

'Just you wait!' he warned Kerry. 'I'm telling Dad about this, and you know what he'll do!'

It was as if he'd waved a magic wand; the Kerry that had been screaming and fighting just moments before suddenly became far calmer and quieter. 'No, Sam! You won't tell, will you?' she spluttered, clearly afraid now. 'We were just messing about.'

'It didn't look like messing about to me; just look at the state of her!' he exclaimed in disgust. 'Too right I'm telling; now get on home before I get our dad to drag you home!'

Kerry began to grizzle and scuttled off, doing her utmost to rustle up a few crocodile tears – knowing full well that if her father got wind of what had just happened she'd be howling for a week.

Sam picked up his school bag – having discarded it hastily earlier – and went over to Sara and Lily. 'I'm really sorry about that, Lily. Are you okay?'

'She's obviously *not*, Sam!' snapped Sara. 'You need to sort your sister out – she can't go around attacking people like this. She's nothing more than a common bully!'

Sam shook his head; he was embarrassed and ashamed of what they'd just witnessed. He liked Sara – a lot – and was friends with both her and Lily as they all attended the drama club together. He knew that if he *did* tell his dad about Kerry, she'd suffer a lot more. He chose, however, not to share this. Instead he placed his hand briefly on Lily's arm and dipped his head. 'I'll speak to her and try to ensure it doesn't happen again, I promise. Okay?' Lily nodded briefly. 'I'm sorry,' he added, 'but I've got to go now. I'll catch you guys later!' he called out as he set off towards home.

Having managed to stop Lily crying, Sara rummaged through her school satchel and pulled out a wad of tissues, some hand sanitiser, and her water bottle. Smiling, she held up the bottle of hand sanitiser so Lily could see it. 'Do you know, I'm the only one in the whole village who carries this stuff around with me? My mother's crazy, you see; she thinks I'm going to get some sort of infectious disease.' She spoke in a humorous fashion, which made Lily laugh. 'That's better,' soothed Sara, soaking a wad of tissue with water, which she then used to clean up Lily's knees. 'It looks like you've got some gravel stuck in there. What are you going to tell your mum?'

Lily bit her lip. If her parents knew about this they'd be furious. 'I just got back from netball practice so I could say I did it there?'

'Brilliant,' replied Sara. 'Now, let me get some more tissues for your face and we'll have you sorted in no time, then we can walk back together.'

Lily smiled again at hearing this, feeling safe. Sara lived just across the green from Hampton Manor House and she knew she'd see her right to her front door.

'There we are, all done,' Sara said, picking up all the used tissues and putting everything back into her bag. 'Right, come on!' She linked her arm through Lily's as they started walking. 'Have you heard about the majorettes competition?' she asked, trying to keep Lily's mind off what just happened. 'Apparently, we've got someone really famous coming to teach us all how to dance!'

They chatted and giggled as they walked along, and for the first time that day, Lily felt really happy. Although Sara was four years older than her, she regularly chatted to Lily at drama club, and at weekends they often hung out together with Louisa and Lottie Sable and their horses. In fact, Lily got along with everyone, which made it harder for her to understand why Kerry Madison had suddenly started hating her. She pushed that thought aside for now.

When they reached Lily's house, Sara decided to go inside with her. She knew Lily was scared to tell her parents what had happened and Sara wanted to support her.

Of course, Poppy noticed Lily's bloodied knees and socks straight away. 'Lily!' she shouted. 'Where have you been and what on earth's happened?' She guided her daughter to a chair and greeted Sara, who immediately explained what had happened. 'Oh my goodness, did I forget to pick you up? Hang on, where was Rachel?'

Sara managed to smooth out the confusion whilst Poppy fetched the girls a welcome drink and set about cleaning up Lily's wounds. 'Well, I'm most grateful to you, Sara, for coming to Lily's rescue, so to speak.' Little did she know just how true her words were. 'Would you like to join us for dinner?' Poppy asked. 'Nothing fancy, I'm afraid – just fish fingers, chips, and peas – but you'll be most welcome.'

'Sounds yummy,' Sara responded, hanging up her school satchel and taking a seat at the table, 'I'm starving.'

She slipped her hand under the table, giving Lily's a squeeze of encouragement. She only wished her own home was as welcoming.

* * *

Charlotte felt sick.

She picked up the telephone and then put it down again. *You're being ridiculous!*

Or was she? After all, she'd seen both Dylan and Thomas Davies arrive home over ten minutes ago and still Sara wasn't home. She looked out of the upstairs window again – it gave her the best view – but still she couldn't see her. Charlotte usually watched the school bus arrive from this spot, but as she'd been distracted today she wasn't certain that Sara was even on it.

Where is she?!

She picked up the phone and, pausing, put it down again. *This can't go on.*

She sat down on the edge of the bed and placed her face in her hands. *She probably stopped off to feed that wretched horse again, that's probably where she is.* This made her feel slightly better, but not much. *I'll give her another half an hour, then that's it.*

Her phone burst into life at that moment, ringing loudly and causing her to scream out in surprise before she quickly answered it. 'Hello?'

'Hello Charlotte, it's Poppy. How are you?'

Charlotte's heart sank a little; she'd hoped it was going to be Sara. 'Oh fine... fine thanks. What can I do for you?'

'I was just calling to check if it's okay for Sara to join us for dinner? She came to Lily's rescue earlier – she tripped and fell in netball practice, you know how it is – and they seemed to be getting on so well I thought it would be a nice treat.'

Charlotte closed her eyes, thankful that Sara was safe. 'That's very kind of you,' she replied, 'of course she can. And thanks for letting me know, Poppy. You know what these teenagers are like,' Charlotte added, certain that Sara wouldn't have told her about her change in dinner plans otherwise.

'Yes, I've got that to look forward to,' Poppy replied, laughing slightly. 'I'll make sure Sara gets back by 8 p.m. if that's okay?'

'That's fine, thank you.'

They said their goodbyes, and relieved to learn that her daughter was safe and well, Charlotte made her way downstairs, where she poured herself a very large glass of red wine before sinking onto the nearest sofa – and not for the first time that day either.

CHAPTER NINE

'*Morning Ron, okay to come in?*'

Sadie Alcock looked up from her morning cereal and stared doe-eyed at the giant policeman standing at the back door. Her father mumbled something incoherent and stood aside, allowing their unexpected visitor to enter the property. Sadie had seen the policeman a few times and knew he was friends with her parents.

'*Hello Geoff,*' *greeted her mother Jen as she came bustling in with a basket full of dried washing,* '*cup of tea?*'

'*I need to speak to Ron about last night,*' *came the rather blunt reply.*

Anticipating trouble, Jen placed the basket on the table and pulled out a chair whilst her husband returned to his battered armchair situated in front of the kitchen stove. He lit a cigarette, which caused Jen to sigh disapprovingly, and he threw her a dirty look in return.

'*Would you like to explain what happened, Ron?*' *Geoff asked.*

'Take a seat, Geoff.' Jen indicated the free place at the table, which he gratefully accepted, keeping his focus on Ron at all times who, in turn, was looking down at the floor.

'C'mon Ron,' said Geoff, 'that was one of Councillor Roberts' kids last night and he's kicked off big time – what happened?'

'Nothing!' Ron got up suddenly, causing Geoff to stand up too. 'It's my property for fuck's sake, Geoff! Why should I have to explain myself?'

'Because you threatened to kill someone, didn't you, Ron?'

'Sadie,' Jen said quickly, 'go up to your room, love, and start getting ready for school.' Her mother nudged her towards the hallway door, and after closing it behind her, Sadie fled upstairs.

She knew all about the trouble of the night before because a group of teenagers had turned up at the farm just as she was going to bed and had begun messing about in one of their fields. She'd stood and watched the commotion unfold with her mother at the huge bay window in her bedroom.

They saw her father walk across the yard with the big lamp – the one they always used to check on the cattle at night – and then head out towards the far right field. Of course, there were no late night checks anymore; the land was empty given there was no longer any cattle to care for.

Sadie wasn't sure what had happened next but they'd heard shouting and then her mother had ushered Sadie quickly into bed before drawing the heavy plum-coloured velvet curtains into place and heading back downstairs.

Sensing another row looming, Sadie took her favoured earmuffs from underneath the bed and placed them over her ears. Then, remembering the packet of crisps she'd taken from the larder earlier, she slipped out of bed and rescued them from the bottom drawer. 'Salt and vinegar, my favourite!' Sadie whispered to herself. She loved examining each crisp before *placing it satisfyingly into her mouth, each crunch helping to drown out the noise raging below just a tiny bit more.*

❖ ❖ ❖

Ron Alcock was trying to keep his temper. Reluctantly, he sat down again.

'C'mon, Ron, what happened?' *Geoff pursued, retaking his seat at the table.*

'It was those mouthy little shits off the estate – Mickey, Col, Grant, and... I dunno, but you know who I mean.'

'Mickey? Tall lad, red hair?' *Ron nodded.* 'That's Councillor Roberts' son,' *Geoff confirmed.*

'Whatever, I asked them to leave – nicely,' *he insisted. Jen rolled her eyes in disbelief, causing him to throw her another withering look as he shouted out,* 'I DID!' *He sighed.* 'Look, I heard a commotion, and when I went outside to check I realised there was a bunch of kids in Ryder's field so I went and asked them to move on. I just told 'em, a farm's not the ideal place to be hanging out on a dark, cold night – or any night for that matter.'

'Right, and what happened then?' *Geoff asked. He was taking notes now.*

'Oh, the usual crap, you know. 'Leave us alone, we're not doing anything wrong.' Not a shred of respect for the fact they're on private land.'

'And?'

'Well, they started getting in my face and stuff so I told 'em if they didn't get off my land I'd shoot 'em.'

'Shoot them or kill them?'

'I dunno!' *Ron laughed and threw his hands in the air.* 'Does it matter? Either way they better not come back if they know what's good for 'em.'

Geoff shook his head in dismay. He'd been friends with Ron and Jen Alcock for almost twenty years. 'You can't say that, Ron, not these days – you can't take the law into your own hands. That's threatening behaviour.'

'But it's my land!' Ron roared, causing Jen to stand up anxiously.

'Look, Ron, I know you've had a tough time, mate, but you can't do this. And he's got a witness so I can't ignore it either; I'm going to have to ask you to come down to the station.'

Ron spun around to face Geoff, completely stunned. 'You WHAT?'

'I'm sorry, mate; you've left me no option. Of course, it doesn't help that he's a bloody Councillor's son with a point to prove. I'm going to have to issue you with a caution. Come with me now and I won't have to use the cuffs.'

Ron couldn't believe what he was hearing. He grabbed his coat viciously off the peg on the back of the door and stamped outside into the crisp, cold January morning.

Once he was out of the room Geoff placed a hand comfortingly across Jen's. 'Is everything alright, Jen?' he asked her gently. 'You look awful if you don't mind me saying.'

Jen shook her head. 'It's been hard losing the cows, Geoff – really hard. You know Ron's not a bad man; we're just trying to get back on our feet. It'll pick up once the compensation comes through, I'm sure.'

Geoff nodded knowingly. This was the heart of the farming community and every farm around had all suffered huge losses since the BSE crisis hit. Geoff knew there was a lot of tension in the air and this wasn't the first incident he'd been called to involving one of the farms.

He wasn't sure it would be the last either.

CHAPTER TEN

James Turvey placed his head in his hands in frustration, which went unnoticed, of course, by Rita Denby, who by now was in full swing.

'But he's black, I tell you.' She was referring to Dr Pradeep Chandola who'd just moved into The Haven next door to The Firs, which was where Rita lived with her long-suffering husband, Ralph.

'The new doctor is *not* black, Rita, he's Asian,' James replied, 'and anyway, it shouldn't matter – he's an asset to the practice from what I hear.'

'Well, he's not putting his hands on *my* body, I can tell you that right now!' she huffed disapprovingly, pulling the panels of her blue woollen cardigan closer together across her chest.

'I'm sure he'll be delighted to learn that, Rita,' James replied, clearly getting really irritated now. He'd already met Pradeep and found him to be the perfect gentleman – not that that was the point here. 'You might be interested to know he's more than just a

GP,' he said, trying a different tack, 'he's also a qualified psychotherapist and is offering counselling services too.'

His words, however, fell on deaf ears.

'Goodness knows what they'll be cooking up over there,' Rita replied, ignoring him completely, 'all manner of spicy foods, no doubt – you know what that lot are like. My Ralphie has such a weak constitution, you know; he can only eat bland dishes at the moment.'

'I'm sure your cuisine does it justice too,' James quipped, but she continued ranting on, unperturbed. Ignoring Rita, he returned his attention to the order he was in the middle of packing for Lucy Whittaker. He was aiming to deliver it when his assistant David returned from his morning coffee break with the hope of sharing a spot of lunch with her – if he was lucky.

'... and what's this about Swinford St. George Golf Club?' Rita continued, her words ringing out just as Joy Brooks – another renowned village gossip – entered the store.

'Morning all!' chirped Joy merrily. 'Did I hear you mention the golf club? My Alan says it's already been sold.'

James rolled his eyes discreetly; Alan Brooks considered himself to be something of a guru when it came to golf. Despite the Swinford St. George Hotel being shut for the past year, he'd continued on as an employee, maintaining the golf course until a new buyer was found – and he didn't hesitate to brag about it either.

'That's what I'd heard too,' nodded Rita, 'to some property developer, apparently, who's going to bulldoze the whole lot and turn it all into flats.'

'Well, that's not what my Alan says,' Joy replied, leaning in closer. She was clearly empowered by what she thought was a golden nugget of knowledge that no one else had. 'Keep it to yourself, of course, but it's all being turned into a nursing home.'

'What?' Rita gasped. 'That's terrible! There are far too many care homes around here as it...'

'Morning!' greeted Lizzie Anderson from the doorway, unintentionally interrupting the gathered trio as she reached for a basket on her way in. Being married to the Senior Partner at the Hamptons Medical Practice afforded Lizzie the opportunity to know everyone who lived in the villages, and she was just as popular and well loved as her husband.

'Ah, Lizzie,' began Rita authoritatively, 'we're a bit concerned to hear that Swinford St. George Golf Club is being knocked down. Do you know anything about that?'

Lizzie smiled, knowing full well she wouldn't disclose any such knowledge. 'I didn't even know it was up for sale, to be honest.'

'Well, that can't be true!' sniffed Joy. 'Everyone knows it's been empty for years.'

'Not years, Joy,' corrected Rita smugly, 'it's not been empty for *that* long – surely your Alan would know that.'

Seeing the look on Joy's face, Lizzie quickly cut into the conversation. 'Ladies, you'll have to excuse me, I'm just collecting a few things for a lunch I've organised with a dear friend of mine.' And with that she headed towards the back of the shop, and – much to James' relief – to the deli counter, giving him an excuse to escape the gossips too.

'Sorry about that.' James rolled his eyes again and Lizzie nodded knowingly.

'It's not a problem,' she smiled, 'and clearly they don't have a real clue anyway. Can you put together a selection of cold meats and olives for me, please? Oh, and I'll take a piece of your Cornish brie too; it looks delicious.'

'Fresh in this morning!' James nodded towards the favoured produce and began gathering a nice selection together. 'You going to the dinner tomorrow?' he asked, dropping his voice an octave and winking.

'Oh yes, we can't wait to meet the guest of honour!' She clapped her hands excitedly but quietly, so as not to draw attention.

'I know, and I'm thrilled to have been invited along too.'

'Have you met her before?' Lizzie whispered.

'No, I think she might have popped in here one day, but now I'm not so sure. Anyway, I'm looking forward to it.' He passed Lizzie her produce and returned to the front counter, disappointed to discover Rita and Joy were still moaning on.

'Oh, and another thing, Lizzie,' Rita said, stepping forward into her path as she attempted to approach the cash desk, 'I hear your new GP has got the village rattled.'

Lizzie stepped back in surprise. 'Pradeep, you mean?' Rita nodded. 'Oh, why? He's so lovely, Rita, and such a gentleman, trust me. Actually, you'll see for yourself at the dinner tomorrow night.'

James silently slapped his forehead.

'Dinner? *What* dinner?' Rita was almost shrieking now, causing Lizzie to wish she'd driven over to Swinford St. George and purchased lunch from the food hall at the Hambly-Jones department store instead. 'I've not received an invitation to any dinner –and I'm invited to *everything!* Who is it? *Whose* dinner? Poppy? Ah, Poppy and Richard, *of course*, such dear friends of mine and Ralphie's.' She hurriedly picked up her shopping bag. 'Must go everyone, see you tomorrow!' And with that she flounced out of the door like a woman on a mission.

Sheepishly, Lizzie paid for her shopping – trying her best not to catch James' eye – and after thanking him she went on her way too, making a slight detour to Hampton Manor House along the way.

* * *

'Great work, Francine!' Richard enthused. 'This is going to be the best collection yet.'

Francine smiled, basking in the rarity of Richard's praise. She'd just shown him the final samples she'd selected for the Hambly-Jones exclusive *Magnifique Madame* winter range and it was clear that he was genuinely pleased with her choices.

Finally! It had been a rough few weeks getting settled into her new role as Senior Buyer for the Hambly-Jones Department Store and Richard was a hard nut to crack. She wasn't certain she'd quite earned his trust and respect just yet – but things were definitely going in the right direction.

'I selected some dates for the launch too,' she added, wanting to make the most of his attention while she actually had it. 'I thought we could hold it here, right in the heart of the lingerie department. We could begin with a drinks reception for gold card customers only, then invite our other members to join in a while later on for the fashion show. What do you think?'

'Hmmm...' Richard pondered this for a moment. 'I think it'll be a lot of work... *but* we could open up the tills afterwards, catching people whilst they're hopefully still gushing with enthusiasm. You'll have to ensure we've got plenty of stock.'

'Of course; I had the same thoughts too,' Francine agreed.

'And plenty of gift boxes – our customers like big, shiny, glamorous packaging with lots of colourful tissue paper and ribbons – *lots* of ribbons.'

'Not a problem,' Francine replied, smiling. 'So, can I get the go ahead then, if you're happy?'

'Absolutely,' he exclaimed, leaning over and signing the purchase order she'd placed on the desk in front of him. 'This is a real measure of achievement for your work,' he continued. 'I like the edgy, contemporary feel to the range and I hope our clients do too; great job.'

By this point Francine was practically glowing inside, but despite this she still managed to maintain a professional stance. Taking her smart phone from her pocket, she loaded up the diary. 'Now, let's talk dates,' she said, flipping across several screens while Richard eyed her cautiously.

'You need to liaise with Margaret for that.'

Francine paused and, placing her phone back in her jacket pocket, began to gather her papers together. 'Of course,' she trilled lightly, completely masking her true feelings. She'd no intention of undoing all her good work over the past few weeks. 'It's been great to catch up with you. See you tomorrow.'

Once Francine had left, Richard studied the back of the door for a few moments, frowning. He wasn't sure if the uneasy feeling he was experiencing was because he was allowing someone new into the key areas of the family business or if it was due to something else entirely.

Deciding he was perhaps being too harsh, he pushed his uneasiness aside and reached for the phone to call Poppy. He'd really missed her, and he knew she had her hands full organising tomorrow's dinner, but that was one of the many things he loved about his amazing wife – she took everything in her stride and she never complained about anything.

'Hello, gorgeous!' he greeted Poppy warmly when she answered his call.

'Darling! This is a nice surprise – are you on your way home?'

'I am, and I've rearranged tomorrow's appointments too so I can be home to help out with the dinner.'

'Really? Oh, that's brilliant, Richard, thank you!' she exclaimed, delighted. 'It's going to be such a great night. Anyway, hurry back – I can't wait to show you what we've done so far; Billy's been really creative.'

Richard loved how passionate Poppy was about everything – and every*one*. It wasn't that long ago he'd had grave doubts about Billy Franklin, a waif and stray taken in by Reverend Fisher and his wife, Cathy. But now Billy was a permanent member of the

Hambly-Jones team, so to speak, and a valuable one to boot. *If I was wrong about Billy, maybe I'm wrong about Francine too.*

They said their goodbyes and Richard gathered his things together, slipping in a few of the *Magnifique Madame* winter collection samples for good measure.

* * *

'Aye, aye!' teased Sergeant Phil Harris as PC Laura Benjamin arrived for the afternoon shift, 'Finally come up for air, have you?'

'Well, someone's got to keep you in line, Serge,' Laura quipped, blushing. She'd had to rush to get to the station, literally post-coital, and was still trying to catch her breath.

She made her way to the female locker room — thankful that none of her colleagues appeared to have arrived yet — and began changing into her uniform, trying to settle the lustful butterflies that were still fluttering around her stomach. *I think he's the one!*

She smiled to herself as she buttoned up her white shirt, eager for the shift to be over so she could see him again. This reminded her that they hadn't actually fixed up their next date as yet, so she quickly took her smart phone from her locker and texted him a message before tucking it safely away again. Police officers weren't allowed to use their own phones whilst on duty so she'd have to wait until later to see his reply.

Slipping on her police issue shoes, she collected her hat and went off to join afternoon *roll call*, bouncing with each step she took along the way.

***

'Cathy!' Poppy embraced Cathy Fisher warmly before helping her inside. Cathy and Reverend Fisher were part of their close group of friends and she'd kindly offered to make a couple of her special trifles for the dinner tomorrow night. 'These look absolutely *divine* as usual, thank you so much!' Poppy exclaimed before leading Cathy through to the kitchen and placing her offerings carefully down on the kitchen table.

'You're most welcome!' Cathy gushed. 'We're both excited for tomorrow, although I'm not sure trifle is the best dessert, under the circumstances,' she laughed.

'Oh, I'm sure she likes a sweet treat just like us all, Cathy!' Poppy leaned in closer. 'I do hope you've added a little something,' she said, winking cheekily – something that caused Cathy to shriek with laughter.

'Absolutely – what's a trifle without sherry? – only I must warn you: I think Peter came in whilst I went to fetch the jelly and added a bit extra in as well.'

Poppy started laughing just as the front door bell went, and after going to answer the door she returned with a rather harassed-looking Lizzie Anderson.

'Everything alright, Lizzie?' Cathy asked, concerned, as she embraced their friend.

'Oh, I just think I've put my foot in it as usual!' she sighed, sitting down in the offered seat at the table. Poppy began making coffee whilst Lizzie relayed her earlier exchange at the Hampton Stores with Rita Denby, and a few minutes later Poppy placed a hand soothingly on her friend's shoulder as she handed her a much-welcomed cup. 'The thing is,' Lizzie ranted, 'I've got Charlotte coming for lunch today and I'm supposed to be supporting her – at this rate, she's going to be leaving feeling even more stressed than before.'

'Don't worry about Rita Denby,' Poppy assured her, 'I can't fit in another person anyway, let alone two; we're bordering on another Autumn ball as it is.' Lizzie smiled up at her friend with relief. 'I'll ask Anthony to find her something to do for our stall at the Cotswolds County competition later in the year; that will keep her busy.'

'Great idea,' agreed Cathy, 'but tell me, Lizzie, why do you need to support Charlotte? I hope she's not ill?'

The two of them focused on Lizzie, who blushed and rolled her eyes.

'Here I go again!' she exclaimed, reprimanding herself. 'I'm not supposed to say anything… it's just that Jonathan's been into the surgery and he's pretty worried about her. She's really not been herself since all this business with Tiggy Lawrence and Aster Maxwell.'

'Well, that's understandable,' Cathy empathised. 'It was a huge shock to us all – certainly, Peter's had several visits from concerned villagers – but I didn't realise it had affected Charlotte.'

'Me neither,' Poppy replied. 'Anyway, they're both coming to the dinner tomorrow and she always seems to enjoy herself at these events – as you know – so hopefully that will give her a welcome boost.'

'Hmmm,' said Lizzie, nodding, 'she does usually… but she didn't exactly seem quite herself when I last spoke to her, although she was certainly pleased to receive my invitation. Which reminds me,' she drained the last drop of coffee from her cup and stood up, 'I must get on or I'll be late for our lunch. Thanks ever so much.' She went over and embraced her friends. 'You always make me feel better. See you both tomorrow.'

'Keep us updated about Charlotte!' Poppy called after Lizzie as she let herself out of the front door. 'Right,' she added, smiling across at Cathy, 'let's get these trifles in the chiller and then perhaps we can go and visit Anthony – see if between us we can rustle up something to keep Rita Denby happy.'

* * *

'Ah, Margaret, I'm glad I caught you.'

'Mr. Hambly-Jones has left for the day, I'm afraid,' Margaret informed Francine, a tad bristly.

'It's you I was after, actually – and Richard's diary,' Francine replied, her attempt at light-heartedness falling flat with Margaret, as usual. She might be winning over Richard somewhat, but she'd need to work much harder on his PA. 'I'm just looking to check his availability for the winter fashion show.'

Margaret – who was renowned for her hatred of modern technology – flipped open a large desk diary and began turning the pages, but not before Francine caught sight of the next day's event.

'Sorry, but I couldn't help noticing the dinner you've got down for tomorrow there, Margaret. Is this something I should be involved in? I am the Senior Buyer, after all.'

Although Margaret looked thunderous Francine was oblivious to it, her thoughts elsewhere.

'This is a private family dinner that *I've* been invited to,' Margaret answered pointedly.

'Oh? Is this a Hambly-Jones event? Perhaps I've been overlooked – just give me the details and I can be there.'

Margaret, however, was having none of it. 'As I just said, this is a *private* family dinner, and if your presence was required you would have been notified. Now, if you'll excuse me,' Margaret stood up, unamused, shutting the diary in the process, 'I need to be somewhere; you'll just have to wait until tomorrow to check your dates.'

With that, she began locking things away in her desk drawer, leaving Francine with no choice other than to return to her own office empty-handed.

Once inside, Francine angrily kicked the door shut behind her before kicking the grey metal rubbish bin sitting to the side of the glorious oak desk that took up most of the room. The bin fell to one side, spilling the contents out onto the ruby-coloured deep pile carpet.

Fuck, fuck, FUCK! Things weren't going at all as she'd planned. Pissing Margaret off had been a big mistake; she'd need to get her back on board fast.

After placing her files down on the desk Francine began pacing the floor, tapping the side of her head with her forefinger as if the very action would somehow manifest the answers she was so desperate for.

Frustrated, she returned to her desk and began reorganising the paperwork she'd just been through with Richard. Whatever happened, she needed to get the order for the new collection sent off as soon as possible; they were working to a tight schedule as it was.

She unearthed the purchase order and then... *bingo!* Richard had forgotten to sign off the official order. Purchase order or not, this particular supplier was well known for its meticulousness. No completed paperwork – no deal.

With Richard well on his way home, she now had the perfect excuse to give him a little visit – one way or another she'd be at that family dinner.

* * *

Diana Fortune checked her appearance in the full-length Edwardian mahogany mirror that matched the rest of her bedroom furniture. Despite the heavy troubles that had prevailed over the past year, she was looking healthy again. At one point, her weight had dropped to just under 8 stone, and at only 5 feet 6 inches tall, she'd looked almost skeletal.

Thankfully, she was at a much healthier weight now and her face had filled out again. She certainly looked – and felt – much younger than her 72 years, and she had her new house guest to thank for that. Camilla Barrington-Smythe was a breath of fresh air and her bubbly personality and easy-going manner had certainly chased any remaining gloom away from The Boathouse.

Diana selected a white clutch bag from her dressing room to complement the black chiffon polka dot maxi dress she'd chosen to wear for the evening. She'd reserved a table at *l'angle* – a popular bistro in Swinford St. George – for a welcome dinner, and it was going to be just the two of them. After all, Camilla would be meeting everyone else at the Hambly-Joneses the following night.

'Ready?' Camilla popped her head around Diana's bedroom door, which was ajar. 'Oh, you look lovely in that dress, Diana – it really suits you.'

Diana blushed, not used to receiving such compliments. 'Thank you, Camilla, and likewise.' She nodded towards Camilla's own attire – a pale blue *skater* type dress – which fitted her enviable figure perfectly. 'Right, shall we go?'

They headed downstairs and made their way outside, where they both got into Camilla's red *Fiat 500*. Diana had offered to pay for a taxi so they could share a bottle of wine, but Camilla had preferred to keep a clear head in anticipation of the next day's exciting event.

Victor, the maître d' of *l'angle,* welcomed them eagerly before ushering them inside. His restaurant regularly hosted local celebrities and – with Diana Fortune being one of the most popular right now – he'd ensured to reserve them his best table.

Once seated, he handed them both a menu and the wine list whilst one of the waiters delivered some hot artisan breads together with an olive oil and balsamic dip, which Camilla enthusiastically helped herself to.

'Oh, this is such good balsamic vinegar,' she exclaimed, breaking off small pieces of the malted bread and dipping it into the unctuous oil as she decided what to order. 'I'm really feeling the bread tonight so I think I'll start with the pâté.' She nodded at the maître d', and Victor – who'd been hovering nearby – approached their table, ready to take their order.

'I think I'll start with the soup please, Victor,' said Diana, 'followed by the salmon fillet – but could you change the ratatouille side for new potatoes, please?'

'Certainly, Madame,' Victor nodded, 'and for Mademoiselle?'

'The pâté for starters, then I'll have the salmon too, please.'

'Can you also bring a jug of water, please? We don't fancy wine tonight,' Diana joked, receiving a warm smile in return.

Victor removed their menus and made his way to the kitchen with their order.

'So,' Diana clasped her hands together, bringing them up in front of her face as she rested her elbows on the table, 'how did your date with the Hamptons' most eligible bachelor go?' Her fingernails were painted almost exactly the same shade of red as her lipstick, which momentarily distracted Camilla.

'Oh, do you mean Matt? He's certainly easy on the eye, isn't he? And a bachelor, you say, at his age – I assumed he must've been divorced or something.'

Diana paused, rather surprised at how quickly Camilla appeared to draw conclusions about him. 'Well,' she replied after a moment, 'I suppose it's fair to say that he *has* been married – to his career, that is. He joined the force as a young PC, you know, and has done extremely well for himself. He's actually only 46 and trying to make Inspector this year; I wouldn't be at all surprised if he gets it too.'

'Yes, he told me about that last night; his earlier exam seemed to go well, which is promising.'

'Oh, that is good to hear.' Diana smiled. 'Actually, you might be interested to know that Poppy Hambly-

Jones dated Matt for a while; I believe he was quite fond of her too.'

'Poppy? The one who's hosting the party tomorrow night?'

Diana nodded. 'Yes, that's right. Poppy and her husband Richard are a wonderful couple – you're going to love them. They both do an awful lot for the community, and not just here in the Hamptons but much further afield too.'

Camilla raised her eyebrows but didn't comment further. She'd heard a lot about Poppy in the short time she'd been in the Hamptons and she just couldn't wait to see if she was as *amazing* as everyone claimed she was.

'So, are you seeing him again, then?' Diana probed, hopeful.

'Oh yes,' said Camilla. 'Of course, I'll see him tomorrow at the dinner anyhow, and we'll no doubt hook up again after that.'

As Diana sank back, deflated, into her seat, Camilla fished her smart phone out of her bag and began flicking distractedly through the screens until Victor appeared a short time later with their first course.

'I'm excited for the first *Fortunettes* rehearsal, Camilla,' Diana said in between mouthfuls of her starter, 'have you had any ideas yet about the music?'

'I have,' Camilla enthused between bites of the delicious pâté, which was served with thinly toasted slices of the artisan bread she'd enjoyed earlier, 'a close friend of mine, Daz Rice – who's a brilliant musician and singer, by the way – has been working on releasing his debut album. It's a mix of Americana meets Country and there's a song on it that would be perfect for the competition. He's kindly given his permission for us to use it. I'll play it for you tomorrow and you can tell me what you think.'

Diana smiled. 'Really? That does sound exciting, and hopefully it'll give your friend some free publicity too – it's a wonderful opportunity to support a local artist.'

'Exactly, and we could ask him to come along to do a gig or something – I think it would go down really well here.'

They continued to enthusiastically exchange ideas for the rest of the evening whilst enjoying the finest cuisine *l'angle* had to offer – with Victor on hand close by to attend to their every need.

They'd just finished coffee when Camilla leaned in closer to discreetly whisper to Diana, 'I think that chap over there's recognised me,' before sitting back and relishing the attention. 'To be honest, I don't mind as long as they don't follow me. Do you think I should go and offer him an autograph?'

Diana pursed her lips, bowing her head slightly to hide her amusement. Whilst Camilla was indeed a highly successful actor, Lydia Cooper – the character she played in *Northern Rights* – couldn't look more different, as Diana had discovered when she'd first researched Camilla. The Lydia Cooper most people knew was a washed-out, ex-drug addict with pale, mottled skin and long, black straggly hair who bore a thick northern accent – a complete contrast to the well-groomed, elegant lady seated before her. However, Diana chose not to comment further. She wasn't one to court attention herself, despite knowing full well she was the reason they'd been given the best table – and the utmost attention – in the restaurant.

She also knew how high maintenance actors could be, and her thoughts returned to Matt again. *I sincerely hope he doesn't get hurt.* It was well known that he'd never really got over his relationship with Poppy, and although he deserved to move on, Diana didn't believe Camilla was the one for him.

At the end of the day, she's only here for a few months – she'll be gone before we know it.

However, it was what Camilla might get up to in that short space of time that began to raise concerns for Diana.

CHAPTER ELEVEN

Ron Alcock poured himself another large whiskey whilst his wife Jen put their daughter Sadie to bed. He was sitting in his usual chair in front of the roaring log fire.

Slowly, he took a gulp of the smooth amber liquid, enjoying the sweetness as the bitter warmth washed over his tongue while he stared sadly into the flickering flames. 'Poor Sadie.' Ron loved his daughter deeply and he hated that he was unable to properly provide for her and Jen anymore.

As he brought his fist down angrily against the arm of the chair Jen returned to the kitchen, immediately rolling her eyes at her husband.

'Drinking that's not going to make things any better,' she snapped as she began clearing away the dinner plates. She was getting sick and tired of this scenario — it was always the same thing, night after night. 'I don't know how we can afford to pay for all the bottles of that stuff you're getting through either.'

Ron tapped his fingers impatiently on the arm of the chair. He really didn't want another argument with Jen but she was clearly pushing for one. 'Don't start.' He flashed her a warning *look. He was in no mood for this. 'And, just so we're clear. it's 'me' who affords it, not you – you need to remember that.'*

'Oh, here we go!' She slammed down the tea cloth she'd just wiped her hands on and lunged across the kitchen towards him, poking the air angrily with her finger. 'It's all about you, isn't it, Ron? It's always all about you! Your farm, your house, your money – I've done more than my fair share over the years, you know; I'm entitled to every penny, just as much as you are.'

'BUT THERE ARE NO MORE PENNIES!' Ron screamed, suddenly jumping up out of his chair. His face was bright red and he was shaking with rage, clenching his fists angrily.

Jen placed a hand against her chest, having been caught off guard, and began to back up. She'd never seen Ron more furious than at that moment.

'Why don't you just give it a rest, woman!' he raged. 'I've enough on my plate without your constant nagging, so just back off, Jen – leave me be!'

She swallowed nervously, unable to remember a time when he'd raised his voice to her quite like that. Slowly, she retraced her steps back to the sink and began washing the dishes, her eyes moving left to right as all manner of thoughts raced through her mind. Mostly – as usual – her thoughts were about money. The compensation they'd been promised still hadn't materialised and funds were running low. Jen shook her head, recalling how different things had been just a year or so ago.

The farm had been doing really well and they'd been excited by their decision to invest some of the profits into having a state-of-the-art milking parlour installed, something that quickly proved its worth. Jen had even begun looking into the possibility of making their own cheese with a view to selling it at the local farmers' markets. They used to look forward to their evenings together, which were spent excitedly discussing their ideas to grow the farm further and renovate the tired-looking farmhouse and outbuildings — so much so that they were completely blindsided when the BSE crisis hit. Of course, it was all made worse by the fact they weren't at their best financially, and certainly, no one was interested in buying a dairy farm with no cattle.

Jen sneaked a sideways glance at Ron as he poured himself another drink, and after finishing up the dishes she took herself quietly off to bed, imbued with feelings of hopelessness and despair.

She wasn't sure what woke her up first — the music or the shouting.

Whatever it had been, Jen's eyes danced in the darkness as she tried to focus on the commotion unfolding outside.

Throwing back the heavy covers — still warm from her deep slumber — she sat up groggily, straining to make sense of what was going on. When she heard the gunshot her blood ran cold.

Suddenly, it seemed that all hell had broken loose.

There was screaming and shouting and she clambered desperately for her dressing gown and slippers. Settling for just the gown, she raced down the stairs and out through the back door, into the yard. The earth was freezing beneath her bare feet but she hardly noticed. She could just make out some figures running towards her from the direction of Ryder's field — they were screaming and shouting but it was difficult to hear them clearly with all the commotion that was going on behind them, causing her to think she'd heard another shot ring out.

'We need help!' one of them shouted. 'Our friend's been shot — there's blood everywhere!'

Jen steeled herself, trying to calm the young man down whilst his friends caught up — they were frantic.

'We need an ambulance,' one of them yelled. 'Quick! He's been badly injured!'

Jen panicked, wondering where Ron was, but with no time to spare she rushed back inside the house and called an ambulance before following the others back to the injured boy. It seemed that the teenagers from the other night had returned and this time they'd brought quite the party along with them. The far corner of Ryder's field was lit up with a multitude of torches and lamps and there were bottles and cans littered everywhere.

Far from the chaotic rave that appeared to have been going on earlier, however, a very sombre group was now huddled around a figure lying on the ground.

Jen could tell he was dead even before she reached him, such were the injuries to his head, suggesting he'd been shot at close range.

Trembling, she put a hand to her mouth, knowing there was nothing more she could do for him.

CHAPTER TWELVE

The phone rang just as Lucy Whittaker began searching for the house keys in her handbag and she tutted, annoyed at the distraction.

She was trying to get on her way to the Hamptons Hair and Beauty salon; James Turvey had invited her to accompany him as his guest at the Hambly-Joneses' dinner that evening and by all accounts it was going to be quite the event, so she'd booked herself an emergency hair appointment.

She snapped up the receiver, silently praying it would be a quick call, then relaxed with delight at hearing her son's voice. 'Ian! I wasn't expecting to hear from you today. Is everything alright? I'm just on my way to have my hair done, actually; I've been invited to a special dinner tonight,' she breezed merrily.

'A *special* dinner, eh? Sounds intriguing, Mother. What's all that about then?'

'James has asked me to accompany him to the Hambly-Joneses tonight as they're hosting a dinner for someone famous, apparently.'

'The Hambly-Joneses?' came Ian's reply. 'You do know they're famous in their own right, Mother?'

'Yes, yes of course I do – I've known Anthony Sullivan for years – but I haven't seen him since he remarried so I'm really looking forward to catching up with him.'

'Who is this James anyway?' Ian asked. Lucy could hear the irritation in his voice.

'James Turvey, the owner of the Hampton Stores – I told you about him. We've been out a couple of times already.' She smiled to herself; *I'm quite keen on him too.*

'A shopkeeper? Are you kidding me?' Ian questioned, grunting down the phone in disgust, 'And what sort of name is *Turvey*, anyway? Sounds a bit pervy to me, Mother,' he mocked.

'Honestly, Ian,' replied Lucy, exasperated. 'There's no need to be so rude, you know, and let me tell you – there's absolutely nothing wrong with being a shopkeeper. What are you ringing for anyway?' Lucy was beginning to feel quite rattled; whenever she got enthusiastic about anything Ian always seemed to find some way to put a dampener on it.

'I thought you might like to know that I'm coming home for the Easter holidays,' he retorted, equally rattled.

His words nevertheless lifted her spirits. 'Really? Oh, that's wonderful news, Ian! I can't wait to see you, and you'll be able to meet James too.'

'Hmmm,' he replied, clearly annoyed, 'well, we'll see about that. Anyway, just be careful tonight – I presume you've got some form of contraception?'

Lucy almost gagged at hearing this. 'For God's sake, Ian! What sort of woman do you think I am?'

'Just saying – after all, that's how I came along, remember?'

Lucy felt her cheeks burn. They'd never discussed this before, but it seemed Ian was more bothered about his parentage than she'd previously realised. She floundered for a moment, not quite knowing what to say. 'Uh... well, I-I'd better get on then, Ian, or I'll be late,' she stammered. 'Enjoy the weekend, darling – I'm really looking forward to seeing you.'

'Okay, Mother,' he responded, a tad patronisingly; she could sense the satisfied smirk on his face – could picture it too. 'See you in a few weeks then.' And he was gone.

Lucy held the telephone against her chin for a few moments afterwards, concerned that she hadn't handled their conversation very well. They'd had many long discussions over the years about Ian's father – certainly Lucy had never been secretive or ashamed of her liaison with Raoul De'ath; far from it – however, this was the first time Ian had ever referred to the situation himself, and Lucy wondered if there was more to it. After all, he was well aware that she'd enjoyed plenty of dates over the years, and it hadn't seemed to bother him before. Certainly, it had been her choice not to become too involved with anyone – Ian was her first priority, her work second. She didn't have room for anything else at the time. But now things were different; now she wanted more.

Perhaps he feels threatened. I'll call him back later today or tomorrow – I could suggest picking him up from University to save him getting the train. These thoughts buoyed her slightly and she replaced the phone in its charger before gathering her things together, focussing on the day – and evening – ahead.

She felt that after today her life was going to be very different – and she really hoped James would become a part of that life too.

* * *

Francine Dubois checked her appearance in the rear-view mirror, adding just a touch more pink lipstick; the shade complemented her flame red hair perfectly. She also couldn't resist turning her head left and then right again, relishing the swish of the sleek new bob haircut she'd had styled that morning at the exclusive *Marco Francesco* Italian hair stylists based in Swinford St. George – *and it was worth every penny too.*

After checking for flecks of stray mascara and eyeliner, she stepped out of the car and smoothed down the skirt of her black cocktail dress. She was completely overdressed for that time of day, of course, but she was envisaging that once Richard set eyes on her, he'd be gushing to include her on this evening's guest list.

After retrieving the documents from the back of her car – the ones she was hoping would assist her in her quest – Francine made her way towards Hampton Manor House, soaking up the scenery as she took one graceful step after another.

* * *

'Poppy!' her father Percy called out as he answered the front door of Hampton Manor House for what seemed like the umpteenth time that morning, 'Where do you want these flowers?'

His wife Rosie came bustling in from the kitchen. 'I'll deal with this, Percy love, why don't you go and make us all a nice cup of tea?'

Not needing to be asked twice, he made his way back to the kitchen with relief, and whilst he filled the kettle he couldn't help smiling as he listened to Rosie animatedly chatting with the delivery lady. She was so friendly and welcoming, and hearing her like this always reminded him of the first time they met.

It was several years after his first wife – and Poppy's mother – Grace had unexpectedly died. With Poppy no longer living at home then, the huge three-bedroomed property he owned in King's Oak suddenly seemed so vast and he was struggling to manage it. Then, after seeing an advert in the Midford County Gazette, Poppy had gone with him to visit a new housing development on the edge of Swinford St. George to take a look at a new retirement village that was being built there. Rosie was working for the developers at the time and whilst they'd hit it off straight away, it took a while longer for their friendship to develop. After all, Grace had been the love of Percy's life; no one could hold a candle to her. She'd been an excellent wife, mother, sister, and friend, and was sorely missed by everyone.

Over the years, as his and Rosie's friendship developed, he was taken aback by the depth of feelings he felt growing for her. It wasn't the same love he and Grace had shared, and it was this that allowed him to pursue his feelings further, being mindful of Poppy's feelings too. She'd lost her mother at a very young age and had gone on to experience more tragedy of her own. As his only child, his first thought was always for her.

He couldn't have been happier, therefore, when Poppy welcomed Rosie into their life, and over the years they'd grown extremely close. When Poppy married Richard, Rosie was there to support her, not as a replacement mother but as a much beloved and dear friend.

'You making tea, Dad?' The sound of Poppy's voice brought Percy out of his reminiscing and he turned his attention back to the job in hand. It was panic stations as usual at *Chez* Hambly-Jones – and they all loved it! There was a buzz of excitement in the air already with everyone anticipating how the guest of honour would be received that evening, amazed they'd managed to keep it under wraps thus far.

'Here you are, love,' Percy said, handing his daughter a steaming mug of tea and pushing a place of biscuits towards her, 'take a couple of these too. You've been running around all morning and I've not seen you eat yet.'

'Thanks, Dad,' Poppy said, smiling as she picked up a biscuit.

'I've taken the flower arrangements through to the dining room, Poppy – you're going to be really pleased when you see them, love,' Rosie said as she came into the kitchen and joined them at the table, gratefully accepting a mug of tea too. 'Beautiful pinks, purples, and the most gorgeous dahlias – huge they are.'

'That's perfect, Rosie, and just what I wanted. I'll go and take a look when I've finished my tea.' Poppy glanced at her watch. 'Has the chef arrived yet?'

As it wasn't unusual for Poppy and Richard to be hosting a special dinner or a gathering for one of the many charity events they supported, they'd therefore installed a full working kitchen in the basement of Hampton Manor House to cater for such occasions. Previously, they'd hired staff from the Swinford St. George Hotel and Golf Club before it closed down, and more recently, Piers and Marcus from the Maide of Honour had provided excellent cuisine for several of their parties. Sadly, though, they could only cater for numbers of up to fifteen and so recently Poppy had begun using a prestigious agency based in Chipping Melbury to supply staff. This had worked out fine so far, but as they never seemed to get the same person twice, she never knew what to expect.

'Yes, about an hour ago,' Rosie replied, 'and I took him straight down to the kitchen.' She looked across at Poppy, concerned. 'Strange-looking bloke, though – and a bit young too in my opinion. There was no one else with him either.'

'Oh?' Poppy asked, eyebrows raised. 'Perhaps they're on the way. I'll go and check in with him first then. Did the butcher call, Dad?'

'Yes, love,' replied Percy, 'and I got him to put everything in the chiller just like you told me. *And* Brenda's been – picked the veg fresh herself this morning, she told me – so that's all ready downstairs too.'

Poppy smiled fondly; her father knew her too well.

They all focussed their attention towards the door then as Richard came striding in – quite unexpectedly

– with a huge roll of carpet on his shoulder. Despite his muscular frame he was sweating from the exertion and the fringe of his dark hair – which clearly needed a trim – had fallen forward into his eyes.

'What on earth have you got there?' Poppy stood up and went to pour him a cup of tea whilst glancing curiously in his direction as he proceeded to slip the heavy load from his shoulder. He cut the string around it, which then released the most vibrant red floor covering they'd ever seen.

'It's for tonight,' he grinned, 'for our special guest – I thought we could roll out the red carpet for her.'

They fell about laughing at his artfulness.

'Oh, she'll love that,' enthused Poppy. 'It's a good touch, actually – well done!'

'Thanks, I think she'll appreciate the humour behind it for sure.'

They were interrupted then by the front door bell.

'Here we go again!' Percy made to get up but Richard intervened. 'You stay where you are; I'm closer.'

* * *

'Where are you going, Sara?' Charlotte Palmer-Reid called out from the kitchen, her eye having caught the front door opening. She noted Sara's shoulders droop sadly, followed by a long sigh of frustration. She was wearing slim-fitting blue jeans complemented by a fuchsia pink short-sleeved t-shirt. Her honey blonde hair was swept back into a ponytail and even though she didn't have a shred of make-up on, she looked older than her 14 years.

She turned her head at an angle – just enough so she could see her mother, while still keeping her body halfway out of the doorway.

'Lily's!' she cried. 'Poppy asked if I could spend some time with her and Roderick today whilst they get organised for tonight's dinner – *remember?*'

Charlotte felt a pang of hurt – she hadn't remembered at all. 'That's fine, Sara, and what time will you be bringing them back here?'

Sara turned further towards her mother, glaring at her. 'Honestly, Mummy! We went through all this last night – at 4 p.m. I'll bring Lily and Roderick back here, then Dylan's coming over with Tom and Anna-Maria. Mrs Anderson will be bringing over her daughters just before 7 p.m. and Sam said he'll come over early evening.'

'What about the Fitzgeralds?'

Sara rolled her eyes. 'Sorry, I forgot about them. Mrs Fitzgerald said that Aaron's old enough to bring Jemima over with him and that'll be around 7 p.m. too.'

Charlotte smiled as she took all this in. 'Alright, darling. See you later.'

Sara walked out of the house and closed the door behind her, thankful to be outside in the fresh air. She was actually looking forward to the day ahead. Usually, whenever there was a party or a dinner going on, most people hired a babysitter for the evening, but that didn't seem appropriate anymore now that most of the village children were teenagers. So, they'd arranged for Sara to look after several of their neighbours' children – whose parents were also attending the dinner – supported by Dylan, Rachel Davis' oldest son, and Sam Madison. His parents weren't going to the dinner, but he was part of their friendship circle and Charlotte quite liked him. He was a polite young man – if a little rough around the edges – but nevertheless a good influence on Sara, who seemed to enjoy his company too.

'Hello, darling!' Charlotte greeted her husband whilst she continued preparing them a light lunch. 'Did you get the car sorted?'

Jonathan kissed her affectionately before going to wash his hands in the kitchen sink.

'I wish you'd use the downstairs bathroom,' she complained, missing the hurt look that crossed his face at her words.

'It's just hand washing, Charlotte. I like being near you; the bathroom's right down the hallway.' He tore off a few sheets from a nearby kitchen roll – not feeling brave enough to try and wrestle away the tea cloth nestled on the kitchen surface nearby – then sat down at the kitchen table. He was pleased to see she'd already set out cutlery and napkins and hoped this was a sign that she was feeling better. He knew she'd been to lunch with Lizzie Anderson but as she hadn't actually mentioned it to him herself just yet, he was reluctant to bring it up. The last thing he wanted was for her to think he was spying on her.

'Here are we.' She turned around, smiling, and handed him a plate whilst placing her own opposite him.

'This looks lovely, Charlotte.' He smiled and reached for her hand as she sat down to join him at the table.

'It's just a ham salad.' She reached for a bottle of wine and went to pour him a glass.

'Not for me thanks, darling,' he said, causing her to raise an eyebrow in surprise. 'I want to keep a bit of a clear head for tonight.' He smiled sheepishly, knowing it wouldn't wash with her.

'Oh, because we rarely over indulge at such events,' she commented drily before taking a large gulp of white wine from her own glass.

He hesitated for a brief moment, trying to summon up the words he'd been rehearsing over and over since his meeting with Dr Anderson. 'To be honest,' he blurted out, 'I've been struggling in Court recently – some of these new cases, you know how it is. I really have to be certain that I'm completely crystal clear about every tiny detail when I'm representing a client.' He paused. 'I've noticed that when I've not had any alcohol the night before, my thinking process is much sharper.' Relieved to have finally spoken out, he looked up to meet her gaze. He could see, however, that she still wasn't convinced.

'Really, Jonathan? I thought you lot went out most days for long, boozy lunches – indeed, isn't that where some of your best work is done?'

'Things are different these days, Charlotte,' Jonathan sighed. 'Boozy lunches are very much frowned upon; you really have to be on your game. I'm not as young as I used to be, either, and there's plenty of new blood coming through – the competition is strong.'

She surprised him then by nodding in understanding. 'Yes, I suppose I do get it when you put it like that – to be honest, I think we could both do with cutting back a bit more.' Placing her cutlery down onto her plate she looked up at him despondently, sucking in her bottom lip. 'Actually,

Jonathan…' she paused, clearly struggling to find the right words, 'I've found myself enjoying one or two glasses of wine most lunchtimes myself recently.' She hesitated, and then, quite unexpectedly, she began to cry.

As huge sobs racked through her tiny frame Jonathan went to scoop her up in his arms, holding her tightly against him. He stroked her hair, desperate to comfort her. 'It's okay, darling, I've got you,' he murmured.

The lunch now abandoned, he knew this was an opening from which they could not turn back.

Slowly, and with some difficulty, she started to reveal how she'd been consoling herself more and more each day with an extra glass of wine, then two – and then more.

Jonathan listened, saddened that he hadn't appreciated just how much she was struggling, and disheartened that they hadn't felt able to open up to each other much earlier. He knew how upset she'd been after the ghastly events of last year – but he hadn't truly appreciated just how deeply affected she clearly was.

Of course, he now had his own health issues that needed addressing, but he was glad then not to have burdened her further with them. He certainly wasn't going to miss making the most of this opportunity now, though, to help sort out her own troubles.

'It's alright, Charlotte,' he whispered, turning her face so she was looking into his. 'I love you, darling, more than anything – you know that – and we can get through this. We *will* get through this. I promise.' He gathered up her hands comfortingly. He knew they both had huge hurdles to jump over, and despite his previous concerns, he now believed there was every chance of overcoming these too – together.

* * *

'Hello, you must be Gavin,' Poppy greeted the guest chef brightly. 'I'm Poppy, the host for the evening.' She tried to keep the concern out of her voice as she took in his appearance, preferring to give him the benefit of the doubt. *First impressions aren't always what they may appear to be.* He looked about 18 – although she sensed he was probably in his early 20s at least – and he also looked as though he could do with a good meal inside him. He certainly didn't look like he could cook four courses for 34 guests. His chef whites were already heavily stained with a mosaic of colours and his trousers and trainers had seen much better days. *Hardly in keeping with the professional and well-presented staff usually sent to us.*

'Alright, missus,' he greeted her, wiping a hand across his apron before taking her own, 'big place this, ain't it?' He grinned whilst gesturing with his hands – one of which held the knife he'd just been chopping vegetables with – very much giving the impression that he might be casing the joint. 'Right posh too – are you famous or somefing?'

Poppy smiled politely as a wave of uneasiness swept over her. 'Err... I assume your colleagues are on their way?' she asked, ignoring his question. 'There's quite a lot to do, I'm afraid.'

He grinned again, nodding whilst he took the outer skin off an onion. 'Oh yeah, right, they should be 'ere soon. We had an event over at Chipping Melbury last night – that were a big posh do as well – so we're running a bit late. Don't worry, love, they'll be here soon.'

Poppy, however, wasn't convinced. 'Right... well, shall we go through the menu?' She smiled cheerily, trying to raise the energy positively as she took a seat opposite him.

'Oh right, well, I'm doing vegetable soup for starters,' he began, pointing to the selection of vegetables in front of him that he was in the middle of preparing, 'and I'm gonna do a chicken pie with celeriac mash for...'

Poppy interrupted him. 'Vegetable soup?' She frowned, confused. 'That's not on the menu; you're supposed to be cooking seared scallops with a minted pea puree and crispy pancetta, followed by chargrilled lemon chicken with Mediterranean couscous, ratatouille, and a basil cream.' She looked up, unamused at his returned look of total confusion.

'I don't know nuffin' about that, love; I've just been told to come 'ere and cook dinner for a big group. I've been through the cupboards an' all that and this is what I've come up with – I can't do none of that fancy stuff you're goin' on about.'

Very rarely did Poppy get angry but at that moment she was finding it extremely difficult to keep calm. 'Surely you *cannot* expect our guests to slurp soup dressed in all their finery, and chicken pie – that's what I serve our children for tea; it's certainly *not* fine dining!' Without uttering another word, she slipped off the pine stool she'd been sitting on and made her way back upstairs, leaving chef Gavin grinning aimlessly to himself.

'I'll be back!' she called out at the last minute as she made her way towards the study. *Prestigious agency!*

she fumed. *We'll see just how prestigious they are by the time I've finished with them!*

* * *

'I am *not* going tonight and that's final!'

Pradeep Chandola sighed, bowing his head to cover his frustration. Despite being a qualified GP and psychotherapist, at that moment he was at a complete loss as to what to say or do.

He watched as his beloved wife Esha continued ranting and raving, angrily pulling out random drawers from the oak dressers in their bedroom and throwing the contents on the floor before collapsing into a heap on the magnificent queen-sized sleigh bed that dominated the room.

Her cries ripped through his soul, and when he went to reach for her she pushed him savagely away. '*Leave me alone!*' she screamed, beginning to sob helplessly.

Exasperated, Pradeep brushed a hand across his furrowed brow and decided to step out of the room to give her some space. He pulled the door silently shut behind him, the thickness of the carpet helping to silence the movement.

Downstairs, Bronwyn – the nanny they'd employed to help care for their baby daughter – was folding up the washing, trying to act as if she hadn't overheard the events of moments ago.

Pradeep sat down at the table of the contemporary kitchen breakfast set they'd recently had delivered from the Hambly-Jones department store, placing his head in his hands, oblivious of Bronwyn's presence.

She watched him for several moments, uncertain whether to speak; she'd only been with them a short time and she didn't want to overstep the mark. However, her comforting Welsh heritage soon got the better of her and she started making them both a cup of tea, adding an extra spoonful of sugar for Pradeep. Slowly, she carried it over to the table, taking the seat next to him.

'Salena's sound asleep,' she said quietly, not wishing to disturb Salena or to revive Esha's anger, 'she took all eight ounces today too – she's coming along nicely, she is.'

Pradeep looked up and gratefully accepted the hot beverage. She offered him a biscuit but he declined; his stomach was in knots.

'Has she been like this before?' He spoke softly, looking straight ahead.

'Just a few times, lovely – nothing major – she tends to go and sleep it off and then comes back refreshed.'

He pondered her words for a moment. 'I suspected she wasn't well before we moved,' he admitted, sighing deeply. 'I should have trusted my instincts and left her back in London – she felt safe there.'

'She's safe here.' Bronwyn placed a hand gently on his arm. 'You know what this is. Give her time – she's been through a lot.'

Pradeep smiled briefly, wanting to appear thankful for her support, but inside he felt sick and tortured. *She needs professional help.*

'The dinner tonight is a huge opportunity,' he explained, 'not just for me but for Esha as well – to connect with our neighbours and make friends. I don't want to go without her but it's going to look odd not turning up at all, what with me being the new village doctor. I mean, there are enough rumours going around as it is.' He sighed helplessly.

'Look, lovely,' said Bronwyn, 'it's still early, right? Let's leave her to rest – don't worry about Selena, I've got it all covered – and let's have a think about what she might like to wear if she does decide to go. When she wakes up, I'll run her a nice bath and offer to do her hair for tonight. We can see how the land lies then – what do you think?'

Pradeep smiled, slightly hopeful now. *Who'd have thought it? The new village doctor taking advice from a 21-year-old nanny.*

This time he reached out and placed a hand on her arm. 'You're a gem.'

* * *

Richard wiped the tears from his eyes, his stomach aching from laughing so much. 'But I like chicken pie!' he gasped breathlessly, quite unable to contain his mirth. Rosie had forced her handkerchief halfway into her mouth to stifle her giggles and Percy was hiding behind the Midford County Gazette – though the shaking of the pages gave him away.

'It's not funny, Richard!' Poppy fumed.

She was standing in front of the huge bay kitchen window with her hands firmly on her hips, and despite her obvious rage Richard thought she looked beautiful. She'd scooped up her long, dark unruly hair into a makeshift bun earlier that morning but several tendrils had since slipped out and were now framing her tiny face. Her whole being was illuminated by the rays of the morning sunshine bursting through the windows; the shards of light that filtered around her outline resembled a giant hand engulfing her in a comforting hug. Richard's heart swelled with longing, and after going over to reassure her, he soon had her laughing along with them.

'I mean – you couldn't make this up, right?' Poppy asked, still laughing. 'The Hambly-Joneses entertaining one of the UK's most famous – as well as some of the Hamptons' most prestigious residents – and we can't even rustle up a decent dinner!' This set them all off again just as Monty came bounding in, getting more excited than usual by the energy their high spirits were creating. He began barking, reminding Poppy it was his lunchtime. 'Well, we'll just have to see what the agency come up with next – at this rate I'll be cooking the dinner myself!'

This thought sobered them all up.

'Don't be ridiculous, darling,' Richard cut in. 'I want you up here with me, not skivvying away downstairs.'

'I suppose I could step in if needs be,' volunteered Rosie, suddenly taking to the idea, 'it's appalling for the agency to let you down like this.'

'Oh no you don't,' complained Percy, 'I'm only here because of these two.' He gestured with his thumb towards Poppy and Richard. 'I need you to be here with me – you know how tongue twisted all this pomp and fuss makes me.'

'No, the only people cooking tonight will be Gav and whoever else they can rustle up at short notice,' Richard cut in. 'One way or another we'll just have to make do.'

'You're right, darling.' Poppy gave Monty his food before going over to kiss her husband. 'At least we've got Cathy's trifle for dessert – and knowing the Fishers there'll be so much booze in it no one will even remember the rest of the meal anyway!'

They were interrupted then by the front door bell.

'I'll get it,' Richard offered, walking down the hallway with a huge smile spread across his face, a smile which soon dried up when he discovered the identity of the caller.

* * *

'There's a lot of activity across the way,' Ralph Denby pointed out as he came through the door having collected the morning papers, 'looks like someone's having a party.' Without looking up, his wife Rita continued her computer search, seemingly unconcerned – but Ralph knew better. 'Shall I go and get my shirt out to be ironed?' he smirked. 'Or have you pressed it already?'

Rita slammed the computer mouse hard against the top of the faux pine desk she was sitting at and glared at him.

'I've already told you that I've been asked to undertake some important research for Anthony – there's a lot involved, Ralphie – and as stall manager I have a lot of responsibility on my shoulders. I don't have time for social gatherings right now.'

Ralph had his back to her at this point, and as he began to fill the kettle to make some coffee, he took the opportunity to smile like the cat that had got the cream.

Usually not one to miss anything, Rita liked to sit near the front windows of The Firs as much as possible, affording her the perfect viewing place in order to watch all the goings-on in Hampton Waters. The fact that she was currently ensconced in the corner of their dining room, therefore, spoke volumes.

However, he'd had enough fun now. He'd heard all about the fancy dinner that was going on across at Hampton Manor House, and whilst he usually thoroughly enjoyed going to such events, Ralph was glad not to be going to this one. There was a supposed well-known celebrity attending and he really didn't enjoy having to put on airs and graces – but Rita did, and he hadn't appreciated just how disappointed she was until that morning. Being fobbed off with the position of stall manager was no compensation either. As he handed her a cup of hot coffee, he couldn't mistake the sadness in her eyes. *She might be a busybody, but she's my busybody.*

'I fancy a meal out tonight, Rita,' he said suddenly. 'There's a new place that's just opened at Chipping Melbury, what do you think?'

She looked up, completely astonished. 'Chipping Melbury? That's miles away – we'll need another meal by the time we get back home!' she scoffed.

'It's not that far – and I heard a lot of celebrities eat there frequently too.'

She sipped her coffee nonchalantly, considering his offer. 'To be honest, Ralphie, this really is going to be quite full on today,' she gestured towards the computer and the papers she had scattered across the keyboard, 'and I don't think I'll have time to cook tonight, so why don't we give it a try?'

He smiled and nodded before taking himself off to the lounge with his own coffee, together with the papers he'd brought earlier. *Good job I already booked.*

* * *

'Hello Richard,' Francine greeted, a tad breathless, as she flashed him her best smile.

For a brief moment he was taken aback, but then he quickly recognised the Hambly-Jones' *Magnifique Madame* senior buyer – such was the extent of her makeover – and he was not best pleased. 'I take it you've got a very good excuse for turning up at my private residence – unannounced – Francine?'

'I'm *so* sorry Richard,' she said, just about managing to hide her disappointment at his reaction, 'having to bother you at home like this – honestly – but Margaret assured me you wouldn't mind. In fact, she suggested it. It's about the paperwork for the *Magnifique Madame* winter order – you didn't sign it properly.'

Richard raised an eyebrow curiously – he wasn't usually one to make such mistakes. 'Didn't sign it or didn't see it, Francine?' Her blushes proved otherwise. 'Either way it doesn't warrant you needing to visit my home.'

'That's exactly what my thoughts were, Richard,' she replied, 'but as I said, when I explained to Margaret about the urgency of the order she thought it best that I bring it in person. Of course,' she paused and smiled coyly, 'she was rather surprised that I wasn't coming this evening anyway – you know, for the dinner.'

Richard knew better than that, but he failed to materialise his thoughts as at that moment his parents arrived.

Anthony – being ever the charmer – could never resist a beautiful young lady. 'Hello, my dear,' he greeted Francine, his blue eyes twinkling mischievously.

She seemingly had no time to appreciate his greeting, however. 'Listen, guys,' she said, holding up her hands and beginning to back away, 'my apologies for disturbing you, I'll let you all get on. I really need to be somewhere else anyway.'

Richard briefly wondered if that was the reason she was all dressed up and not – as he'd first assumed – a cheeky attempt at getting invited to the dinner. 'I'll see you on Monday, Richard!' she called out, leaving before anyone could get another word in.

'You scared her off, darling,' Ianthe teased.

Anthony chuckled in response as they went inside to join the others, 'I told you, it's this aftershave – it's gone out of date. They don't keep for years like they used to.'

Despite the peals of excited laughter coming from inside, Richard stood on the doorstep for a few moments, replaying the bizarre interaction he'd just witnessed in his head. He wasn't sure what was going on with Francine, but one way or another he was going to get to the bottom of it.

* * *

Winnie Vagas stepped off the number 47 bus and paused to catch her breath, grateful to have the use of her canvas shopping trolley for support. 'Thanks

Stan!' she called out to the driver before he closed the doors and drove off.

She glanced around, attempting to gather her bearings. It'd been a long time since she'd ventured out to the Hamptons and there seemed to be a lot more houses around than the last time she'd visited. The bus stop was just outside what used to be known as The Swan Public House, but that was all boarded up now, scaffolding having been erected all around the building. *Another fancy house on the horizon, no doubt.* She could see St. Michael's Church in the distance – its spectacular spire was amongst one of the tallest medieval structures in the UK, making it a familiar landmark – and she knew that Hampton Manor House was situated just next door.

She crossed over the Hampton Ash Road and shuffled her way towards the village green. It was quite a pleasant day considering the weather of late, and she set her mind to thinking of the task in hand.

Ever since she'd taken early retirement fifteen months ago, Winnie had been inundated with agency work. She was a qualified chef, and at the top of her game had run one of the busiest restaurant kitchens in London's West End – favoured by theatregoers and inundated with tourists.

She'd met her late husband Eric there too; he'd arrived late one evening just before last orders, and as she was training up a new chef she'd offered to go and take his order – nothing to do with his striking good looks, of course. He told her he ran a training company whose offices were just off Pall Mall and that he'd come in for a bite to eat following a recommendation from one of his clients earlier that week.

His visits soon became regular after that, and within a few months they'd begun dating. As their relationship had developed so did Eric's business, and soon he was opening offices all throughout the UK, eventually setting up his headquarters in Swinford St. George. They were quite smitten with each other by this time and the long absences only made Eric's heart grow fonder. Two years after their first encounter he made Winnie an offer she couldn't refuse – to become his wife – something she didn't need asking twice.

After they were married she left the restaurant in London and took up agency work until she found a permanent posting locally. As Eric became more successful, Winnie cut down on her hours and travelled with him whenever possible. Overall, they'd enjoyed a very happy and fulfilling marriage. *Until he went and died on me, that is.*

Winnie sighed as she always did when she thought about how lonely life was since she'd lost her dear husband. Despite Eric having provided well for her, Winnie had recently signed up with a local catering agency – it was more for the company than anything else – and she hadn't expected to be quite so busy.

Just before she got to St. Michael's Church Winnie stopped to catch her breath again, taking out a paper handkerchief to mop her brow. She liked to blame her hot flushes on the menopause, but deep down she knew that being heavily overweight – and unfit to boot – really wasn't helping. She was 5 foot 4 inches tall but her rotund figure made her appear much smaller and dumpy. She'd pinned her greying hair up into a small bun at the back of her head and her silver metal-framed glasses kept sliding annoyingly down her nose as beads of sweat dropped off her brow from her overexertion. *I'll need a nice cup of tea once I get inside.*

Gathering herself together, she took the last few steps towards Hampton Manor House.

* * *

'Oh Richard, before I forget,' Anthony said, catching up with his son in the dining room. The waiting staff for the evening had finally arrived and Richard was helping them with the finishing touches.

'Yes, Dad? What can I do for you?' He smiled, grateful that his parents had arrived early to help out.

'That girl from before – the one at the door earlier – who is she?'

'Girl?' Richard flitted through that morning's visitors in his mind before answering, 'Oh, do you mean Francine?'

'Oh, it *is* Francine then, I did...'

'Richard!' squealed Poppy with excitement, rushing in happily to their delighted surprise, 'Sorry to interrupt you, Anthony, but you must come and meet our chef for the evening – I think we're onto a winner!' She pulled at their hands, her elation contagious.

Their conversation forgotten, they followed her through to the kitchen to be greeted by a large, friendly lady who was already sipping a cup of tea at the table and chatting away happily with the others like they were old friends.

She stood up when they entered and went to shake Richard's hand. 'It's lovely to meet you, sir,' she began politely.

'Welcome, Winnie. You've no idea how pleased we are to have you here, and call me Richard, please.'

Anthony stepped forward to greet her too, engulfing her small hand with his much larger one.

'I'm delighted to be here,' she replied, looking around at the gathered group. 'Now, I don't want any of you worrying about tonight – I'm fully qualified and I know exactly what you're after, trust me. I'll just finish my tea before getting started. And I'll knock young Gavin into shape in the meantime!' She laughed then, the others laughing along with her.

Smiling, Poppy brought her hands together in a prayer motion. 'You've no idea how grateful we are to you, Winnie, for coming over to help us out at such short notice. I understand that you recently retired; I hope we didn't spoil any plans you might've had for today.'

Winnie took another sip of tea, shaking her head. 'Not at all. I was glad of the distraction. I'm looking forward to cooking for a large group again. These days I don't get called in for numbers above ten and I'm at my best when there's lots of work to be done.'

With the tea finished, she gathered up her things and followed Poppy downstairs to the basement kitchen, which was to become her home for the next few hours.

CHAPTER THIRTEEN

*S*adie Alcock sat perfectly still. She was wearing her
Sunday best. The polished wood of the long seat felt hard
beneath her, the distinct musty smell of the familiar old
building seeping into her nostrils and making them tingle; she
wiggled her nose, attempting to stem a sneeze that was
threatening to explode out of her.

The creaking of the heavy wooden doors of the grade I
building caught her attention as yet more people came in and
scrabbled to find a seat. Her mother was sitting beside her,
sobbing inconsolably. Resting to her right – at the front of the
church – was the coffin they'd followed in just moments before,
the shiny wood reminding her of her mother's dressing table. It
was covered in pretty red roses that had been woven together,
causing her to wonder how such a thing had been created.

Just then Reverend Collins stepped forward and everyone
rose to their feet as the first hymn was played, the sounds from
the organ echoing around the stone walls of the small church.

She hadn't been to a funeral before, and she thought it
might be a bit like the Christingle service they'd attended a few

months earlier. I wonder if we'll be given an orange with sweets like last time. *Her stomach growled hungrily.*

Reverend Collins began speaking and everyone sat down again. Sadie sneaked another glance towards the coffin, quite unable to believe her father was lying dead inside.

* * *

By the time the ambulance and police had arrived, the teenagers were frantic and Jen was struggling to hold it all together.

It was impossible for the paramedics to get the ambulance into the field so they started running as quickly as they could towards the group, carrying a stretcher between them. There were four or five policemen running besides them too from what Jen could see.

Although it was still quite dark, the sun was just beginning its morning descent into the sky and first light was lingering on the horizon.

Having also seen them arrive, the boys began shouting and screaming out for help again, several of the group still crying hysterically. Thankfully, the police soon took control of the situation and one of the officers took Jen aside to ascertain what had happened. He introduced himself as Sergeant Bill Wilson and listened intently while she spoke, noting that Ron was still missing. Then he instructed his officers to move the group away from the body and out of Ryder's field to allow the paramedics to deal with the injured boy.

'Once we've taken statements and got them home safely, we'll start looking for your husband,' he explained calmly, knowing they'd need the morning light to help them navigate around the farm. It was well known that there were ditches and steep banks situated all around the area and he couldn't chance anyone else getting injured in the meantime.

He escorted Jen back to the farmhouse and helped her inside before putting on the kettle. She was clearly in shock, her legs and bare feet covered in thick, sticky mud.

He handed her a cup of hot, sweet tea – which she gratefully accepted with shaking hands – and they drank in silence for a while. He then suggested she go and clean herself up (and check on her daughter) before he took a statement from her.

In the meantime, he reported back to the station to request more officers to help with the search. Now they had light they needed to find Ron as soon as possible, given that he was carrying a loaded gun.

By the time Jen returned, two more officers had arrived at the door and Sergeant Wilson went off with them. He came back a short while later, removing his hat and looking at Jen woefully.

Her bottom lip was trembling violently as the tears began to roll down her face. She was shaking again and he caught her just before she crumpled to the ground.

'I'm so very sorry.'

Ron had been dead for some time when they found him; they think he ran off and shot himself soon after the fracas. A few of the boys shamefully admitted to having gone to Upper Pethewick Farm that night to deliberately wind Ron up just for a laugh – specifically Councillor Roberts' son Mickey, who'd been wound up by his own father earlier that evening, claiming Ron had no right to stop them going onto the land and that the police were on their side.

Knowing full well that Ron had already received a caution, they didn't think he'd want to risk any further trouble. However, they didn't bargain for the fact that after having put his life and soul into his beloved family farm – only to suddenly lose everything to something that was completely out of his control – he was in the depths of deep despair and wasn't *thinking straight. He'd been drinking heavily that night too and they think he went to confront them with the intention of firing a warning shot, just to scare the kids away. Only in his inebriated state, he hadn't held the gun completely upright.*

Instead, he'd fired point blank.

Mickey Roberts had died instantly.

CHAPTER FOURTEEN

Leon and Vinny – two of Midford County
Security's best guys, and not just for their good
looks – took their place at the entrance to
Hampton Manor House, ready to greet the evening's
guests.

At over six foot tall each (and both being regular
gym users) they looked every inch the handsome
bodyguards, an image they'd so carefully worked to
create. Both dressed in tuxedos, and with perfect
white smiles, they weren't averse to receiving the odd
cheeky comment from excitable ladies – or men – on
their way in, but they were no pushovers either. Well
spoken and mild mannered, they were renowned for
never leaving an assignment until the very last person
had gone home; when they had a job to do, they did it
properly.

'Aye up,' Vinny nudged Leon, 'they must've got
wind of our special guest.'

The two of them carefully watched the cameraman and reporter that had seemed to appear from nowhere. They were busy setting up their equipment, just minutes before another photographer's sudden arrival, who begun setting up his own camera too.

Together, they walked towards the quickly growing group, who were lurking just metres away from the gates.

'We're going to have to ask you to move much further back, please; you're causing an obstruction.' Vinny gestured with his hands as his spoke, directing them further onto the green.

'Says who?' challenged the reporter cockily, pushing his dark-rimmed glasses back up onto his nose. He reminded Vinny of a young *Louis Theroux*.

'Says me,' Vinny said as he and Leon stepped further forward. 'Our guests will be coming along here,' he pointed toward St. Michael's Church, 'or from there,' indicating Ashton Abbey, as permission had been given to use the car park for the evening. 'And, as you are *here*, you're right in the way, so move further back please or we'll move your equipment for you.'

The reporter grunted something incoherent but the others had already begun to make the move, knowing full well that they'd chanced their luck in the first place.

Satisfied, Vinny and Leon returned to their post, flicking their eyes every now and then towards the growing group of Paparazzi, something that was becoming a much more familiar sight in the Hamptons of late. This hadn't been helped by Richard and Anthony's calls earlier that day either, although their intentions had been coming from a good place.

Just then a hum of voices brought along the first guests and Vinny and Leon jumped into action.

* * *

Francine Dubois paced the floor of Orchard Cottage like a cat on a hot tin roof. *I should never have gone there! And with all the extra effort I'd put in these past few weeks too!* She was truly beside herself.

She continued to march up and down the hallway, the heels of her black stilettos tapping on the flagstones as she went, the noise echoing loudly around the tiny stone cottage she was renting from Poppy and Richard.

When she caught sight of her reflection in the large ornate mirror positioned at the foot of the staircase, she sighed heavily. *All dressed up with nowhere to go – the story of my life!* She sneered at her reflection, unable to erase the morning's confrontation.

Suddenly Francine grabbed her keys and purse from the hall table and went outside, taking a moment to admire the beauty of the brand new Audi A5 Richard had organised for her. *I'm not giving up without a fight, not for anyone.* And with that she slipped into the driver's seat and headed back towards the Hamptons.

Time for this girl to have some fun!

* * *

'Whoa! Don't you look a picture?'

Poppy blushed at Richard's compliment. Having spent much of the day red faced with frustration, she was pleased to have taken herself off a couple of hours ago for a long soak in a hot bath, which she'd generously scattered with several drops of Lavender and Frankincense oils. She'd opted to wear her dark hair down for a change and had swept it to the side; huge loose curls perfected the look and complemented the midnight blue sequinned maxi dress she'd chosen to wear, which had straps that criss-crossed at the back and clung luxuriously to her curves.

Richard, resplendent in his black tuxedo, pulled her closer towards him. 'We've still got half an hour, you know,' he teased, and she feigned pushing him away.

'Later!' she giggled as he began nuzzling her neck. 'We need to get ready for our special guest.'

'Okay,' he replied, grinning. 'It's worth waiting for.' He kissed her hand whilst looking deep into her eyes, a gesture he knew she appreciated. Then, referring to the evening in hand he added, 'It's going to make a huge change having her back here; I hope she receives the warm welcome she deserves.'

Poppy agreed. 'She's worked hard to get where she is today – and think of how many lives she's changed in the process. I'm *so* excited she's chosen our dinner to make the formal announcement too. Which reminds me, did you call the Gazette?'

He nodded and smiled. 'I did, and Dad phoned several of his old contacts too – she's going to get quite the welcome.'

Poppy took a deep breath before holding her hand out towards him, smiling. 'Brilliant! Well then, let the evening – and the fun – begin!'

* * *

Chipping Melbury was approximately 15 miles from the Hamptons, and Rita and Ralph Denby were currently making their way to The Melbury Fox, a popular bistro and wine bar that was reported to be a frequent watering hole for the rich and famous who lived in and around the local area.

Sitting in the passenger seat, Rita smoothed the skirt of the floral print dress she'd picked out to wear for the occasion, admiring the swirls of green, pink, and yellow.

Ralph glanced across at her. 'Everything okay?'

She smiled. 'I was just thinking that spring is just around the corner. I do love seeing everything coming back to life – especially after the dreadful winter we had this year.'

'Yes, we haven't had high winds like that for a long time.' He paused, wanting to expand further, then decided to leave it at that for the time being.

They seemed to arrive in no time and after parking the car close to the entrance, Ralph got out and stretched his legs before going around the other side to help Rita out. It didn't take many minutes of sitting still for both of them to suffer with stiff joints – they were in their 60s, after all.

The bistro looked like it had recently been refurbished, and Rita stood to admire it for a moment. 'Look at that sign, Ralph,' she said, 'what a colourful fox they've got there.' The hand-painted sign depicted a very regal-looking fox, dressed akin to a gentleman from Victorian times; his top hat was set at a jaunty angle, his cane by his side and a broad smile stretched across his furry face. The richness of the fox's red fur was beguiling.

'Let's hope the food's as good as he looks,' quipped Ralph, opening the main door for Rita.

Once inside they were warmly greeted by the front of house manager, who checked their booking before leading them to the bar area. 'Please take a seat and make yourselves comfortable.' He took their coats and handed them both a menu. 'Would you care for a drink whilst you peruse the menu? I'll lead you through to the restaurant once your first course is ready.'

Rita was most impressed; she hadn't received such attention for a long time. 'May I have a glass of dry white wine please?'

'Just an orange juice for me please,' added Ralph. 'I'm driving.'

'Certainly, sir. I'll get the waiter to bring your drinks straight over.'

They watched him as he walked off towards the bar and passed their order over to a waiting colleague.

'Well, this all looks very nice,' smiled Rita, suddenly immensely grateful for Ralph's suggestion. 'Isn't it nice? Plush red carpets, fancy tables and leather seating… I could get used to this, Ralphie.'

He smiled, appreciating her enthusiasm. 'We should get ourselves out more,' he suggested. 'Sitting around that house all day… it's no good for anyone. There's more to life than the bloody parish council, you know.'

Rita raised her eyebrows in surprise at her husband's sudden outburst, but as the waiter appeared with their drinks she chose not to comment further, concentrating on the menu instead.

* * *

Quite a hubbub of chatter was underway when Poppy and Richard joined their guests in the great hall at Hampton Manor House. Being popular, they were quickly swept up into the waiting crowd.

'Peter, Cathy!' Poppy greeted Reverend Fisher and his wife warmly. 'It's lovely to see you both.' They were soon joined by Charlotte and Jonathan Palmer-Reid, both of whom Poppy was pleased to note were looking much happier than they had done of late.

'Evening all,' remarked Charlotte, 'you're all looking lovely as usual.'

Everyone knew such compliments from Charlotte were rare and they nodded in appreciation.

'I'm looking forward to dinner!' Reverend Fisher smiled brightly, his protruding teeth glistening from the reflecting light of the overhead chandeliers as he gave a cheeky wink. 'The good Lord guided me to bless the trifle for the benefit of us all.' This was followed by several guffaws of laughter.

Marnie and Greg Sable had now joined them, and Alexander and Skye Harvey, having just arrived, were making their way towards the group too.

'We all know how heavy-handed you are with the booze, Reverend,' teased Anthony Sullivan. 'Why do you think Sunday Communion is so popular?'

The crowd roared with laughter again, kicking off what they knew was going to be a fun and entertaining night ahead.

* * *

Camilla Barrington–Smythe sprayed a further covering of hairspray, ensuring her ash blonde locks were held securely in place. *I need to look my absolute best tonight!*

She was excited to be meeting some of the most influential residents of the Hamptons who were to become her neighbours for the next few months – and, hopefully, friends. Apart from Matt Hudson – and Diana, of course – she'd yet to meet anyone else, having squirrelled herself away in The Boathouse preparing for the first rehearsal of *The Fortunettes*. The majorette competition was several months off, affording them plenty of time in the coming weeks to practice.

Diana entered the guest bedroom she was currently using. 'That dress is very *Marilyn Monroe*, Camilla,' she commented. 'It suits you.'

Camilla smiled before applying a coat of rich, red lipstick. 'Are you ready to leave?'

'Yes, but first – could you clasp this for me please?' She held out her left arm and handed Camilla a sapphire and diamond bracelet.

'Oh, this is heavy, and so pretty,' Camilla said as she clicked the clasp into place. 'It matches your eyes, Diana, and complements your dress too.' She was wearing a long-sleeved navy blue evening gown, and she'd swept her grey hair into a *chignon.*

Camilla popped the lipstick into her evening bag and zipped it shut. 'Right, if we're finally ready – our public are waiting.'

* * *

'Don't you give me any of your lip, young man, or I'll clip you round the ear!'

Miffed at Winnie's arrival, and his subsequent enforced demotion from chef to kitchen boy, Gavin was being as slow – and as difficult – as possible.

'Think yourself lucky that you haven't already been given your marching orders! If it wasn't for decent people like the Hambly-Joneses you'd be on the next bus back to Chipping Melbury right now and you know it.'

He mumbled as he went to fetch the scallops, then stood there watching sulkily as Winnie showed him how to prepare them.

'Right, your turn,' she encouraged, much to his surprise.

He reached for a scallop, then, as directed, he began to carefully remove the side muscle and the coral-coloured roe before carefully washing and patting it dry.

'Good lad,' she told him. 'See, you can do it when you try. Right, we're almost ready to go, so you carry on with the rest of these – don't forget to give them a nice bit of seasoning – and I'll go and get the pans ready, okay?'

He nodded, feeling a little guilty that he'd played her up. He hadn't expected to be allowed to get this involved considering how she'd arrived earlier. *Gave me a right telling off too.*

She came back into the kitchen carrying two heavy frying pans. 'And, just so you know, after today I'll be having a word with the agency about tonight – make no mistake. It's absolutely disgusting sending an inexperienced young chef to cook for such esteemed guests.'

'I did tell 'em, like, but they told me to wing it,' he explained, exasperated.

'Don't worry about it – we'll get you sorted, even if I have to train you myself.'

He watched her walk off back towards the chiller, silently wishing he really could find someone like her to train him.

'Pre-dinner drinks are underway, Winnie!' shouted one of the waiters from the stairway.

A moment later she came back through to the kitchen again and washed her hands. 'Right, sunshine!' She smiled at Gavin. 'Let the games begin.'

* * *

Although The Boathouse wasn't far from the Hambly-Joneses', Diana had arranged for a chauffeur-driven Bentley to ferry them to and from the event. With her popularity having grown exponentially, she wanted to play the part of being an ex-Hollywood icon with as much grace and style as possible. Besides which, she didn't really relish walking the distance – no matter how short – in a long, fluid evening gown while having to use a walking stick for support.

Camilla slipped into the back of the chauffeur-driven Bentley, sinking into the sumptuous white leather upholstery that perfectly complemented the black shiny exterior of the impressive vehicle, then waited for Diana to join her.

Once she was in, the driver took his time as he carefully closed the car doors before retaking his position behind the wheel. Slowly, he guided the powerful vehicle along the King's Oak Road and towards the village green, where quite a number of waiting paparazzi had gathered.

Camilla nervously took a deep breath and smiled, prepared to meet her public.

* * *

Francine – who was completely aware of the attention her presence was attracting – took a long, slow drink from her glass, relishing the taste of the sweet, fruity Merlot wine.

'Mind if I join you?'

'Please do.' She gestured with her hand to the seat opposite, watching him as he smoothly pulled out the chair before sitting down, keeping his eyes fixed firmly on her the whole time.

He laughed. 'I was going to ask if you came here often, but that's a bit clichéd, right?'

She laughed too. 'My first time actually,' she responded artfully. 'You?'

'Oh, I'm a regular – I'll have to show you the ropes,' he said while maintaining eye contact, completely at ease with their flirtatious banter. He nodded towards her empty glass. 'Another? Glass or bottle?'

'Bottle, of course – if we're sharing, that is.'

He smiled knowingly and went off to the bar.

They say a little bit of what you fancy does you good. She glanced over at him again, a smile playing on her lips. She wasn't averse to picking up one-night stands, but although this guy seemed to be a player, he was unusually well turned out. Expensive suit – bespoke, she fancied – well groomed, and no wedding ring in sight.

Don't lose focus, Francine. She took a satisfying deep breath. *One little ship won't sink the whole battle.*

* * *

'Tiggy, Harry, come over here!' Poppy gestured to her friends, who'd just arrived, and grasped two glasses of champagne for them from a nearby waiter. 'You look amazing, Tiggy,' she greeted her friend, 'it's so lovely to see you both – thanks for coming tonight.'

'Wouldn't miss one of your events for the world!' Harry chuckled and took a sip of his drink. 'They're becoming infamous!'

'Well, let's hope tonight's not going to be *quite* so debaucherous, given our guest of honour – speaking of which...' There appeared to be significant interest coming from the front entrance. 'Excuse me for a moment, won't you – I think she's arrived.' And, collecting Richard and his parents along the way, Poppy went to welcome their special guest.

* * *

'Oh, this is gorgeous, Ralphie!' They'd both ordered the light smoked salmon starter that was served with a beetroot medley, and Rita was relishing the horseradish cream. 'I don't think I've ever tried this before.'

'Me either; I always thought horseradish was far too hot for my palate.'

They continued eating in silence, wanting to savour every mouthful whilst basking in the pleasant atmosphere around them. There was a gentle hum of conversation in the air, but nothing too distracting that prevented other diners from enjoying their own interactions.

Rita had a good look around the restaurant every now and then, her eagle eye keen to spot any celebrities they might be rubbing shoulders with that night.

At the same time, Ralph sat back and took a drink from his glass. 'I really enjoyed that; let's hope the main course lives up to the same standard.'

The waiting staff discreetly removed their finished plates, leaving them for a good few minutes more to savour their first course before bringing the next.

'Chicken parmigiana for you, Madame.'

Rita's face lit up like a Christmas tree as the waiter placed her food in front of her. The flattened chicken breast almost covered the whole plate and the smell from the tomato sauce combined with the mozzarella and parmesan cheeses were making her mouth water.

'And spiced duck leg confit for you, sir,' he said, placing Ralph's order gently in front of him on the table, 'with plum compote. Now, can I bring you anything else?'

'No, this is wonderful, thank you,' Ralph replied.

The waiter nodded politely and left them to enjoy their food.

'I don't know how I'm going to manage to eat all this as well as the potatoes and vegetables they've brought us,' said Rita as she eyed up all the food.

'Eat what you want, love,' Ralph soothed. 'We've got all night so there's no rush – just enjoy yourself. Have another glass of wine too if you like.'

Rita smiled at him gratefully, and then – from over Ralph's shoulder – someone caught her eye.

'Oooh, look towards the bar!' she whispered. 'I think I recognise that chap wearing the fancy suit, the one sitting with the redhead.'

Ralph craned his neck to follow her view. 'He doesn't ring any bells for me.'

Rita gave a little jiggle of excitement, certain it was someone off the television, such was his familiarity. 'Well, it's still early yet, who knows who else might join us!' she exclaimed.

Ralph smiled. He was enjoying seeing his wife relaxing and he hoped this change of scenery would turn into a regular outing for them both.

* * *

'Hello, Diana!' Alexander Harvey exclaimed, embracing his friend. 'You're looking as fabulous as ever.'

She pushed him away playfully before exchanging greetings with his wife, Skye. Everyone was in high spirits and there was a lot of laughter ringing out.

'May I introduce Camilla Barrington-Smythe?'

Camilla – who was currently inwardly seething – attempted to put on her best smile as Diana made her introduction.

'Oh, you're working with Diana for the competition, aren't you?' enthused Alexander. 'You'll have the joy of our three little darlings then,' he joked.

'Take no notice of him,' Skye soothed, mistaking the sour look on Camilla's face. 'They're all lovely kids – just like their mother!' she quipped, before continuing to share how excited all the village children were at having the opportunity to get involved with the competition.

Camilla wasn't listening, though; she'd been led to believe that tonight was a welcome dinner just for her. Discovering otherwise was currently a very bitter pill she was finding extremely difficult to swallow.

* * *

Archie Sloane – the reporter who'd been tackled earlier by Vinny and Leon – had now been joined by a few more news anchors, all of whom had managed to muscle their way to the front, much to his annoyance. He'd only been with the Midford County Gazette a few months and he wanted to get the best picture of the night; he knew that if he filed a great copy it would earn him major brownie points with his editor.

Several cheers rang out as she came into view, Georgina Fame smiling and waving brightly as her car approached the descent towards Hampton Manor House.

As she stepped out of the car, the bespoke turquoise evening dress she was wearing floated gracefully into place, emphasising her enviable figure. Her hair had been fashioned into a contemporary up do, showing off perfect cheekbones and a long, slender neck.

She posed for several photographs before enthusiastically greeting Vinny and Leon – much to their delight – and she even posed for a few pictures with them.

She smiled broadly when she noted that Richard had, as promised, literally rolled out the red carpet for her.

* * *

Francine watched him head off into the night in the taxi she'd ordered a short while before, the red tail lights glowing ominously in the dark night. She then went back inside Orchard Cottage and carefully shut the heavy wooden door behind her, taking a moment to lean up against it.

Through closed eyes she relished the events of the past few hours and sighed, satiated. She didn't usually invite one-night stands back to her home – in case they were of the stalker variety – preferring to be in complete control of any liaison. However, he didn't strike her as being from that ilk. He was a player, alright – he'd charmed his way into her knickers in no time at all, so to speak – but this one was different. He'd been every inch the gentleman, not once displaying any of the self-centred traits she was used to experiencing from her romantic interludes.

He's a keeper, for sure – but not for me. Maybe if they'd met a few years ago she might have been tempted to try and tame him, but not now. *I've bigger fish to fry.*

With that thought she took herself off to bed. She needed to get a good night's sleep – there'd be a lot of damage control to handle in the morning and this wasn't the time for distractions.

* * *

Poppy and Richard exchanged welcoming embraces with Georgina – along with Anthony and Ianthe – who she'd known for many years. Most of their guests had no prior knowledge that they'd be dining with someone so famous that evening and the air was electric with the excitement it had generated.

'I can't say I'm familiar with her myself,' sniffed Camilla, 'what's she even been in?'

Diana diverted her attention towards Camilla for a brief moment, her eyebrows raised. 'Really? She's a very famous weight loss guru and self-made millionaire – or billionaire, I shouldn't wonder, given that she's now international.'

'Oh, that'll be why I don't recognise her then; I've never had a weight problem.'

Diana pursed her lips, unimpressed. She'd seen this side of Camilla several times now and she didn't like it one bit. However, given her reason for being in the Hamptons she didn't want to rock the boat, so she decided to dismiss her catty behaviour for now.

'So, that's the *amazing* Poppy over there, is it? The one with no bra on?'

Diana glared at her this time. 'Trust me, Camilla; don't make waves where there's no water,' she said icily, before walking off to join the others.

* * *

'Who the hell are you?' Winnie had to shout to make herself heard above the noise coming from the extractor fans and the three pans of scallops that were in the middle of searing.

Billy Franklin smiled. 'I'm Billy.'

'Well, *Billy*, what are you doing in my kitchen?'

Billy hesitated, confused. He was used to random staff coming in and out of Hampton Manor House – and it didn't usually bother him – but then, they didn't usually challenge him either.

'I work here,' was all he said as he proceeded to walk through the kitchen and into the storeroom at the far back of the basement. A couple of the garden lights had blown and he was fetching replacement bulbs.

'You can't come in here dressed like that when I'm cooking food,' Winnie commanded. 'Now, get out before I throw you out!'

Having achieved his task Billy left the kitchen, light bulbs in hand, throwing her a withering look along the way.

* * *

Matt Hudson took his place at the dining table. He'd been seated between Camilla and Esha Chandola, noting that the latter looked almost as pale as the pink dress she was wearing.

Camilla smiled briefly; she was still festering over not being the centre of attention, which was further fuelled by Matt then directing his attention towards Esha.

'Hello, I'm Matt – Matt Hudson – I'm a Sergeant at Midford County Police Station,' he said, introducing himself. Esha accepted his hand nervously. 'You've just moved into The Haven, haven't you?'

'Yes, that's right,' she replied. 'I'm Esha and this is my husband, Pradeep.' She sat back to allow the two men to shake hands. 'He's the new doctor at the Hamptons Medical Practice,' she finished proudly.

The trio exchanged pleasantries whilst they waited for the first course to be served.

Camilla, meanwhile, focussed her attention on her smart phone, much to the annoyance of Robert Fitzgerald, who was sitting to her right and who very much wanted to get to know the stunning blonde on his left.

* * *

'Oh, that chap's gone now,' Rita noted as she drained the last dregs from her coffee cup and set it down again. She rubbed her eyes wearily. She'd thoroughly enjoyed the evening but it was getting quite late now. Combined with the magnificent food and wine, it was all beginning to take its toll.

'Before we go…' Ralph smiled, reaching across the table and taking her hand, a gesture that completely surprised her and made her wonder if he was feeling amorous, though the very thought at that moment made her feel even more exhausted than before. 'I was going to mention this earlier, but with all this fine dining I got distracted.' He finished off his coffee too, the cup gently rattling in the saucer as he replaced it, somewhat distracted. 'What do you think about going on holiday?'

'Holiday?'

'Yes, what do you think about it?'

She shook her head, looking confused. 'We haven't had a holiday since before you retired, Ralphie – I mean, our life is one long holiday now.'

'But we need to get away, Rita – treat ourselves a bit more, get a bit of sunshine on us, soothe our aching bones. It'll do us both the world of good.'

She perked up at the idea then, having considered it a bit more. 'But where would we go?'

'Anywhere we bloody like!' he chuckled. 'What's the point of sitting around day after day in that big old house? We never really go anywhere other than to Church, the Maide of Honour, or a party – and there's not been too much of that lately.'

'Are you bored, Ralph?' Rita bit her lip nervously, the thought suddenly occurring to her for the first time.

'Not *bored*, love.' He looked up, frustrated. 'I know you like to be involved in anything and everything in the Hamptons, Rita, but I think they're taking you for a ride, love, and I've had enough – we've both had enough, haven't we? You've done so much for that bloody village over the years, and what real thanks do you get for it? Look at all the effort you put into helping out with the Hampton Players last year – you were exhausted at the end of it, remember? That was when the chest infection started.'

She nodded her head knowingly, beginning to cough as the memory of the bronchitis she'd suffered around the same time the previous year flooded back into her mind – it had given them a big scare too.

'Has it ever occurred to you that whilst you're running around, the rest of them are off enjoying themselves elsewhere?'

'I like getting involved, Ralph,' she said defensively. 'There are fun times too, you know.'

'Yes, but we've lived here for over 30 years, Rita; it's time someone else got involved.'

She nodded, knowing he was right. 'Well, I don't see why not. To be honest, all that computer stuff I was doing earlier gave me a headache anyway – I could've been watching *A Touch of Frost* on *ITV3* instead.

This buoyed Ralph somewhat. 'Well, there you are, you see!' he exclaimed. 'A perfect example of what I'm saying – you're beginning to sacrifice your own pleasures just to please everyone else.' He reached over again, patting her hand lovingly. 'Let some of these youngsters who've moved into the Hamptons recently have a go instead; you've earned your stripes now.'

On the way home, Rita kept running their conversation over and over in her head. She'd long forgotten the excitement of going on holiday – from choosing a destination to buying insect repellent at the airport, and she'd always had to fight excited butterflies as the days counted down to their summer breaks.

'Shall we start looking online tomorrow?' she asked. Her excitement matched Ralph's now and he lifted a hand briefly from the steering wheel to pat her leg affectionately.

'We certainly can, and the sooner the better! There's nothing stopping us.'

'I hadn't thought of that!' she squealed and he laughed out loud; she was reminding him of the Rita he'd married.

'I do love you, you know,' he said quietly.

A small thrill ran through her then; Rita couldn't remember the last time she'd heard him utter those words. This was turning out to be quite the day.

Maybe I won't be too tired when we get home after all.

* * *

The waiting staff served each guest a plate of perfectly seared scallops and crispy pancetta aside a sea of vibrant green minted pea puree subtly decorated with fresh pea shoots. It was well received and seemed to be polished off in no time.

The pause between courses was merely for the benefit of the guests, and soon the plates of steaming chargrilled lemon chicken with Mediterranean couscous, ratatouille, and a basil cream began to make their way out of the kitchen.

Lucy Whittaker and James Turvey were being kept entertained by Jon Anderson, who was sharing anecdotes from his days as a medical student. His wife, Lizzie – sitting to his right – was being entertained in a similar fashion by Alexander Harvey.

Poppy took a moment to scan her eyes around the table, soaking up the happiness and laughter that emanated from her guests. She briefly caught sight of Matt Hudson, who returned her smile before continuing his discussion with the Chandolas. *I'm looking forward to getting to know them better.*

Her eyes then came upon Camilla Barrington-Smythe, who was staring gloomily into her meal and pushing the couscous around with her fork. Having heard that Matt had gone on a few dates with her, Poppy wondered if she was feeling a bit left out. Having *rub-your-bum* Robert Fitzgerald the other side probably didn't help much either.

She made a mental note to single her out after the dinner, when they'd be in a more informal setting.

'Ladies and gentlemen, if I might have your attention!' Richard stood up, gently tapping the side of his crystal wine glass with a spoon. A raucous roar rang around the room in response – as had been expected, and as was usual for such events. He laughed, trying to calm the excited howls. 'As you know we are *most* fortunate to have the lovely Georgina Fame with us this evening...' He broke off, laughing again as their guests made their pleasure known; a few had even begun banging the table with their hands now. 'Thank you, thank you.' He gestured with his hands to quieten them down. 'Well, she has some exciting news to share with you all, so I'll hand you over to her now – Georgina Fame!'

She stood up to great applause, which she found deeply heartening. She only hoped her announcement would be just as well received.

'Good evening!' she began warmly. 'It's a pleasure to be here tonight, and I'd just like to thank Poppy and Richard – along with Anthony and Ianthe – for hosting such a fabulous dinner this evening.' She paused, allowing time for some applause from the other guests. 'I've known Anthony for a number of years – in fact, I used to work for him.' This brought forth a surge of inappropriate, but humorous, jeers. 'Now, now,' she said, laughing along with them, 'it's all perfectly innocent, I assure you. When I first met Anthony, I was *not* working as a waitress in a cocktail bar,' she quipped, referring to the favoured and well-known hit single *Don't You Want Me* by the popular 70s group *Human League,* 'I was, in fact, working as a temporary secretary, and 14 stone overweight too – that's a whopping 196 pounds if you want to go sterling.'

Gasps of disbelief swept around the room then and everyone hushed, focussing all their attention towards her.

'It took me almost three years not just to lose the weight, but to get fit too. Carefully and methodically, I researched and planned every single step until I'd created a weight loss system that delivered results. This became the brand you're all familiar with today. Yes, *Nourish and Gain with Georgina Fame* was born. It was Anthony who helped me secure the funding to get my first weight loss centre off the ground, and later, his clever investment in the profits afforded me the opportunity to offer my brand not just in the UK but internationally too. And so now I'm bringing it back home; I've bought the Swinford St. George Hotel and Golf Club – lock, stock, and barrel – and I'm turning it into a state-of-the-art health and fitness retreat, not just for weight loss but for wellbeing too. It will be the first of its kind – and you're all invited to join me at the grand opening next month.'

A chorus of cheers went up at this, and the speech completed, Georgina stepped aside to allow Richard to come forward.

'Now, everyone please join me in a toast – not just for the success of her new business but also to welcome her home; here's to Georgina!'

Matt Hudson sank back down into his seat, his eyes very much on the guest of honour. *What an amazing woman.* Several people had already clambered up to congratulate her and he watched her work the front of the room with grace and ease. She oozed confidence and charm and her natural beauty was certainly compelling. He didn't imagine for one moment that this had all come easy for her.

'I bet she's got a gastric band,' Camilla sniped.

Matt glanced across at her. She'd been in a weird mood all evening and it didn't look like it was going to improve anytime soon. *Not even the trifle had managed to put a smile on her face.*

Not wishing to get drawn into a negative conversation, Matt excused himself and went to join the others.

* * *

'Oh, you're back, are you?'

Billy stopped in his tracks. He really didn't want another confrontation; it was getting late and he was hungry.

'I saved a meal for you.' She pointed to one of the pine stools opposite her. 'Take a seat and I'll fetch it.'

He hesitated for a moment more, not wanting to be on the receiving end of her fiery temper again, but she did seem quite a bit calmer now. *Why not?*

She put a plate of the lemon chicken in front of him, the aroma of the roasted vegetables and basil cream soon getting his taste buds going. He ate heartily while she poured them both a drink.

'It's okay,' she said, responding to his look of concern, 'Poppy brought it down earlier. I thought you might like a glass too.'

He accepted the offered wine gratefully, and when she noted his empty plate she went to fetch him another helping, suddenly realising he'd probably not eaten for hours.

'I'm sorry about earlier,' she said, placing a big spoon of couscous next to another helping of the chicken, 'it was all go in here and I was feeling a bit, you know, stressed what with the lad and everything.'

'Where is he?' Billy looked around.

'Oh, I sent him off home after the final course was served. I can manage the clearing up on my own, and by all accounts he'd been working until the early hours the previous night too – he was shattered, poor lad.'

Billy continued with his meal. It was much better than the microwave hotpot he'd planned earlier. *But never got a chance to cook.*

'Do you work here then?' She took a sip from her own glass and kicked off her shoes; her feet were beginning to throb.

'Yes, been here over a year or so now. Lovely family, they are – they've looked after me very well. I take care of the outside mostly, and sometimes clean the windows inside or tend to anything that goes wrong – you know, like the toilet getting blocked or a light not working. I live just up the road so it's quite convenient.'

'Oh? That is handy. I'm all the way over at Swinford St. George. In fact,' she glanced at her watch, 'I'd better get going or I'll miss the last bus.'

'Bus has gone.' Billy looked up, and catching sight of her disappointed face, felt suddenly bad for her. 'They changed the timetable a few months ago and took the night bus off because no one was using it.'

'Typical,' she tutted. 'Well, never mind. I'll call a taxi.' She slipped off the stool she'd been sitting on and walked over to her shopping trolley to retrieve her purse. 'I always carry their number just in case.'

'That'll cost you.'

'Yes, I know.' She rolled her eyes. 'It's at times like this I really miss my late husband, Eric. He was always on hand to chauffer me around, bless him, no matter how late the time or how long the distance.'

Billy finished up his meal and, gathering up his plate, carried it over to the sink to begin washing it up.

'Hello, you two!' Poppy beamed. They hadn't heard her coming down the stairs. Despite the party going on above, the kitchen below was now quiet, having served its purpose for the day. 'Fabulous dinner, Winnie, I can't thank you enough – you literally saved our bacon.'

She laughed as Poppy went over to hug her. 'You're most welcome – I actually enjoyed myself. It's been a long time since I cooked for such a large number.'

'Everyone was raving about the scallops and the chicken,' Poppy gushed, placing her hands over her heart and raising her eyes with pleasure as she recalled just how well received Winnie's lemon chicken had been. 'Now, how are you getting home tonight, Winnie? Your job here is done for the evening.'

'She's phoning a taxi,' Billy cut in.

'A taxi? At this time of night?'

'The last bus has gone,' explained Winnie, 'but it's alright, I use a local firm.'

Poppy frowned; she didn't feel happy about that.

'At this hour? No, I'm not having that, not at this time of night. We've loads of spare rooms available, Winnie – you can spend the night here and I'll drive you home in the morning.'

Winnie smiled wearily. 'To be honest, I'm too tired to argue. I just need a bath and me bed and a good night's sleep.'

'Well, let's get you upstairs then – I'll run a nice hot bath for you.'

After bidding Billy goodnight, Poppy helped Winnie upstairs with her shopping trolley, which seemed to house all her worldly goods.

Billy went to switch off the lights, pondering a moment. Despite being used to the comings and goings of the various catering staff Richard and Poppy regularly hired, there was something about having Winnie there tonight that just seemed so right.

He clicked off the lights and made his way towards his own home. For the first time that day he had a full belly and a happy smile, and he had something else too – hope in his heart.

* * *

Lucy Whittaker and James Turvey practically floated along the King's Oak Road on their way back home from Hampton Manor House. The evening had been so enjoyable, and as they walked they continued to exchange anecdotes from the evening, causing them to fall about laughing every now and then – fuelled by several drinks they'd enjoyed throughout the night.

'It was great catching up with Anthony again,' Lucy gushed. 'His wife Ianthe is such a delight; we must invite them over for dinner one evening.'

James stopped in his tracks, turning to face her head-on. 'You make us sound like a couple,' he teased, awaiting her reaction.

'Oh! Well, I sort of...' She was briefly horrified at her apparent misunderstanding but James soon eased her concerns.

'To be honest, Lucy,' he began earnestly, 'I was hoping you wanted to place our relationship on a more firmer footing.' He seemed embarrassed then, looking down at the ground for a second or two. 'I don't know about you, but dating at our age seems awkward somehow – it's hard to tell if someone's just looking for a night out or whether it's something more.'

They held hands and gazed into each other's eyes.

'Which one are you?' Lucy was fishing, not wanting to reveal her true intentions right away.

'I'm in it for the long run,' he said gently, breaking his hand away and gently stroking the side of her face. 'There's just something about you, Lucy Whittaker. It got under my skin the moment we met and I've wanted to get to know you better ever since.'

Lucy looked back at him, hesitating for a moment before replying. 'It's been some time since I've ventured out into the dating scene myself, James. Spending time with you these past few weeks has been wonderful – I find myself thinking about you more and more.' She smiled coyly. 'When I'm not trying to think of a reason to visit the Hampton stores, that is.'

She thought back to the conversation she'd had with her son, Ian, earlier that morning. Spending time with James had indeed brought forth an awareness that she wanted to take their relationship to the next level, and tonight that desire had increased further. He was quite the entertainer, and the perfect dinner guest. He possessed impeccable manners and was clearly a favourite amongst the Hamptons set. *And he's so very handsome too.*

'Let's give it a go, shall we?' he whispered before leaning in and placing his mouth against hers.

A thrill surged through her and she revelled in his embrace, wanting it to go on forever. When they reluctantly pulled apart he held her close to him, gently stroking her hair.

'I think we'd better move along,' he quipped, kissing the top of her head, 'before we get arrested for indecent behaviour.' He reached for her hand and they continued their journey home.

Lucy didn't necessarily have any expectations of what might lie ahead, but at that moment she was certainly pleased she'd taken Ian's advice from earlier!

CHAPTER FIFTEEN

It was notably warm for April. The trees were blooming with blossom and all the bright, vibrant flowers were springing into life, bringing an abundance of colour along with them as nature began to wake up, ready for the warmer months ahead. The Hampton woods were covered in a blanket of glorious bluebells, which had already begun attracting the usual deluge of visitors keen to witness this glorious phenomenon. Daffodils were bursting into life all around the Hamptons too, lifting the gloomiest of spirits with their dancing yellow heads, bobbing gently in the breeze. The brighter weather had brought forth a spate of activity too.

An excited Diana Fortune welcomed everyone to the first rehearsal of the Hamptons *Fortunettes*. An invitation had been issued to every child living in the villages – via their parents – offering them the opportunity to participate and be part of the

Hamptons entry for the Cotswolds County Majorette of the Year competition. From what Diana could see, it looked as though most had accepted too, and certainly all of her drama students were there, she was pleased to note.

'Good morning, everyone!' she welcomed them brightly. 'It's a pleasure to see so many of our young people on this glorious Saturday morning. Thank you for coming.'

They were using the great hall at Ashton Abbey for their rehearsals – as was usual for the drama club meetings too. Although somewhat daunting, the Abbey was a unique medieval building, with the great hall presenting the perfect venue for hosting anything from a bingo evening to a wedding reception for two hundred guests. Or, as today, for rehearsals.

'Now,' Diana continued, 'I'd like to introduce you all to Camilla Barrington-Smythe who's here to help choreograph the majorette routine we're going to be learning.'

Camilla smiled as she waved her right hand to greet them. She was dressed in brightly coloured jogging pants, matched with a black sports top, and had secured her hair in a neat ponytail.

'I'm going to hand you over to Camilla now,' Diana added, 'who will talk us through her plans for the *Fortunettes* and the schedule of rehearsals planned prior to the actual competition, which will take place in August.' She nodded towards Camilla and went over to the left side of the hall – glad to have her stick for support as usual – then took a seat in one of the few armchairs the Abbey had installed. Although these were usually found in the bar area, she'd managed to catch Billy Franklin on her way in that morning and had asked him to move it for her, something he was more than happy to assist with. She positioned herself comfortably in the blue-coloured, plush velvet, high back chair and tuned into Camilla's introduction.

'Right, everyone, before we start I'd like to ask each one of you to come up to the front and take one of these,' she held up a sheet of white oblong stickers, 'and write your name on it, please. Stick it to the front of your jumper – or whatever you're wearing – just by the left shoulder. This way I can get to learn your names quicker.'

The children surged forward and a hubbub of excited chatter rang out whilst they carried out the task in hand.

'Ouch!' Lily Hambly-Jones rubbed her upper arm having just been punched out of the way by Kerry Madison, who turned and poked out her tongue in response. Thankfully, there was no time for her to act further as everyone began returning to their seats.

Gregory Harvey put up his hand.

'Yes, Gregory?' Camilla encouraged.

'Is it true you're an actor, miss?' he began. 'My father says you're on the telly.'

Camilla smiled, relishing the unexpected attention. 'I am indeed an actor and I've been part of a long-running drama for some time now. I don't think any of you would have seen it, though, because it's on quite late at night.'

'My dad says you play a drug addict,' cut in Sam Madison, 'and that your husband's always knocking you about.'

This brought several concerned gasps from the younger children, who looked quite worried for her.

Camilla kept her smile plastered on her face as she answered, 'Well, we're not here to talk about that today – and don't forget, it's not real life. Let's concentrate on our rehearsal and maybe later on I can tell you about some of the other acting parts I've played. I think you'll be quite surprised.'

Whilst relieved at having diverted the discussion, Camilla felt frustrated that she seemed to have fallen foul again, given Sam's negative spin on her career. However, she knew she needed to push those feelings aside for now. 'Right!' she exclaimed. 'Jump up, everyone, and push your chairs to the side, please. Let's get warmed up!'

The children, who were keen to get going, scrambled to move their chairs while Camilla went over to the tables she'd placed along the back wall and switched on the CD player she'd brought along. Music began booming out, echoing around the huge room, causing the children to giggle with excitement at what was to come. They began jumping about immediately, anxious to get moving.

'Everyone ready?' They nodded their heads eagerly. 'Okay then, just follow me!' She began walking on the spot, her arms swinging by her sides, whilst keeping an eye on her protégés, ensuring they were following her every move and not overexerting themselves. As she put them through their paces, she began to really enjoy the session and soon forgot about her earlier discomfort.

So far, since she'd arrived in the village, nothing seemed to have worked out as she'd expected it to, and she'd been feeling somewhat disheartened of late. Certainly her relationship with Matt Hudson had cooled, although she was reminded then that they'd arranged to meet up later that week.

She brought her attention back to the group, to the huge smiles beaming back at her from every face.

Perhaps my time in the Hamptons isn't going to be so bad after all.

* * *

Rupert Coombes slapped his wife playfully on the bottom before scampering off to jump in the shower. They'd just enjoyed the most remarkable sex they'd had in years and he was still tingling from the intensity. He allowed the cooling water to run over his face and down his toned body, savouring the relaxing sensation until he was distracted by the opening of the door. 'Evie, what are you doing?' He laughed before becoming consumed with her again as she pulled him towards her and wrapped herself around him.

'Coffee?' Evie glanced up seductively as she poured them both a cup of the steaming beverage. She was dressed in a white silk negligee – which left little to the imagination – and, momentarily distracted, he went over and scooped her towards him for another embrace.

'You'll be the death of me.' He nuzzled her neck before finding his way to her mouth, then abruptly pulled away. 'I need to go, darling.'

She pouted sulkily. 'But it's Saturday.'

'I know, darling, but when you're the boss it's not a 9 to 5 job anymore.' He took a quick drink from his cup. 'Don't forget, those little trips to the South of

France and Geneva we've enjoyed recently are all off the back of this deal I've been working on, and there's plenty more where that came from too.' He slipped on his suit jacket before collecting his keys and briefcase. 'But I have to work to earn the pennies, my love.'

'I know, and I appreciate it,' Evie replied, smiling, before walking towards the front door to see him off. 'Will you be back for dinner tonight?'

He paused, rubbing his chin with his free hand. 'Depends on what time Luca's flight is – I can hardly leave him to amuse himself, can I? – but I'll call you later, promise.' He gave her a quick peck on the lips before getting into his car, and then he was gone.

Evie went inside and closed the front door again, humming merrily to herself. Luca Meier was the President of one of Switzerland's largest retail pharmacies and she fully understood the importance of his recent visit. This could be extremely lucrative for Rupert's company, and would no doubt set him far out in front of some of his major competitors. With that in mind, she was more than happy for him to be off working at weekends – or whenever required. The time they spent together more than made up for it. She smiled, sated from this morning's activities.

The front doorbell chimes rang out then, resounding around the large hallway. She glanced down at her attire, concerned it wasn't wholly appropriate for greeting visitors, but then shrugged her shoulders and answered it anyway.

'Good morning, Mrs. Coombes,' Cathy Fisher trilled, 'I hope I'm not disturbing you on this beautiful morning.' She was, of course, referring to the glorious weather and not the Coombes' morning activities.

'Not at all, do come in!' Evie clasped her negligee in front to afford herself at least some decency and stepped back to allow Cathy inside. 'If you give me a quick moment, I'll just go and change and make us some coffee. Please go through to the kitchen and make yourself at home.'

Delighted at receiving such a cheerful reception, Cathy went to settle herself at the table, gasping in surprise along the way as she entered the recently refurbished kitchen. A set of bi-folding doors had been installed at the far end of the room, giving them an incredible vista of the well-manicured lawns and gardens beyond. They were a delight to look out onto and she was momentarily distracted by the mix of birds outside, busy pairing up for the nesting season. She admired the traditional oak kitchen they'd had installed, and when the ornate country butler sink caught her eye she just had to go and run her fingers across the brightly patterned bowl.

'Sorry about that, Cathy.' Evie breezed in, having changed into a lavender sundress. She'd also scooped her unruly long red curls into a banana clip that was almost the same colour as her hair. 'I've been treating myself to a late morning today.'

'You deserve to, dear; I know you both work long hours.' Cathy had been one of the first residents to welcome the Coombes' just after they'd first moved in, bringing an invitation to a dinner that the Hambly-Joneses were hosting. Sadly, it clashed with their recent travel plans, much to their disappointment. 'I'm here on the take actually,' she joked whilst Evie made them some fresh coffee. 'We're holding a craft fair on the village green next weekend, with all the proceeds going to support homeless families this Easter. I wondered if you'd be happy to donate one or two of your paintings?' She hesitated, hoping she wasn't overstepping the mark. Whilst the locals were renowned for their generosity, Cathy never took anything for granted.

'Really? I'd be delighted to!' Evie exclaimed. 'As a matter of fact I've been playing about with painting some of these gorgeous spring flowers that have started to appear in the garden. I've used much smaller canvasses than my usual ones, but they've turned out quite well. I'd be happy for you to take some. When we've had our coffee I'll take you through to my studio and you can pick out the best ones. Now, tell me,' she added, offering Cathy a chocolate biscuit to go with her coffee, 'how did the dinner go?'

* * *

Laura Benjamin threw her phone across the bed, disappointed at having yet another date cancelled. This was the first weekend she'd had free in ages and the plan was for her to cook dinner for her new beau, followed by an amorous night of passion.

She sighed deeply, annoyed at the sudden change of plan. *Perhaps I've been playing things too cool – either that or he's going off me.* She wasn't a particularly emotional person; feminine, yes, but she wasn't one to sit around blubbering just because things didn't go her way. She idly toyed with the idea of calling the station to see if she could change shifts with someone else –

giving them the chance of a weekend off – but quickly decided against it.

Her phone beeped then, indicating a new message, and she rushed to wrestle it free from the duvet, wondering if he'd changed his mind.

She scanned the text and laughed out loud. *Cheeky sod.* It was from Phil Harris, one of her colleagues from the station. She pressed the call button and he answered almost instantly. 'You're up early, Sarge, did you get pushed out of bed?'

He chuckled. 'Thought you'd have your hands full at this time of the morning,' he returned, 'and it's Phil when we're off duty. Look, you're not the only one who can manage to pull a two-day break; I wondered if you fancied joining a few of us for a drink tonight? We're off to that wine bar over at Chipping Melbury.'

'I know the one you mean, The Melbury Fox? It's proper decent actually.' She hesitated, thinking for a moment. 'Yeah, I'll come along – thanks.'

'No worries, we'll be there from around 7 p.m., so whatever suits.' He paused before adding cheekily, 'There's a spare bed going at mine too if you want to have a drink.'

'You should be so lucky! I'll just grab a taxi, thanks. See you later.'

It wasn't unusual for police colleagues to date each other – in fact, many of the staff at Midford County Police station were either married, in a relationship, or had been involved in one at some point – and Laura wasn't averse to the idea at all. It's just that, until then, Laura hadn't been certain if Phil was winding her up or not. She didn't know many women who *weren't* attracted to him, but with his charm and good looks, everyone assumed he was already taken; he certainly didn't talk about his private life – not to her, anyhow.

Enthused at the unexpected invitation, she hopped out of bed and got into the shower. *If I get my skates on I'll have time to do a bit of shopping.* It'd been ages since she'd treated herself to something new – and why not? If wasn't as if she had anything better to do that evening.

* * *

'Wow, what a transformation!' Tiggy and Harry were spending the morning over at LC's bar, together with Sheridan and Mary Rose. 'You'd never guess this used to be a pub,' she continued, impressed.

'I'm glad you like it. Tawfique's excelled himself with the design – I don't think there'll be another place like it for miles around,' Sheldon shared proudly, the others nodding their heads in agreement.

When it had been The Swan Public House, it had offered little to entice people in; having been built in the early 70s, it had been all cold-looking painted cement walls and stone flooring, and the only thing the remaining furniture was fit for was a skip.

'They've really pulled out all the stops on this too, haven't they?' mused Harry. 'It looks almost complete.'

'Don't forget, Harry, the building's solid,' Sheldon replied. 'It's basically all fixtures and fittings. After we'd gutted the place and removed the Crittall windows, we installed solid hardwood double glazing, then laid new flooring – all reclaimed oak – and then the staircase was added and, finally, the mezzanine floor. Whilst all that was happening we had chippies replacing all the doorframes, doors, and all that malarkey – again using reclaimed timber – and then the toilets were completed gutted and renovated. You won't recognise them.'

'It looks much bigger, though,' Tiggy commented, wondering if they'd built an extension.

'Ah, that's because we've moved the bar right to the very far wall,' Sheldon explained. 'It was halfway across this room – diagonally – before, which took up most of the space. Tawfique has commissioned a bespoke bar in the shape of a scroll – beautiful it is, solid mahogany. The clever thing is that it will stretch from the far wall, all the way across and into the restaurant. This means that not only does it serve as a bar, but the bottom end will also act as a reception desk for the maitre'd – he can check guests in and there'll be a till and everything installed there for taking payments too. Clever, eh?' They nodded enthusiastically again as he continued, eager to complete the overall picture. 'Whilst we'll have some tables and chairs in this bar area, there'll be two huge leather Chesterfield sofas either side of the fireplace – and there are more on order for the mezzanine floor, along with a smaller bar. Perfect for private dining or drinks receptions, don't you think?'

'It's fabulous, Sheldon, really,' gushed Tiggy. 'What's left to do apart from the furniture?'

'The kitchen fitters are in next week, and that'll be completed by next Friday. Then it's the accommodation on the top floor, which again, is just going to be a case of redecorating and replacement furnishings.'

'Has Barnaby seen it?'

'He has, Tiggy, and he was going to join us today but he's had to go over to the golf club to help Georgina Fame with something or other. Between you and me,' he added, lowering his voice and winking, 'I think he's sweet on her.'

'Well, in that case, we'd better get this finished so he'll have more time on his hands!' Tiggy joked.

'I've every confidence we'll be ready to open next month,' Sheldon continued. 'The liquor licences have all been approved and we just need to get someone in to spruce up the gardens – you know, a few hanging baskets here and there. Make the place look pretty.'

'It's beginning to look quite the picture already – has the sign been organised?' Harry questioned.

'Funny you should ask that,' Sheldon replied. 'Mary and I went over to The Melbury Fox last night, you know, just to check out the competition, and they've got a fabulous-looking sign so I got the number of the chap who made it; I'll call him later and see what he can do for us. What we really need now – and this is where you two come in – is to find a chef and get the menu sorted. Oh, and some wines would help,' he added with a chuckle.

'I think we can handle that!' Harry looked towards Tiggy, who was nodding again in approval. 'Why don't we work on ideas over the coming week and have a get-together next Saturday? For dinner?' The latter question was aimed at Tiggy.

'Great idea,' she responded eagerly. 'Check with Barnaby, and if there are any problems, let me know. In the meantime, I can give Sidney Moffat a call, if you like; he did the gardens for us at Riverside Hall.'

'Of course he did, and he's a lovely chap too – retired, I think, but he welcomed the distraction. He was getting bored sitting at home all day.'

'Brilliant – thanks, Sheldon.' Tiggy went over to embrace him and then Mary. 'I can't believe this is actually happening, to be honest! Thank so much for all your hard work.'

'My pleasure; it's great to see it all coming together.'

'Just a quick thought,' Harry interjected, 'isn't Georgina reopening the country club soon? We wouldn't want to clash with that.'

Sheldon tapped his forefinger against his nose. 'I've got an inside man on the job, have no fear!'

They parted on high spirits.

CHAPTER SIXTEEN

'Come on, Sadie, you'll be late!' Jen yelled up the stairs before making her way back to the kitchen to finish off her packed lunch. Knowing it was quite a walk down the hill to the school bus stop, she added an extra mini roll before clicking shut the lid of the large oblong plastic box.

'I can't find my PE kit!' Sadie moaned. 'I'll get detention again. Did you wash it?'

Jen thought for a moment. 'Can't remember seeing it to be honest, love, but don't worry – I'll write you a note. Now, get your lunch and get going or you'll be late!'

Sadie started getting her things together and was already waiting by the door by the time Jen brought the note through.

'Here you are.' She handed her daughter the note and the lunchbox, kissed her goodbye, and watched her go before shutting the door and returning to bed.

Their life was very different to how it had been six years ago. Following the devastating death of Jen's husband Ron –

not to mention the manslaughter of Mickey Roberts – Jen and Sadie had made their escape to Wales, setting up a new life for themselves in a small village just outside of Cardiff. They'd rented a tiny two-up two-down terraced house, which was all Jen could afford until Upper Pethewick farm was sold. It was a fresh new start for them both, the main thing being that no one knew anything about them or their past. It was a clean slate from which to rebuild their lives – and Ron was never mentioned again.

Jen had taken up part-time secretarial work whilst Sadie was at school, and it was during this time that she met Mervyn 'Merv' Davies, an IT expert who'd used his skills to make a small fortune. Apart from divulging that she was a widow with a young child, Jen never referred to her tainted past again and it didn't occur to Merv to give it a second thought.

He'd told her he was divorced – having married far too young – and had also admitted that as he spent most of his time at work in those days, rather than at home, his party-loving wife had soon given him the elbow.

When Jen introduced Merv to Sadie, they seemed to get on well enough, although her daughter was incredibly shy and spent most of the time gazing at him, doe-eyed, through her thick fringe. Nevertheless, she didn't seem to find his company unpleasant, so when he asked Jen if they'd like to move in with him, she didn't give it a second thought.

Merv lived in an affluent part of Cardiff in an eight bedroom mansion, all with en-suite bathrooms. They married just before Sadie's 12th birthday, a huge affair that they'd held at a nearby castle, no one thinking to question the lack of guests from Jen's side of the family.

It was just after this time that Merv announced he was launching a new call centre business, which took off practically overnight. They became quite the celebrity couple around the *local area, with their fake tans, bleached hair, and whitened teeth, and they regularly entertained or attended a variety of functions and parties. It was during this time that they lost their focus.*

Having suffered so much trauma in such a short space of time, little Sadie Alcock began to show signs of having inherited her father's addictive personality, only her addiction was to food.

Before she'd even reached the age of 14, she weighed over 16 stone.

CHAPTER SEVENTEEN

'Hi, Ian, it's only me – just calling to see what time you want picking up on Thursday? Give me a call back when you get this message, darling. Love you.'

Lucy replaced the phone into the electric charger, her face etched with concern. That was the fourth time she'd tried to get hold of Ian and he still hadn't returned her call. She thought back to their last conversation and, although he'd seemed a bit miffed about her dating James, it hadn't appeared to greatly upset him. *Knowing him, he'll just turn up unannounced.*

Lucy was reminded that it wasn't the first time she'd had difficulty getting in contact with him, and with Easter just around the corner, she decided to simply wait and see what happened.

* * *

'Good morning, Margaret,' Richard greeted his PA as he headed towards his office, 'is Francine in yet?'

'No, apparently she's due in this afternoon,' came the reply.

Richard stood there opened-mouthed, clearly not impressed. 'I'm not sure what she thinks she's playing at but it's been two whole weeks since she's been in the office, out on supposed supplier visits – just how many suppliers does the lingerie department need, for Christ's sake?' He stormed off, slamming his office door behind him.

Margaret shook her head. Having a bone of her own to pick with Francine, she completely shared his frustration. Just then, the intercom buzzed unexpectedly on her desk. 'Yes, Richard?' she answered promptly.

'Can you call HR and ask them to come up to my office? I want to check our position with Francine's employment.'

'Yes, of course,' Margaret replied, a little surprised but not at all unhappy with this development.

There was silence for a moment before Richard added, 'I'm certainly not going to stand by and let her take us for a ride.'

* * *

Laura Benjamin had a spring in her step as she walked her regular beat that morning, stopping every now and then to chat to the local traders, checking everything was in order. There'd been a spate of shoplifting in the area and Sergeant Phil Harris had asked her and PC Danny King to step up police presence, hoping to nip it in the bud.

She checked her watch – keen for the shift to end as she had a date planned for that evening – and as she rounded the corner of Midford County High Street she came face to face with Danny.

'Everything okay your end, Laura?' he asked.

'Looking good, there doesn't seem to have been any problems over the weekend. You?'

'Yeah, all good. I went along Mill Street and then up towards Mason's butchers; no one had anything to report along there either.'

'Great news!' Laura replied. 'Let's head off towards the library next, then; we can stop off at *Delightful Dolls* for a well-earned cuppa.'

Danny fell into step beside her and they began chatting about the night out she'd joined in with a couple of weeks ago.

'It was a right laugh, wasn't it?' Danny asked. 'Especially when Sarge kept doing his impressions of Jill.' Jill Swift was another Sergeant at Midford County Police station, along with Matt Hudson – each of them heading up a different shift. She was renowned for two things: her thick Yorkshire accent and her flame red hair. It was the former that Phil Harris had managed to perfect.

'I know,' giggled Laura, 'and when that woman asked for his autograph because she thought she'd seen him off the television, I almost wet myself!'

'Yeah, me too! We should definitely meet up more often; it was the perfect stress reliever.'

Laura agreed. 'You can count me in.'

They were distracted then by a suspicious-looking trio of teenage boys who'd just walked out of Bishop's Court, a small courtyard set back off the high street. There was only one shop open there – the

Eclectic Electronics Emporium – which was run by an elderly Greek gentleman called Kiki. He sold everything from capacitors to bread makers, the shop being a treasure trove of antique and modern components. Having recently branched out into mobile phones, he was getting more than the usual footfall of late and had been targeted on several occasions by the mystery shoplifter.

The trio were walking with their backs towards the young PCs, not having seen them as they turned the corner back onto the high street. They were all wearing hoodies and faded jeans, and their expensive branded trainers stood out like sore thumbs. Laura had momentarily seen the middle boy holding his arms against his chest – like he was hiding something – and she shared her concerns with her colleague.

'Let's keep following them and radio in our suspicions along the way,' he suggested.

Laura nodded in acknowledgement and they stepped up their pace. *I do love my job but I hope this doesn't drag on – I've got a date to prepare for.*

* * *

Francine Dubois knew she'd been pushing her luck, but if the next meeting went as planned, she hoped it would give her sufficient leverage to avoid Richard's wrath.

Having turned up at Hampton Manor House to try and wangle an invitation to dinner, she hadn't expected things to turn out as they did, and she couldn't believe she'd made such a fool of herself. The only thing she could think of to repair the damage was to stay away from the office completely until things had settled down – or so she thought.

The weekend distraction certainly hadn't helped.

As she drove along, her mind wandered to the past couple of days when, quite unexpectedly, her one-night stand from a couple of weeks ago had turned up unannounced – something she didn't appreciate. Usually.

A flutter of lustful butterflies surged through her as she recalled their very steamy encounter. Although he'd presented an unexpected but nevertheless welcomed distraction at the time, despite their fervour, it was just sex – *albeit very good sex!* – and when he'd finally left she'd made it very clear to him not to call on her again.

Her goal was closer now than it had ever been before and she needed to remain focussed on the road ahead.

* * *

It was the end of morning surgery and Jon Anderson made his way to Pradeep Chandola's consultation room, knocking lightly on the door before entering.

'Jon,' he welcomed, 'come on in and take a seat.'

Jon sat down opposite him. 'I just wanted to know how you've been getting on; Steph tells me your list has been full every day this week?'

Pradeep smiled proudly. 'Yes, it has, and I've had some returning patients too, which is always a good sign!' he laughed.

'Indeed,' Jon acknowledged. 'I hear the psychotherapy is warming up too?'

'Yes, I've had a good mix of private and NHS patients, so it seems to be really taking off. I've a couple of interesting cases, actually – one of which is *PTSD* – and we've made some progress already.'

'Excellent,' said Jon, standing up to leave, 'I've got a GP meeting over in Chipping Melbury so I have to be going, but let me know if there's anything you need. You can always call me at home too; we've often got the kettle on or a bottle open.' He smirked, then suddenly remembered something else. 'I nearly forgot, how's Esha? It was lovely to see her at the Hambly-Jones dinner but she didn't look herself if you don't mind me saying.'

Pradeep frowned, looking concerned too. 'Not at all, Jon,' he said. 'She's had a bit of postnatal depression but she won't speak to anyone about it.' He looked down at his hands and Jon retook his seat.

'Ah, that would explain it. I'm sorry to hear that, Pradeep; it must be hard for all of you, what with starting a new job, moving house, and having a new baby to care for. I'm more than happy to give you some time off if you think that would help?'

Pradeep smiled at him, grateful for the suggestion. 'Thanks, but my presence seems to make her worse at the moment – I'm just not sure what to do for the best. We've an excellent nanny,' he smiled, 'she takes care of Salena and most of the housework so that Esha can go out and about, but she finds it hard to leave the house.'

Jon nodded knowingly. 'Would you mind if I asked Lizzie to pay Esha a visit?' he asked. 'Discreetly, of course. It's just that Lizzie suffered with postnatal depression after our second child was born, and sometimes when women recognise it in others it can often help them to unburden. What do you think?'

Pradeep smiled gratefully again, holding his head up as if a weight had been lifted from his shoulders. 'Thank you. I think that's just what the doctor ordered.'

* * *

'Where have you been?'

Francine jumped at Richard's unexpected presence, placing a hand on her chest. 'You made me jump,' she laughed graciously. He stood in front of her desk, glaring at her and waiting for an explanation. 'I've been busy building up some exclusive suppliers for us, Richard,' she explained, beckoning with her hand. 'Come around here and I'll show you.'

As intrigue always seemed to get the better of Richard he begrudgingly went around to her side of the desk whilst she clicked madly with the computer mouse, having loaded up a number of websites she was keen to share with him.

He scanned his eyes across the screen as several major brands such as *Dimarcos, enchantée, Millbrook* and *Louise Carter* screamed out at him, and he leaned in to take a closer look at some of their products. He didn't realise, however, that the action caused his arm to slip along the back of the chair she was sitting in – something that didn't go unnoticed by Francine. Her heart was pounding in her chest as the musky aroma from his favoured aftershave permeated her nostrils, and she leaned back, savouring the touch of his warm arm against her back.

'Oh, excuse me.' He snatched his arm away, repulsed, and she quelled the surge of disappointment that seared through her before managing to draw him in again with yet another exclusive designer.

'So, what's with all this, Francine?' Richard asked eventually. 'Are you trying to tell me you've been driving around the UK visiting some of our finest suppliers? With what purpose, exactly?'

She laughed cunningly. 'It's not exactly been a busman's holiday, Richard – I've been oiling wheels that have long been rusted.'

'Let's dispense with the metaphors shall we? And?'

'*And* I've secured exclusivity for Hambly-Jones for the next two years' spring and summer ranges with three of them.' She sat back smugly in her chair, waiting for her words to sink in.

'Is *Süsse* one of them?' She nodded in acknowledgement and he let out a gasp of disbelief. 'Well, I need to see evidence of this before any decisions are made, and samples too – everything they've got.'

She smiled, opening out her arms. 'No problem at all,' she reassured Richard, knowing she'd finally hooked him. 'Actually, you're invited to join us for dinner tonight – I'm meeting up with Emilia Weber, the MD of *Süsse*.'

'I know who Emilia is,' he interrupted, 'I'll be there. Leave the details with Margaret.'

'Don't you want to travel together? Save fuel and all that?'

He turned and glared at her with disdain. 'Leave the details with Margaret and I'll meet you there.'

Francine nodded, smiling. In truth, she wasn't really bothered whether they travelled together or not.

I have an ace up my sleeve, and now I'm the one holding all the cards.

CHAPTER EIGHTEEN

Camilla Barrington-Smythe was leading another rehearsal for the *Fortunettes* at Ashton Abbey. 'Great warm up, guys – now stretch those muscles out!'

They were all well practiced at this by now and she kept an eye on them as she went to change the CD and grab some song sheets. 'Okay, today we're going to listen to the song you'll be dancing to for the competition.' A hubbub of excitement spun around the room as she handed them each a song sheet.

'Who's Daz Rice?' Aaron Fitzgerald called out – the living image of his wayward father both in looks and personality.

'Daz Rice is a very good friend of mine and a renowned musician,' Camilla explained. 'He's very kindly given us permission to use one of the songs from his Americana debut album, *Precious Times*,' she continued, delighting in their excited response, '*and* he said if we win the competition, he'll come and play for us – right here in the Hamptons.' This announcement was met with great enthusiasm, and as they were clearly keen to get on she went over to switch the CD player on. 'Let's all listen to the song first and then I'll go through the routine step by step, okay? The song's called *Emily's Child*. Here we go!'

As the melody played out, Daz Rice's must-hear voice soon had the children nodding their heads and jiggling about in time to the music. As the song came to a close Camilla switched the player off and turned around to face them. 'Well, did you like it?'

'YEESSSSS!' they screamed. The age range went from 6 to 16 years, and the younger ones jumped up and down, waving their hands in the air.

'Brilliant!' She returned their wave, beaming at them. 'Let's begin then! I want to start by putting everyone in a formation, and you'll stay in these places from now on, okay? So, if you can all move over towards the right side of the room, then come over when I call your name, that'd be great.'

The group reformed by the wall as requested, still fired up from the song they'd just heard – the tune was really upbeat and motivational.

'Dylan!' Camilla called. 'You're here. Next row. Sam, here and Sara, thank you. Next row, Louisa, Aaron, Kerry,' she indicated where she wanted each of them to stand, 'next row then, James, Lily, Thom...'

'Camilla.' Diana Fortune got up out of the comfortable chair that was becoming her second home, such was the amount of time she'd spent sitting in it of late.

'Yes, Diana?' Camilla threw her a frustrated look from across the other side of the room. *What's wrong now?*

'A word.' She motioned with her finger and they stepped outside the door of the Great Hall so they wouldn't be overheard. 'I thought I'd asked you to put Lily Hambly-Jones up at the very front,' she said, expressing her disappointment – particularly as they'd spent several times over the past week perfecting the formation.

'I disagree.' Camilla put her hands on her hips and jutted out her jaw. 'I'm the choreographer and I think otherwise.'

Diana was not impressed. 'She's the only one in the group that can twirl a baton,' she persisted.

'Anyone can learn how to do that – it's a piece of cake – and anyway, we're practicing with pom-poms to begin with, and I say she's best off towards the back.'

'Whilst I value your input, this is *my* gig and these are *my Fortunettes,*' Diana insisted. 'You are to place Lily at the front as I requested, and that's the end of it.' She paused for a moment, catching her breath. 'I must say, Camilla,' she added brusquely, 'you've become very difficult of late. Whatever's the matter?'

She shrugged her shoulders. 'I'm sorry you feel that way, Diana. I suppose I'm just getting fed up with you calling all the shots – why bother calling me in at all if you're going to continually undermine my decisions? I'm just doing what you're paying me for.'

'That's right.' Diana leaned closer, lowering her voice. 'I'm paying you a lot of money too. And, if you recall, your contract clearly states that I can terminate it at any time, so I'll just leave that with you.' With that Diana headed back inside, feeling somewhat shaken by their altercation.

'Right, everyone!' Camilla breezed in a few moments later, forcing a smile onto her face. 'Let's begin that last row again, shall we? James, stay where you are. Anna-Maria change with Lily, Thomas stay, Crystal – let's have you over here – next row Daisy, Gregory, and Millie, leaving Isabella here please. Jemima and Lily, you're at the front.'

Once everyone was in place Camilla flounced off to start the music again. Fortunately, her displeasure wasn't easily noted and the group excitedly accepted their given places without question.

'Well done, Lily!' Sara Palmer-Reid called out from behind, indicating the favoured spot, and Lily turned and smiled at her. She was grateful for Sara's support but it earned her a scowl from Kerry Madison in the process. Camilla was also scowling, but as she was still facing away from them, there was no one to witness it.

Through no fault of her own, Lily had acquired herself another enemy that day, only this one had greater consequences – ones that were far worse than anything Kerry Madison could do to her.

CHAPTER NINETEEN

adie Alcock was standing outside the home she shared with her mother and stepfather and was gasping for breath, having struggled to walk up the steep hill from the bus stop. Knowing that Jen and Merv were out for the evening at a launch party for a local restaurant, she let herself in and made her way towards the kitchen, where she kicked off her worn trainers and flopped down at the kitchen table, catching sight of a note from her mother.

'Won't be back until late – don't wait up! Merv went down the chippy so your tea's in the oven.'

She threw it back down on the table in disgust. Talk about ironic – this morning's she's having a go at me about my weight, saying I'm letting the family down, and the next moment she's forcing junk food on me!

It was a familiar pattern that Sadie was becoming more than a little tired of. At 25 and almost 23 stone her life was becoming a daily struggle; even the simplest of tasks seemed almost impossible, and her personal hygiene was rapidly suffering. She seemed to constantly be the brunt of Jen's jibes

194

and was fed up of being continually nagged for being overweight, yet every time she attempted to address it, Jen became oblivious and continued to buy all the wrong foods, knowing full well that in doing so it scuppered any efforts Sadie made to lose the weight.

After regaining her breath, she gathered the still warm package from the oven and opened it to find two steak and kidney pies and a large portion of chips staring back at her.

Suddenly, in the cold light of day, she had an epiphany: the realisation that on most days she would polish this all off without a second thought suddenly made her feel very sick indeed.

Her attention was drawn then to the day's post resting on the kitchen counter, and she opened a thick embossed envelope to find an invitation addressed to her. It seemed yet another one of her friends was getting married. In fact, Sadie suddenly realised, most of her friends were now either married or coupled up, and some even had children.

Sadie wanted that. She wanted all of that. It's not as if she hadn't tried to discuss this with her mother, either, but each time Sadie attempted to address her weight and appearance, Jen just laughed and brushed her words aside, presenting her instead with yet another pizza or making her a special tuna and cheese melt – or, as with today, sending Merv off to the chippy. It seemed that Jen just didn't want her daughter to get a life of her own, yet she also seemed intent on making her life as miserable as possible.

Sadie placed her head in her hands, confused. Was it her mother? Or is it me who's struggling to face the real truth? *She knew she was the one who ate all the wrong foods; she had the ability to change that, at least. So, instead of wolfing down the food in front of her like she usually would, she stood up and threw the pie and chips in the bin before heading upstairs for a shower.*

The next morning, renewed with a sense of determination, Sadie set off for work earlier than usual, leaving Jen and Merv snoring in the land of nod after enjoying yet another late night out on the town. She smiled as she went. Today is the start of a new life.

Having worked for Roberts, Lewis & Hughes steelworks since she left school – and achieving a promotion to Senior Secretary a few years ago – she'd recently applied for the position of PA to Emlyn Lewis, one of the founding members and CEO, as his current PA Stella Briggs was leaving to pursue a career in Australia. Sadie truly believed that not only would this finally impress her mother and give her something to be proud of, but that it would also give her just the incentive she needed to embark on a proper weight loss program, especially with all the extra travel the new position involved – meaning time away from Jen, and therefore temptation.

Imbued with self-confidence she headed to her office, certain she'd secure the promotion that day. She was, after all, the most experienced of all the other candidates by far.

Stopping off at the ladies restroom, she'd just taken herself into one of the toilet cubicles when she was alerted to the sound of the main door opening, immediately followed by two familiar voices. She smiled to herself, recognising the voices of her friends, and was just about to shout out a cheeky greeting when their words stopped her dead in her tracks.

'So, is Emlyn telling her today then, Stella, or what?'

'Yes, I told you – it'll all be signed and sealed by the end of the day, don't you worry. It'll be after his lunch meeting, though. He said he'll need a pint or two before dealing with that lard arse!' They fell about laughing whilst touching up their make-up, oblivious to anyone else that might be there. 'It's bad enough having to cope with the smell, Chlo, but the size of

it! I mean, how could she ever think she's PA material, looking like that?' They were giggling like silly schoolgirls now.

'Minging is what it is, Stella – minging, I tell you. Me and the rest of the girls are all sick of it too.'

'Well, with any luck, Chlo, she'll take the hint and fuck off! We can't sack her, after all, but who wants people like her working for 'em, eh?'

With that they left the toilet, shrieking with more laughter along the way.

Sadie felt sick to her stomach. Her face was wet with involuntary tears, which were still streaming down her face, and realising that she'd been holding her breath the whole time her 'friends' had been in the toilets, she took a deep breath in. Chloe Thomas has only been with the company a year and a bit; I've worked here for over nine! *But she also knew that not only was Chloe bright and bubbly; she was also keen to get ahead.* She's also petite, blonde, and beautiful – something I'll never be.

Or so she thought.

Having washed her tear-stained face Sadie finally left the bathroom, but instead of heading towards her desk as usual, she turned around and walked back through the reception area and out of the front door.

Finding herself at a safe distance away from the building, she stopped to collect her thoughts.

Her legs felt like jelly, something that reminded her of the time she'd been hauled off to the head teacher's office at secondary school for eating in class; her legs had turned to jelly that time too. She'd never received such a savage telling off before, so much so it almost caused her to lose control of her bladder.

Sadie knew that if she returned home she would be faced with her mother's wrath, but she also knew that once Jen had calmed down she'd just ply Sadie with more food than you could shake a stick at. It was simply her way. Of course, she would no doubt then use it as another opportunity to tell her – as she'd done a million times before – that she didn't even need to work; Merv had plenty of money to provide for them all. But that wasn't something Sadie wanted. She wanted to carve out a life of her own.

Without consciously choosing to, she found herself at the bus station, taking a seat on one of the metal benches just inside the ticket hall. As the rush hour had been and gone it was fairly quiet, presenting her with the ideal opportunity to try and clear her head. About 10 minutes later, she took herself over to the counter, suddenly thankful that Jen and Merv hadn't taken a single penny off her since she'd started working; whilst it could be said that she might not be in the best of health, her finances certainly were.

'Can I book a ticket on the next coach out, please?'

'The 9.20's just left for Swansea, love. It'll be an hour until the next,' the grey-haired cashier kindly informed her.

'No, that's alright; I'm not wanting Swansea. Where's the next bus going, please?'

'Well, there's a coach leaving for St. Albans shortly; it's on a two-day trip to the Cathedral and Roman ruins.'

Sadie gasped inwardly; surely this was a sign!

After her mother had married Merv, his father Randall used to come over and babysit her whilst they were out and about socialising and building up their 'celebrity' profile. Sadie loved her Grandpa Davies dearly and used to listen wide-eyed as he regaled her with tales from his youth.

With his 16th birthday looming (he told her) he feared having to go down the mines to work as was expected in those days, taking on a 'job for life' – or so they thought. As each day passed, he grew more and more fearful until one day, gripped by the impending doom of being trapped underground, he upped and left without a word. He ended up in St. Albans of all places, quickly gaining a job as a kitchen hand in a local hotel.

'One to St. Albans please,' *Sadie requested, a huge smile on her face for the first time that day. Suddenly, she was somehow filled with the knowledge that everything was going to be just fine.*

CHAPTER TWENTY

Not only was the May bank holiday the perfect date for Georgina Fame to have chosen to launch her refurbished health and country club, but the weather had turned out perfectly too.

May had welcomed warmer sunshine and the locals had taken the opportunity to dust off their summer clothes – or treat themselves to some new attire, judging by the stylish outfits Georgina had seen so far that morning.

'There's quite the crowd gathering outside,' remarked Marcie Moon, Georgina's PA, as she gazed out of their office window. Georgina had chosen to convert a room at the far corner of the East Wing to use as her office; it had previously been used as a reading room, and being on the ground floor, it presented the perfect angle from which to view the impressive hotel entrance and grounds.

'Well, if the online bookings are anything to go by, this place will be heaving in a few hours,' Georgina replied, happy with how things were going so far.

They'd had a lot to organise in preparation for today's event, including a new look website that had been launched a couple of weeks prior; its crisp, contemporary design perfectly showcased the impressive venue and the many services on offer, and they'd also introduced an easy-to-use booking system for the various talks and presentations that were on offer throughout the day – including a mini taster session in the Westbrooke restaurant, which had been the first to sell out. As Georgina was due to lead four sessions, giving an introduction to her famous weight loss system, she was relying on Marcie to be her eyes and ears when she was otherwise engaged.

The grand opening was due to commence at 11 a.m. and a huge cornflower-coloured silk ribbon had already been placed across the hotel's main doors, ready for Georgina to cut when she formerly opened her flagship property. She'd invited Reverend Peter Fisher to perform a blessing prior to this; he was currently ensconced in the restaurant with his wife, Cathy, both of them enjoying a complimentary full English breakfast before the proceedings began.

* * *

'Will you *stop,* Pradeep!' Esha shouted, placing her hands over her ears and crouching down on the floor.

Pradeep followed suit, wanting to be on the same level as his wife. 'Esha,' he pleaded gently, 'we need to discuss this.'

She began crying then, and when he reached out in an attempt to comfort her she pushed him hastily away, glaring at him as though he'd just tried to attack her.

Just a few hours ago they'd been enjoying a leisurely breakfast with their nanny, Bronwyn, whilst baby Salena was sleeping peacefully in her nursery. They'd been chatting excitedly about the open day they were all looking forward to attending, giving Bronwyn a chance to mingle with some of her own friends. After they'd finished eating, Pradeep had offered to clear away the dishes whilst the girls got ready, humming merrily to himself as he worked, excited to finally be able to show off his beautiful wife and daughter in public. Apart from attending the Hambly-Jones dinner several weeks ago, they hadn't been out together since – and getting Esha to attend that event had been challenging to say the least.

As Bronwyn had been busy carefully securing Salena in her car seat, Pradeep had ventured upstairs to see what was keeping Esha. He'd found her pacing the floor of their bedroom, seeming extremely anxious. This had concerned him, but – as usual – he hadn't been sure how best to broach the issue.

'I'm not going,' she'd said, beginning to panic and sounding breathless, 'and you can't make me!'

Pradeep had held out his arms to try and soothe her, but the motion had made her even more agitated, leading to their current stand-off.

More worryingly, as he'd discovered through Bronwyn, Lizzie Anderson had called in the week and Esha had feigned a headache, asking Bronwyn to pass on her apologies. So much for that plan.

'You can't go on like this, Esha,' he urged gently. 'You need help.'

She flung her hands off her face and glared up at him, causing him to become unbalanced from his crouching position and forcing him to stand up again.

'Oh, here we go – don't play the bloody mind doctor with me, Pradeep!' she raged, also getting to her feet. 'If you have your way, you'll soon have me locked up in the funny farm!'

Pradeep stared at his wife, horrified that she could even suggest such a thing. 'Darling, no – no, that's not what I meant at all!' He reached out to reassure her but she began backing away from him.

'I bet you told Dr Anderson about me, didn't you?' she asked, before understanding washed over her face. The penny had clearly dropped. 'Oh my god, that's why his wife came over, isn't it? *Isn't it?*' she screamed. 'What did you tell him, Pradeep? Does he think I'm crazy too?' She was becoming more and more agitated and was now backing out of their bedroom in apparent fear. It hurt Pradeep to see her like this, more than he could express.

'Esha, no! I didn't say anything of the sort – I mean, I can see you're struggling to cope, and I...'

'*Struggling!*' She was becoming manic with rage now whilst Pradeep was mentally cursing himself, wishing he'd never mentioned anything to Jon at all. 'You think I can't cope? You have *no idea!*' She was still backing away from him, neither of them having realised that she'd now reached the edge of the stairs.

Suddenly and without warning, she tumbled backwards down the staircase.

'*Esha!*' Pradeep screamed. He made to grab her but it was too late.

As he watched in horror, a sickening thud rang out as Esha's head came into contact with the wall.

* * *

Whilst the focus of Georgina Fame's Hotel and Country Club was primarily health and fitness, she was keen to communicate that the venue was open to everyone, and that there was plenty on offer for all.

The hotel boasted an impressive 102 bedrooms, and every single one of them had been given at least a fresh lick of paint; a total of 65 rooms had been completely refurbished, with the remaining currently underway. The previously tired Spa area had been considerably extended, the transformation dramatic. There were 10 new treatment rooms offering a full range of alternative and massage therapies – together with a range of beauty treatments – and a state-of-the-art hot tub and sauna had been installed upon a decked platform outside, affording the most glorious views across the beguiling Cotswolds countryside. A full Olympic-sized swimming pool was currently in the process of being built, and whilst guests would have to make use of the old pool in the meantime, the surrounding area had also been substantially refurbished. A sea of wooden sun loungers had been installed there, all fitted with plush waterproof cushions of the same glorious cornflower blue that had been used throughout all of Georgina Fame's branding. The next step was to turn this area into a full working gym, once the other pool was ready.

The golf course had also received a makeover; Rory Harrington, a former professional golfer – and the new club manager – had taken the lead in redesigning the 18-hole golf course, making it far more challenging than it had been before. He was hopeful this would attract more members – particularly given that the new clubhouse now had a generous lounge bar for players to relax in both before and after their game.

The empty land towards the back of the property – which Georgina had originally questioned – was where the *Nourish and Gain Rendezvous Village* had been built. All of oak timber structure, five *Rendezvous Rooms* had been crafted and placed together to create a pentagon, with the centre structure forming the main reception area. It was the jewel in Georgina's crown and she couldn't wait to show it off.

'It's almost time to begin!' Marcie reminded Georgina as she began gathering the papers together detailing the day's itinerary, which she then secured on a wooden-backed clipboard.

'Has the bouncy castle been set up? What about the giant slide?'

Marcie nodded in confirmation to Georgina's questions. 'Cheryl called me about 10 minutes ago to confirm it's all in place and to say that the Midford County Donkey Sanctuary has finally arrived too. We don't need to worry about that, though, because by the time the opening speeches are complete they'll be ready to go.'

The planning of today's event had been extensive and Georgina was grateful to have Marcie's support. She wanted to ensure that there was something for everyone to enjoy throughout the day, therefore the hotel grounds were bursting with a colourful combination of food and drink stalls, fairground rides, and an assortment of play areas – all fully staffed – to keep the younger generation entertained whilst she and her team worked their charm on the rest.

Slowly, Georgina rose from her chair and smoothed down her dress; she'd complemented the cornflower blue linen with a floral scarf depicting tiny grey and blue buds on a white background.

'Right,' she said, smiling at her assistant, 'let the show begin!'

* * *

Rita and Ralph Denby were strolling, hand in hand, along a paved mountain road in Samos, a Greek island in the eastern Aegean Sea. They'd spent the morning at Megali Panagia, one of the island's most stunning monasteries, founded in 1586 by two brothers: the monks Nilos and Dionysius. They'd stopped for lunch on the way back, having spotted a quaint taverna nestled on the edge of a charming mountain village. After feasting on fresh octopus served with a delicious Greek salad and homemade bread, they were now soaking up the glorious views across the mountain and the sea whilst making their way back to the car they'd hired that morning.

'Isn't the weather glorious?' Rita asked her husband, waving a decorated fan in front of her face.

Ralph nodded, agreeing. 'It's so quiet here too; imagine waking up to this view every morning.' They'd been on the island for almost a week and had embraced the locals' slow pace of life. They were looking quite tanned too – despite the sunscreen Rita kept applying in copious amounts – and it suited them both.

'Quite different from our own vista at home, Ralphie!' she mused.

He nodded in acknowledgement, the mention of home serving as a reminder. 'I wonder how the opening's going today.'

Rita stopped fanning herself for a moment. 'What opening?'

'James Turvey told me that the fancy dinner we weren't invited to at the Hambly-Joneses several weeks back was to host Georgina Fame – she's the one who's bought the golf club over at Swinford St. George.'

'Georgina Fame – the weight loss lady?'

'That's right, love; she's had it all done up apparently and the big reveal is today.' He glanced at his watch. 'It should be well underway by now.'

Rita sniffed. 'I'm not really interested in all that; thankfully, we don't need to worry about being overweight.'

'It's not all lettuce and exercise bikes by all accounts, love,' Ralph said, rather defensively. 'The golf course is going to be accepting members again and they're building a decent swimming pool too – it's about time we had somewhere to go that isn't continually invaded by kids, don't you think?'

He unlocked the car and they both got inside, Ralph immediately turning on the engine to kick-start the air conditioning, which they took a moment to appreciate.

Ralph's referral to the Hamptons certainly wasn't making Rita homesick. She was thoroughly enjoying herself and it wasn't just due to the change of scenery, either; here, they didn't have the distraction of village life – or the TV. They were simply enjoying the lazy days and their pleasant chats over dinner that went long into the night, sharing a bottle or two of wine in the process. It was divine, and like the honeymoon they'd never had.

'We can go and have a look around there when we get back, if you like – it'll give us another thing to enjoy together,' Ralph pointed out.

Rita hadn't thought of it like that, and after a moment she treated her husband to one of her rare, lingering smiles.

They say you should embrace life in your 60s, and if I've got anything to do with it, that's exactly what life in the Denby household is going to be like from now on.

* * *

'Slow *down*, Kerry!' barked Derek Madison. Never one to miss a freebie, he'd taken his family along to the open day and, courtesy of Georgina Fame, they'd all just enjoyed a tasty hot dog – only his daughter Kerry had nipped behind their backs and helped herself to another one. 'Look at the state of you!' he ranted. 'You've spilt tomato ketchup all down your dress now.'

His wife, Beryl, rolled her eyes and rooted around her handbag for some wet wipes, inwardly praying that he wasn't about to kick off.

'It's not my fault!' Kerry argued back, her bravery having been fuelled by the sugar rush from the candy floss she'd consumed when they'd first arrived.

'It's alright, Derek, I can deal with this,' Beryl said as she began rubbing at the stain on Kerry's gingham blue dress. She only made it worse, however.

'For God's sake, look at her! Why do you always have to show us up like this, Kerry?' Derek ranted, shaking his head in exasperation.

The Madisons ran the butcher's shop in Hampton Ash, which was very popular due to their range of organic meats and their award-winning sausages. He was hoping to add Georgina Fame's country club to their client list, especially as their website claimed they '*use local produce wherever possible*', and he kept looking around, eager to find a member of her staff to approach in order to introduce himself.

'Would you leave it, Derek? I'll take her to the bathroom and sort it out there,' Beryl said. She made to walk away, grabbing Kerry by the arm, but apparently Derek hadn't finished.

'Why can't you be more like your other friends?' he questioned his daughter. 'Take that Lily Hambly-Jones, for instance – such a lovely, well-mannered girl she is. You could learn a lot from someone like her.'

He was too beside himself with anger to notice the look of hurt starting to form in Kerry's big brown eyes, and she stamped alongside her mother as they made their way towards the hotel.

I can't do anything right, and we all know whose fault that is!

* * *

Georgina Fame was delivering the third of the four presentations she'd planned for that day and her audience were spellbound.

The opening ceremony had gone better than anticipated as Reverend Fisher – ever the comedian – gave an excellent speech that had everyone roaring with laughter before he carried out the serious task of performing a blessing on Georgina's new venture.

Since then the day seemed to have flown by as she was whisked from one meeting to another, still trying to keep on top of the day and ensuring that everything was running as smoothly as possible.

The audience gasped as a photograph of Georgina prior to her successful weight loss appeared on the screen in front of them – a far cry from the glamorous blonde with the enviable figure who stood in front of them now. Her younger self had very short, dark hair, and apart from the eyes – which were framed by unusually long lashes – and petite nose, it was hard to believe she was even the same person.

She walked confidently across the stage, coming to rest by the side of the photograph. 'This was me 12 years ago,' she announced, causing a hum of disbelief to buzz around the room. She smiled, being used to receiving such a shocked reaction. She was wearing a wireless mike and her clear, well-spoken voice held everyone's attention as she continued. 'At my heaviest I weighed in at 23 stone – yes,' she responded to her surprised audience, 'that's right – 23 stone – and I lost a total of 13 and a half stone!' A spontaneous round of applause rang out. 'The extra weight affected me in many ways,' she explained. 'I struggled to breathe, I struggled to walk anywhere, and even the basics of personal care became a daily struggle. I knew I needed to do something, but I was far too ashamed to seek professional help.'

She paused, letting her words sink in before carrying on. 'As I began to accept that I needed to address my health issues, I undertook my own research, spending hours and hours trawling through websites and visiting libraries. I invested a huge proportion of my time experimenting with food and exercise until I finally found what worked, and that's how *Nourish and Gain with Georgina Fame* was born.' She smiled as the crowd applauded. When they were done, she continued, 'I *nourished* my body with healthy food and *gained* better health by losing weight and getting fit.'

She looked out at the impressed, fascinated faces before her. Whilst not all members of the crowd in front of her were necessarily in need of such a drastic weight loss, they were all in awe of learning about her personal battle.

'I was borderline diabetic and my blood pressure was sky high, but I managed to reverse it all through my now famous system.' She smiled widely. 'But don't just take it from me – let me introduce you to some of my successes. These people have since become *Nourish and Gain* Ambassadors, and they'll be helping me run the rendezvous meetings. Okay, let's welcome Molly Cipriani!' Applause rang out again as her colleague joined her on the stage, dressed in the now familiar cornflower blue uniform. 'This was Molly just three years ago, weighing in at over 20 stone.' Again, a gush of disbelief was expressed as a picture of Molly at her heaviest was displayed on the screen – a far cry from the elegant brunette standing nearby.

'Hello everyone,' Molly said as she addressed the crowd. 'I lost 11 stone with the *Nourish and Gain* plan and I've never looked back. From someone who seemed to be continually visiting the doctors with one problem or another, I'm now enjoying full health, and I make the most of each day.' Yet again the crowd applauded.

Georgina went on to introduce the three other *Nourish and Gain* Ambassadors she'd employed, each one proud to share their journey with the people in front of them. Each time, the crowd gave them their full attention.

Several minutes later, Georgina brought the meeting to a close. 'Right, ladies and gentlemen, I hope that's given you all some food for thought!' she quipped. 'If you'd like to find out more – or if you're interested in signing up to our plan – Jack and Liam will be giving a guided tour of our unique *Weight Loss Rendezvous Village* starting in a few minutes. I'd like to thank you for joining me today and for giving me your time.'

Georgina was treated to a standing ovation as she left the stage and went to join Marcie.

'Well, that was pretty impressive,' remarked Charlotte Palmer-Reid.

'She looks amazing,' enthused Skye Harvey as she gazed lovingly towards her husband, Alexander. He perfectly understood the need to shed a few pounds; he'd experienced his own health problems in the past and Skye had helped him get back into shape.

'Well, I'm up for joining the health club,' he added, with several others from the Hamptons' group expressing their keenness too.

'I do miss my morning swims,' added Poppy. 'When I worked in London, there was a pool nearby that I used most days.'

Jonathan Palmer-Reid was sitting on the periphery, carefully taking in every word. He was uncomfortable joining in the discussion – given his own heath concerns – and he wasn't happy to admit to his own failings.

'Well, I don't know about you lot, but I fancy a drink,' Richard said, slipping an arm around his wife's waist.

'But some of us have to drive back,' moaned Rachel Davies, the comment aimed at herself, given that her husband Don had already sunk several glasses of the complimentary champagne.

'Why don't we all go back to the Maide of Honour?' suggested Reverend Fisher with glee as he stroked his hands across his well-rounded stomach. 'We could ask Piers and Marcus to rustle up an impromptu barbecue – you know, those evenings are always the best.'

This was met with a chorus of approval, and the group began gathering together their things – and their children – before heading off back home.

'Come on, Jonathan!' called out Charlotte. 'Sara wants to stay a bit longer; she says she'll get a lift back with the Madisons.'

Jonathan raised his eyebrows in surprise, though he was pleased she was allowing their daughter a bit more freedom. 'Okay, I'm coming!' he said, smiling.

Nevertheless, he was still dwelling on the theme of the day and had so desperately hoped to have joined in with the tour.

* * *

PC Laura Benjamin and Sergeant Phil Harris were ambling through the grounds of the country club, keeping an eye out for any untoward behaviour the open day might attract.

Other than a few high-spirited children getting into a little trouble, people seemed to be enjoying themselves immensely and were taking full advantage of the opportunity to have a good nose around such a prestigious property. The sound of laughter and excited squeals rang out from the many fun rides that were on offer for people to enjoy, and the aroma of hot dogs and onions soon got their taste buds tingling.

'Good job this is nearly over; the smell of all that food is making me hungry,' Sergeant Harris remarked as they passed yet another stall offering an abundance of tempting treats. 'I suppose you're off out tonight, are you?' He was considerably taller than Laura and he gazed at her from underneath the tip of his hat.

'Nah, not tonight,' she replied, shaking her head.

'Oh, the bank holiday bonk was last night, I guess,' he teased.

'Sarge!' She slapped his arm playfully. She was never sure if he was joking or not. 'I did see him last night, actually, but he's working today.'

'What, on a bank holiday?' he remarked suspiciously.

'Err... hello?' She motioned her arms up and down, indicating their very presence on duty that day.

'Oh, he's one of us, is he?' He nodded knowingly.

'No, actually, he isn't. He's into statistics and all that stuff… some sort of analyst, I think.' She hoped her explanation wouldn't give away the fact that she didn't really know exactly what he did – except that he often got called into his office at short notice.

'Oh, so it's just sex then?' He turned to laugh at her shocked reaction. 'Only kidding,' he assured her. 'I'm pleased for you, actually – I guess you won't be interested in joining us tonight, though?'

She rounded on him. 'Are you kidding, Sarge? We've got two days off; I'm not wasting the evening sitting in on my lonesome.'

'It's a date then.' He nodded, smiling, and they continued on their way.

* * *

Evie Coombes stretched out lazily and rolled over towards her husband. 'We can't lounge around here all day,' she cooed lovingly as Rupert slipped his arm around her, allowing her to nestle into him.

'I guess we should pace ourselves,' he teased.

'Why don't we get up and head over to the open day? It'll give us a chance to get to know some of our neighbours at last,' Evie suggested.

Rupert rubbed his head wearily with his free hand. 'Do you know what? I'd love to say yes, but I'm so shattered. I just want to make the most of having the day off, darling – and spending it with you, of course.' He pulled her gently towards him, dropping tiny kisses along her neck and towards her mouth, which she playfully fought off.

'Seriously, Rupert,' she said after a moment, 'if I don't eat soon I'm going to faint – it's almost 3 p.m.'

'Well, in that case, the open day will be as good as over, won't it? Let's order in some Chinese. I've got a couple of bottles of *Cristal* chilling… we could jump in the hot tub while we wait for our food to be delivered.'

His suggestion was favourably received. 'Oh, that sounds perfect!' Smiling, Evie got up and walked towards the bathroom. 'No need to get dressed then; I'll just fetch our bathrobes.'

Rupert rolled onto his side and picked up his mobile to call the takeaway. He'd switched it to silent earlier, and as he held it in his hands now he noticed the green light was flashing, indicating a new message.

'Oh, you have to be kidding me!' he exclaimed after reading the text. 'You're not going to believe this, Evie – there's a bloody crisis at the office!'

CHAPTER TWENTY-ONE

It was Tuesday afternoon and the children were still tired from all the shenanigans of the previous day, given that most of them had run themselves ragged at the opening. Some of them had also accompanied their parents to the village pub afterwards and had continued to play in the adventure playground well into the night, whilst the adults partied away alongside them.

Thankfully, they had the rest of the week off for the school holidays, but their commitment to *The Fortunettes* still had to be fulfilled and Camilla was rattled at their lack of interest.

'Come on, up on your feet!' she jollied. 'Let's go again.'

The opening bars of *Emily's Child* began to play out from the stereo and the group of children began to move again, though rather half-heartedly.

'Daisy, head up, please!' Camilla called out. 'Sara, you need to keep in time with the music! Here comes the chorus, now *jump*!' She waved her arms about in frustration. 'Come *on*, Lily, wave your pom-poms higher; you're supposed to be the lead!'

The children shook their pom-poms vigorously whilst twisting this way and that, doing their utmost to keep time with the music.

'No, no, *no*!' Camilla screamed, stamping her feet before going over and switching the music off. 'What's the point in me giving you my valuable time if you're not going to listen? This just isn't good enough, I tell you, and you're not just letting yourselves down – you're letting each other down!' She stood there with her hands on her hips, scanning her eyes across the sea of disappointed faces.

'That's not entirely fair,' responded Dylan. At 16 he was the eldest and he thought her words were far too harsh, especially as the younger ones – which included his little sister, Anna-Maria – had put in a lot of effort.

'Excuse me?' Slowly, Camilla began walking towards Dylan, coming to a stop menacingly close to him. 'You're after furthering a career in acting, right?' He nodded slowly in response. 'Well, let me tell you, mister – if you think that's tough just you wait till you get to acting school. Trust me, you won't know what's hit you.'

Unperturbed, Dylan continued to stare ahead, much to Camilla's annoyance – she was spoiling for an argument – and she returned to the front of the hall to address them again.

'Well, I think it's quite clear that we're not going to get any further today. I want you all to go and get changed, go home, and get an early night. We'll start again tomorrow. Lily, you gather up all the pom-poms and put them in the storeroom.'

Lily nodded her head and began to collect up as many as she could carry, which wasn't a lot; she had to make several journeys. By the time they were all safely packed away most of the group had already left, and after picking up her rucksack she went into the ladies changing room.

'Oh, look everyone, here comes mummy's princess!' snarled Kerry, grabbing Lily's rucksack and kicking it across the floor. '*You're* the one to blame for all that back there – you weren't doing it properly. And anyway, it should be *me* up front, not *you*!' She kicked Lily hard in the shin and then began pushing her hands against Lily's chest, causing her to stumble backwards.

'Leave her alone!' cut in Daisy Carey, but at just 8 years old she was no match for such a bully.

Kerry glared at her. 'Shove off or I'll fetch you one too!'

Daisy didn't need telling twice; she went to join her elder sister, who was waiting for her outside.

Meanwhile, Lily went to retrieve her rucksack but Kerry got there first, slamming her foot down on top of it. The dust from her shoes formed a dirty mark on the pale pink material. 'Oh dear, what's pretty princess's mother going to say about that?' she asked in an almost sing-song voice.

Lily shut her eyes for a moment, wishing the ground would open up and swallow her whole. 'I don't know what I've done to upset you, Kerry,' she said quietly. 'I mean, it's not like we've ever been friends or anything.'

'You think you're so perfect, don't you?' Kerry asked, ignoring what Lily had just said. 'You only got the top spot because of who your dad is – only he's not even your real dad, is he? That one's *dead*. My mum said it was a good job there wasn't another brother or your mum would have gone off with him too!'

Lily burst into tears as she sank to the floor, utterly distraught. She'd never heard such cruel and callous words spoken to her before, and although she'd never met her real father, Oliver, she loved Richard just as much – if not more.

She cried pitifully to herself as Kerry – realising she'd finally gone too far – gathered up her own belongings and sneaked out before anyone else could come in.

A while later Lily dragged her heels home, her bottom lip trembling every now and then. She'd never experienced such hatred before and decided that she must have done something terrible to cause Kerry to act in such a spiteful way.

She sighed heavily, unable to see any way forward. It was bad enough having to deal with Kerry at school, but then she'd started acting up at drama club, and now – with them having to spend more and more time at rehearsals – it was getting too much for Lily to cope with.

She sighed as the tears started falling again.

I wish I was dead.

CHAPTER TWENTY-TWO

Georgina Fame had stirred the audience currently seated in *weight loss rendezvous room 1* into a complete frenzy. After commencing the session with her own success story, then having introduced her team of *Nourish and Gain* Ambassadors, she was now talking them through her famous *Nourish and Gain with Georgina Fame* programme. This was one of the first groups that had signed up for the talk following the recent success of the health and country club's open day, and so far it was going incredibly well.

'From now on, ladies and gentlemen,' she began, sweeping her gaze across the room and ensuring she had everyone's attention, 'this is going to be your daily mantra.' She was wearing a close-fitting jumpsuit – in her favoured brand colours, of course – and her long blonde hair had been straightened to an immaculate finish. With just a touch of subtle make-up she looked absolutely stunning, and there wasn't one single person in that room who didn't wish to emulate her. She clicked a button on the small remote she was holding, triggering off the *Nourish and Gain daily mantra* slideshow. As it started, she began reciting the following:

'2 - 4 - 2 - 2
Will create a better you!'

She motioned with her arms, encouraging everyone to stand up. 'Come on, join in with me, please!'

They all stood up and spoke along with her.

'2 - 4 - 2 - 2
Will create a better you!'

'And again...

2 - 4 - 2 - 2
Will create a better you!'

Although no one actually had a clue what the mantra meant yet, it didn't stop them from putting their heart and souls into reciting it over and over again with Georgina; the energy in the room was simply electric.

After switching off the projector she invited everyone to retake their seats, smiling broadly as she asked, 'So, how do you feel?'

'Amazing!' someone shouted out.

'Excellent – and *you've* created that wonderful feeling just by repeating a few simple words. Imagine how *amazing* you're going to feel when you've reached your goal weight.'

She clicked the remote again and moved along with the presentation. 'Okay, let's get into this. 2 – 4 – 2 – 2 stands for 200 – 400 – 200 – 200, representing the amount of calories you're going to consume each day.' Several murmurs of intrigue began to rumble around the room at that. 'You'll consume no more than 200 calories for breakfast, 400 calories are allowed for lunch, 200 calories for an afternoon snack, and 200 calories for your evening meal – and no eating after 7 p.m.' A hand went up. 'Yes?' Georgina encouraged.

'Can you double up? Say, have 400 calories for dinner and cut out the afternoon snack?'

'No,' Georgina replied, 'it's important that you eat this way, hence the mantra. 2 – 4 – 2 – 2 *will create a better you.* As long as you follow that regime, you *will* lose weight. It doesn't matter what time of day you eat, as long as you consume food up to these numbers of calories, and that you don't eat after 7 p.m.' She paused, sweeping her gaze around the room again. 'Now, you're no doubt worried that you're not going to be eating much food, right?' There was a major nodding of heads then, causing her to laugh out loud. '*Wrong!*' With that she set the next presentation off. It was one of her favourites – a slick collection of 200 and 400-calorie recipes – and it was usually all it took to seal the deal.

A plethora of pictures detailing a whole host of delicious-looking food – from sizzling soups to tempting kebabs and mouth-watering stir-frys and curries, not to mention the tempting puddings and desserts – triggered lots of oohs and aahs from the audience. It was the usual reaction she received when she pointed out all the foods they could eat on her plan.

When the presentation drew to a close Georgina turned to face her public. 'The only other addition to this is 30 minutes of compulsory exercise a day – no negotiation. It can be a simple walk, a jog, or any activity that gets you moving for half an hour *every* day. That's why, as part of the *Nourish and Gain with Georgina Fame* membership, you get free access to our health and fitness facilities, including the gym once it's finished. Depending on how much weight you have to lose, we can step up the exercise to 45 minutes a day further along the programme, to help give you that extra boost towards reaching your goal.' She smiled encouragingly, still very much holding their attention. 'You deserve this – each and every one of you. You deserve to be the best *you* can be. So, come and join me now, and make today the first step towards a better you!'

No one needed asking twice; the sound of chairs scraping along the floor resounded around the room as people scrambled towards the front.

Whilst her team began laying out membership packs on the side tables, which had been set up earlier that day, Georgina took a moment to herself; she was coming down from the enormous adrenalin rush that always consumed her during these presentations, so passionate was she about her work.

She'd come a long way in the past 12 years and, before her weight loss, she'd never once imagined she'd ever be able to pull off a presentation like that – let alone be the owner of a much sought-after brand. She felt honoured that she had so many people desperate to share it with her – something she never took for granted.

If they could only see me now...

CHAPTER TWENTY-THREE

Pradeep crept quietly down the stairs. Since Esha's accident, he'd taken to sleeping in one of the guest bedrooms so that he wouldn't disturb her. She'd been very lucky to escape with nothing more than a concussion and a bruised head, but she still needed to rest as much as possible.

It made him sick to the stomach recalling the image of her lifeless body when she lost her footing and fell down the stairs. The fall had knocked her out completely and he'd rushed to her aid whilst Bronwyn telephoned for an ambulance.

I don't know what we'd do without her.

'Morning,' greeted Bronwyn brightly as he took a seat opposite her at the kitchen table. She poured him a cup of tea from a fresh pot she'd just made, which he gratefully accepted.

'Can you listen out for the doctor this morning?' Pradeep asked before taking a drink from his cup. 'She should be arriving sometime after 11 a.m., barring no emergencies.' He raised his eyebrows. *We've had enough of those.*

'No worries, I'll take Esha a cup of tea up in about an hour, check she's alright, you know.' Bronwyn paused for a moment. 'It's for the best – the doctor will get her sorted and she'll be back to her usual self in no time.' She smiled at Pradeep and he attempted to smile back.

Jon Anderson had given Pradeep the name of a female GP from Swinford St. George health centre – a highly respected medical professional who specialised in postnatal depression – and she'd kindly agreed to visit Esha at home, given her recent accident and the fact that Pradeep was a fellow doctor. Pradeep had found her very easy to talk to on the phone; she'd reassured him that she had extensive experience in helping women overcome this debilitating condition and had told him he wasn't to worry.

Even so, his shoulders remained slumped, heavily burdened with guilt. *I should have acted on my concerns sooner – that's what I'm supposed to be trained to do.*

He looked up to meet the gaze of his early morning companion. 'I'm so grateful to you for all your help, Bronwyn,' he told her. 'You really have been a marvellous support.'

'You're okay – it's my job,' she replied, though he wasn't sure that was exactly true. 'You wouldn't believe the carryings-on at my last placement,' she continued, 'constantly rowing they were, usually over money.' She looked up then, worried she'd said too much. 'Not saying that's what's going on here, like.' She shrugged. 'At the end of the day it was my job to look after the children and that's exactly what I did. I developed a way of just letting it wash over me. Your Esha's nothing like that, though; she's lovely, and we're all gonna get through this together.'

She stood up and patted his hand, though Pradeep barely noticed. His attention was drawn to several shards of light from the rays of the early morning sun that were beginning to filter through the kitchen window. The colourful illusion it created reminded Pradeep of a rainbow.

Perhaps this is a sign of better things to come. He certainly hoped so.

*** * ***

'Morning, James!' jollied Joy Brookes. 'Isn't it a lovely day?' she commented before collecting a shopping basket.

James was distracted by his own concerns, though, and he continued unpacking the morning's deliveries instead of getting drawn into conversation.

When the shop bell rang out again, announcing another customer's arrival, he nodded in acknowledgement to Elaine Hall – a fellow shopkeeper who ran *Elaine's Knit & Knatter*, which was a couple of shops along from the Hampton Stores. She was a curious soul, and quite the beauty. Rumour had it that she claimed to be some sort of mystic who guided lost souls back onto their rightful paths – something James dismissed as poppycock. She'd become a good friend, however, and had looked after the shop a few times for him over the years when he'd needed it. She could be a right laugh too.

'Morning, love!' she greeted him in her thick Burnley accent. 'S'alright if I just grab some milk and bread? I'll pop back later when I'm more awake.'

James nodded again; it was a regular thing she did and something that didn't bother him whatsoever. She was a good customer who preferred to shop locally rather than going further afield, which more than made up for the odd pint of milk or loaf of bread. She came to stand in front of him then, a look of concern etched on her face as she asked, 'You alright, chicken?'

He looked up, appreciative of her attention. 'Just a bit tired this morning.'

Elaine – who wasn't at all convinced by his reply – continued to eye him warily for a few moments before heading back to her own place. 'Okay, well I'll see you later!' she called out cheerily.

James went off towards the back of the shop and began unloading the bread and pastry goods, the bell ringing out again just moments later.

'Ooooh, look at you!' commented Joy Brookes to her friend. 'No need to ask if you had a good holiday.'

Rita smiled, basking in the compliment. The holiday had completely rejuvenated both her and Ralph and she really did feel on top of the world. 'It was fabulous,' she gushed. 'We stayed in a hotel right on the edge of the bay, and the food was to die for. You and your Alan should go there, you know – you'd love it.'

'Actually, we've just booked up to go on that retreat with Georgina Fame,' Joy replied.

Rita raised her eyebrows in surprise. 'Retreat, Joy? I never thought of you as spiritual.'

'You'd be surprised!' Joy replied. 'Anyway, it's not all about chia seeds and colonics; it's about freeing yourself from the burden of negativity.'

Rita burst out laughing. 'Have you been at the gin again?' she teased her friend. 'Either that or her fancy hotel is really a front for some sort of cult.'

A look of hurt washed across Joy's face at that; she didn't like being scoffed at. 'It's no such thing, I'll have you know. My Alan says that Georgina Fame's weight loss system is a blessing. They've been packed out up there every day, and he says membership for the golf course has already sold out – they've had to start a reserve list. You should go over and take a look for yourself, Rita; it's completely transformed since old Lord Westbrooke's son ran it – and for the better too. No, we're looking forward to this week away; it's going to be a lot of fun.' She smiled at Rita, as though challenging her to say something else derogatory.

'I didn't mean to upset you,' Rita said, realising how hurt Joy actually was by her comment. 'It just sounded a bit odd, that's all – I guess it's not something we've ever discussed. Where are you going then?'

Joy perked up, excited to share more details. 'Oh, you should see the place we're staying in – Diskwithus Manor it's called. A luxury 4-star hotel in Fowey, Cornwall, promising mesmerising sea views. We can't wait!'

'Sounds like it!' Rita replied earnestly. She was beginning to get drawn in by Joy's enthusiasm. 'We were planning on lunching at the country club today as a matter of fact; I'll speak to Ralph about it and see what he thinks.'

Joy beamed. 'Imagine! You, Ralph, me and my Alan – we could have a jolly good laugh!'

Rita contemplated this as they both went about their business for the day and she began collecting up all the groceries she'd come in for. She was halfway between placing a can of beans into her basket when a thought suddenly struck her. She was reminded of the conversation she'd shared with Ralph during their dinner at The Melbury Fox, and the realisation that they were in the fortunate position to go where they liked, whenever they liked was, apparently, finally sinking in.

She quickly gathered the rest of her shopping and headed towards the till, eager to get home and share her excitement with Ralph.

* * *

'Tiggy!' exclaimed Poppy Hambly-Jones with genuine delight. 'How lovely to see you. Come on in and I'll make us some coffee.' Poppy led the way through to the kitchen and began filling the kettle whilst Tiggy settled herself down at their enormous solid pine kitchen table, soaking up the atmosphere.

Tiggy loved this house. It always seemed to be bursting with positive energy – which was unsurprising given that they were such a lovely, welcoming family. Tiggy was proud that she and Harry were part of their friendship group; you could always rely on any one of them for support no matter what.

'How have you been?' Poppy asked, pouring freshly brewed coffee into two white porcelain cups.

'And how's the wine bar progressing? We can't wait for it to open.'

'That's why I'm here, actually,' Tiggy said, taking a drink from her cup. 'I wanted to ask your advice about hiring staff – specifically a chef.'

Poppy's eyes widened; this was the opportunity she'd been waiting for. 'I'm so glad you asked. Do you remember the chef that cooked for us when we hosted Georgina Fame?'

Tiggy nodded, smiling. 'I certainly do – fabulous scallops that night, and the chicken was just perfection.'

'She's a fantastic cook, Tiggy – Winnie, her name is – and she's worked in some impressive restaurants over the years too. That night she literally saved our bacon; she stepped in at the last minute because the chef the agency originally sent over could hardly boil an egg.'

'That's right,' Tiggy recalled, 'I remember now; Richard had us in hysterics with the chicken pie story.'

Poppy rolled her eyes playfully in recollection and they both laughed. 'Exactly. Well, you might be interested to learn that the agency she's been working for has been taking unfair advantage of her, in my opinion. She's being worked off her feet, and is usually given assignments at the last minute too, which smacks of complete disorganisation. The ironic thing is, she doesn't necessarily need to work, but since she lost her husband she's been incredibly lonely; she told me she only signed up to the agency to get herself out and about more. She really enjoys the company, but they've been sending her all around the county lately and she's had desperate struggles with public transport. I think she'd be ideal for your bistro, and I'm certain she'd welcome the stability.'

Tiggy nodded again. From what she was hearing – and what she'd experienced of her food – she thought so too. 'Oh, this couldn't have come at a better time!' she exclaimed. 'I can't wait to contact her. It's a live-in position too, if she fancies, which by the sounds of it would be right up her street.' Poppy agreed. 'I don't suppose you know of any other places to get good bar and restaurant staff from, do you?' Tiggy asked. 'Georgina Fame's picked up most of the best that were going around here,' she joked, 'and the ground's a bit thin at the moment.'

Poppy shook her head. 'I'm afraid I don't, off-hand, but I was going to put out some feelers myself as I'm not keen to use that agency again – especially if Winnie's not going to be on offer.'

They continued to chat away excitedly, completely oblivious to a third person who was hanging about on the periphery.

Billy Franklin wasn't usually one to poke his nose into other people's business, but he'd heard Winnie's name being mentioned as he made his way back upstairs from the basement and he couldn't help lingering by the kitchen door for a moment to try and understand why they were talking about her.

When he realised what might be afoot a huge smiled stretched across his face; the thought of having another like-minded soul around him filled him with joy.

That day he went about his duties with a slight skip in his step.

* * *

'Hello, darling – lovely to see you!' Georgina Fame embraced her visitor with a light kiss on each cheek. 'How are you getting on?'

It wasn't unusual for her to receive requests for private consultations – which was indeed a lucrative part of her business – she just hadn't expected to have received quite so many requests in such a short amount of time. She wasn't complaining, though.

All appointments were made in the strictest of confidence and the only people who knew about her private offices in Chipping Melbury were Marcie, her PA, and Barnaby Rose, who'd secured the property for her.

'Actually surprisingly well – apart from the booze,' he joked.

Georgina smiled. 'Let's take some measurements and then we can weigh you.'

He slipped off his jacket and she leant behind him with a tape measure, bringing it to meet at the front. Then, after dotting down the readings she took out her digital camera. This was the part of the job Georgina never tired of – the before phase. If she could capture the euphoric feeling her client would experience in a few months' time – when they looked back at the record of their first weigh-in – she'd probably never have to work again.

* * *

'Harry?' Tiggy called out as she let herself back into Riverside Hall. *I could've sworn his car was parked outside the pub.*

It hadn't been unknown for Harry to organise little surprises for Tiggy in the past, and he often parked his car by the Maide of Honour so she wouldn't know he was around. Those days were long gone, however, ever since the attack – and they were something she didn't need reminding of.

Satisfied that she'd been mistaken, Tiggy took herself off to the study, eager to telephone Winnie. Usually she would wait to discuss her plans with the others, but she didn't want them to miss the boat. Besides, she knew full well they'd have faith in her decision.

Almost an hour later, Tiggy had almost finished her discussion when a huge crash rang out. 'I'm going to have to go, Winnie,' she said, hesitating. 'I think my cat's up to no good again. Shall we say 7 p.m. tomorrow? Then you can meet the others.'

After saying goodbye Tiggy rang off and headed anxiously towards the kitchen, imagining Mulbers with all manner of glass shards sticking out of his fur – or worse. When she pushed open the door, however, and quickly scanned the room, she saw nothing. It was in complete silence.

Perplexed, she slowly made her way further inside, creeping past the table and towards the sink before coming upon the source of the crash: a crystal glass lay shattered at her feet. She had a good look around but the usual suspect was nowhere to be seen.

As she went to fetch a dustpan and brush to begin clearing up the mess, her mind was occupied with the possibility of having secured them a chef.

* * *

Laura Benjamin was just beginning to drift off to sleep when the intercom buzzer sounded from downstairs. She glanced at the bedside clock, the luminous green numbers shining out brightly in the dim gloom of her bedroom.

Who on earth is calling at this time of night?

She moodily slipped out of bed and went to answer it; she was on the early shift in the morning, and after having spent a couple of days partying, she needed to catch up on her sleep.

'What are you doing here?' she greeted the midnight caller, but was quickly silenced by his kisses.

CHAPTER TWENTY-FOUR

'Come on, Lily. Finish your breakfast, darling – you still have to clean your teeth before we leave.' Poppy was rushing about that morning, eager to get going. Lizzie Anderson had arranged a spa day at the country club for them both, and they were meeting up straight after they'd dropped their children off at school.

'Have you seen my book bag, Mummy?' Roderick, her 5-year-old, asked as he came into the kitchen, looking somewhat dishevelled.

She went over to him, lovingly straightening out his hair and then adjusting his school uniform. 'You look like you've got dressed in the dark,' she said, kissing him on top of the head before answering his question, 'it's in the drawing room by the coffee table – where you left it last night. Hurry up, now, you haven't had any breakfast yet.'

'Why isn't Richard taking us to school?'

Lily caught Poppy completely off guard and she almost dropped the glass of milk she was pouring. *Richard?*

Poppy placed the glass on the table and looked across at her daughter. She was staring aimlessly into the breakfast bowl before her, one hand supporting her head whilst the other was busy swirling a spoon around and around, creating a chocolatey-milky mush from the cereal she'd poured herself earlier.

'Are you okay, Lily?' Poppy asked, concerned by her daughter's unusual behaviour.

'Yeah, why wouldn't I be?'

'It's yes not yeah, and because… well, look at you. Lift your head up, young lady, when you're speaking to me.'

She did just that, throwing her mother an angry glare in the process and causing Poppy to think she was probably just being a bit moody because she was tired.

Poppy went over to her, putting an arm tenderly around her shoulders before planting kisses across her face and head, a gesture that usually got her giggling – though not today. 'I know you're tired, darling, what with all these blessed *Fortunettes* rehearsals, not to mention being picked for the netball team.' She smiled. 'I guess that's what you get for being so popular!' She thought her words would rally her but Lily just sighed deeply. 'I'll tell you what,' Poppy said, suddenly having an idea, 'why don't we go and eat out at the pizzeria in Midford County tonight? Daddy's got a business dinner to attend so we can go straight after rehearsals? What do you think?'

Lily looked up, meeting her gaze. 'I'd really love that, Mummy.' She paused, biting her bottom lip momentarily before adding, 'Mummy, I'm...'

'I can't find it!' Roderick wailed from the hallway, causing Poppy to roll her eyes.

'I'll be back in a minute, Lily,' she said before rushing off to his aid, desperate to get him moving. By the time she returned their conversation was forgotten as Roderick claimed Poppy's attention yet again – this time by spilling his milk.

Lily sighed desolately.

No one seems to have time for me anymore.

* * *

'Hello Ian, it's me again.' Lucy bit her bottom lip nervously, unsure as to what to say. 'Ummm... I'm getting really worried about you, darling – why aren't you returning my calls?' She floundered; a tight knot was developing in her stomach again. 'I've tried texting *and* reaching you on Skype, and you know how much I hate that blessed thing. If I don't hear from you today I'm going to have to...' she trailed off. *What am I going to do?* 'Just give me a call when you can, will you? I need to know you're okay. Love you,' she added, her voice trembling as she said those last words.

After ending the call, Lucy sank onto the bottom step of the staircase, exhausted. She rubbed her hands across her face, then sat staring into the distance, trying to make sense of the situation. Ian hadn't arrived at Easter as promised – and she hadn't heard a word from him either. There was no landline in the shared house he was renting and she didn't have contact numbers for any of his friends – *that's if I can even remember their names.*

She shook her head in despair. She'd telephoned the local hospitals and all the police stations around the area several times now, to ask if there had been any accidents – or, in particular, if a young male of 20 years had been brought in – but that had drawn a complete blank.

She felt foolish for having made such a fuss, but her instinct urged her on, despite it not being the first time that Ian had taken himself off the radar like this. There'd been a similar incident about two years previously when he'd started dating a girl he'd met at a friend's party. She was older than him, Lucy recalled, and she believed she was his first sexual encounter too. It was almost two weeks before she'd heard from him again.

When he did finally call he'd acted all brazen, like it was *she* who had the problem, and had gone on to tell her in no uncertain terms that she needed to leave him alone and let him get on with his life.

The phone suddenly went off, the shrill screech of the ringtone causing her to jump, and as she made to grab it she could feel her heart hammering hard inside her chest.

'Morning, Lucy.' It was James. He'd spent the night in his own flat as he had to be up bright and early to receive the shop's weekly delivery. 'Is there any news?'

She shook her head, despite knowing he couldn't see her. 'No, nothing,' her voice quivered. 'I rang the University like you suggested and they said they couldn't discuss it with me.'

'What?' James gasped in disbelief; now it was his turn to shake his head. 'Did you explain that you haven't been able to contact him at all?'

'Yes, of course – I told them everything. The chap was very nice but he said,' she paused here to gather her thoughts together, 'well, what he actually said was that he could only discuss it with a member of the police force because of data protection.'

'But that implies they have something to tell…'

'Exactly,' Lucy said, beside herself now. 'I mean, what else could it mean? I'm really beginning to think the worst, but I'm not sure what to do next.'

'I think, given their response, we need to speak to Matt,' James said, beginning to have anxieties of his own now. Although he'd not met Ian as of yet, from what Lucy had told him about her son's behaviour in the past it was highly likely that he'd just gone off somewhere again, maybe having met a new girlfriend. *However, there's always room for an element of doubt, especially given the University's response.* 'Why don't I give Matt a call now and ask him to come over? Then I'll ask David to look after the shop so I can be there with you. I'm not leaving you to deal with this alone, my darling.'

'I'd appreciate that, James,' she croaked. 'I'm not sure I can take much more – not knowing where he is… it's making me frantic with worry.'

'It's okay,' he replied, hoping his words were true. 'It's going to be okay.'

James wasn't certain what to make of Ian's behaviour, but he believed they owed it to him – and to themselves – to act on their concerns, however difficult that decision may turn out to be.

* * *

Camilla Barrington-Smythe hummed merrily to herself as she served up the bacon she'd just been cooking. Having spent the night at Matt Hudson's house, she was now making them one of her power breakfasts – avocado and crispy bacon on hot buttered toast.

'Something smells good!' he exclaimed as he went to join her at the breakfast table.

'I think you'll enjoy it,' she smiled flirtatiously, 'almost as much as last night.'

They were interrupted then by the sound of Matt's mobile ringing loudly. He went into the other room to answer it and returned moments later, shrugging his jacket on.

'Sorry, I've got to go,' he said before kissing her briefly on the lips.

'What, now?' she asked, clearly unimpressed.

'It's a mispers. Just pull the front door up when you're ready to leave, will you? It'll lock itself. I'll give you a call you later.'

Camilla gazed around the room after he'd gone, making the most of her surroundings. Experience had taught her that it was most unusual to meet a single guy who was not only clean and tidy but who clearly shared her expensive tastes too. *I could get quite used to this.*

She poured herself another mug of tea, seemingly in no hurry to begin her day.

* * *

241

'You off?' Evie Coombes was sitting at the kitchen table in her dressing gown, enjoying a cup of morning coffee. She offered up her cheek to her husband, distracted by an article she was reading in *Cotswold Life*.

'I'll be late this evening.' He ignored the cheek and removed the coffee cup gently from her hands so that he could kiss her properly. 'But I'll be back in time for a late supper if that suits?'

She stood up and placed her arms lovingly around his neck. 'Sounds perfect – I shall look forward to it.'

He patted her playfully on her bottom before collecting his briefcase and heading out for the day.

Evie gazed after him, mentally hugging herself. The only thing that seemed to be missing from their lives right now was a child of their own – and if things carried on as they had done of late, she didn't think they'd have to wait much longer for that to happen.

CHAPTER TWENTY-FIVE

*J*en was just cooking up some bacon and eggs when Merv
brought the mail through. She recognised Sadie's
handwriting immediately.

Perplexed, she quickly ripped open the small white envelope
and scanned through the contents of the handwritten note inside.

Dear Mum and Merv,
I know you're both probably beside yourself with worry that I've
not been back home and I'm sorry, I really am. I honestly don't
want to upset either of you but I can't continue the way things
are. Mum, you're my best friend, and I'll never forget all that
you and Merv have done for me, but I need to make a life of my
own. My weight is out of control and if I continue like this I
just can't see a future for myself. Please forgive me. Know that I
love you both to the moon and back, and one day I'll give you
both something to be really proud of.
Lots of love, Sadie xxx

Jen collapsed onto the kitchen floor, shrieking illegibly.

Merv, completely blindsided by Jen's behaviour, hadn't a clue what on earth was going on and it was a good half an hour before he could make any sense of it.

What made it even worse was that they hadn't even noticed Sadie's absence for the past four days; they'd been so busy flitting from one social gathering to another, they'd simply assumed that Sadie had been going back and forth to work and that she'd been tucked up safe and sound in bed by the time they returned home in the early hours of the morning, both of them slightly inebriated and desperate to sleep off the effects of the luxurious food and drink they'd quaffed. There'd not even been a call from anyone at Roberts, Lewis & Hughes where Sadie had worked for the past nine years, despite the fact that she'd never had a day off sick in all that time.

Once Jen had calmed down somewhat she called the police, believing that Sadie must be the victim of some sort of kidnapping.

The police eventually tracked Sadie down, and to this day Jen will never recover from the words the constable from Cardiff Constabulary relayed to her: 'Sadie,' the constable explained, 'has stated that she wants nothing to do with her family and that you are to leave her alone.'

The officer confirmed that Sadie was safe and happy and that she had already begun to establish a new life for herself. She'd requested that neither Jen nor Merv be a part of it.

'Ghosting is what they call it,' the officer explained to a frantic Jen. 'The person just ceases all forms of contact whatsoever with no explanation and the law states that we have to abide by their request.'

Quite unable to come to terms with her daughter's actions, Jen didn't know what to do with herself.

Soon, she found herself suffering from a complete breakdown.

CHAPTER TWENTY-SIX

Having visited Lucy and James earlier that morning, Matt Hudson had returned to Midford Country police station in order to carry out some initial investigations.

Rather than discuss his findings over the phone, he decided to pay them another visit, though he hesitated briefly before knocking on the door of number 34 King's Oak Road. There was nothing necessarily unusual about a missing student – it happened much more frequently than people realised, and it rarely turned out to have dire consequences – but this was a first for him.

James welcomed Matt inside and showed him into the lounge where Lucy was waiting anxiously for news of her missing son. James rejoined her on the sofa and Matt settled himself on the edge of an armchair, facing them.

'Well, I do have some information for you, Lucy,' he began. 'I've spoken to the Head of Student

Services at the University Ian's been attending and they tell me that your son didn't return to his studies after the Easter break.'

Lucy's eyes widened as she gasped in complete shock; James placed an arm comfortingly around her, thinking the worst.

'Why on earth didn't they contact me to find out where he was?' she exclaimed. 'Surely that should have been the first thing they did?'

Matt shook his head, appreciating her frustration. 'Unfortunately, it doesn't quite work like that. The University aren't able to discuss a student without their prior permission due to data protection – even if they have concerns about a student's welfare themselves.'

'But that's ridiculous!' Lucy exclaimed, throwing her hands in the air. 'I'm the one who's been paying for him to take this degree – surely they could have told me he's not been going there this whole time? I mean, where on earth is he?'

'Well, this is what's unusual,' Matt began, taking care to choose his words wisely. 'It seems he vacated his accommodation just before the Easter break, and the day before he was due to return to his studies he accessed his University profile to update his address details.'

'What do you mean, updated his address – to what?' Lucy asked.

Matt took a deep breath. 'I can't tell you that, I'm afraid, not until we've spoken to him. I can tell you, however, that the address he's provided is not based in the UK.'

Both Lucy and James looked at each other in astonishment.

'But that can't be right…' Lucy said, bewildered. 'Are you sure you've got the right person here, Matt? I mean, it can't be my Ian, I'm sure it can't.' Just then a thought struck her. 'Hang on a minute… he was due to go abroad on an internship at the end of May – in the south of France, he told me – is that where he is, Matt? The south of France?' Her eyes darted from side to side as she spoke, trying to make at least some sense of what was happening.

'It's not France, no, but it is a European address – we've had to go through Interpol and request that a local officer be sent to check out the address he's given, to confirm that he's actually there.'

Lucy floundered. 'But why would he go off like that without telling me? I just can't understand it.'

Whilst Matt didn't know Lucy that well – after all, she was a relatively new resident of the Hamptons – he knew she'd been James's guest at the Hambly-Jones dinner and he'd later discovered she was an old friend of Anthony Sullivan's. In fact, since then, Matt had joined them for a drink on more than one occasion at the Maide of Honour and she always appeared to be perfectly lovely. She'd enjoyed a long career in publishing, he seemed to recall… nothing too shocking. Nothing too out of the ordinary.

Though we've all got skeletons in our closet. He sincerely hoped there wasn't anything sinister about her son's disappearance, but as a policeman he had to keep an open mind.

'There's something else,' Matt said, hesitating again. 'I checked out the details for the bank account you said you paid Ian's monthly allowance into, and I can confirm that it's been recently accessed. I also noticed that Ian has been receiving another form of monthly income – did you say he had a job other than the proposed internship he was planning?'

Lucy shook her head, wracking her brains in case she'd missed something. 'Not as far as I'm aware, and I'm certain he would have mentioned it if he did – he couldn't wait to tell me about the internship; he was very excited.'

Matt nodded before asking his next question. 'Do you know a Raoul De'ath?'

Lucy froze, her mouth setting in a thin line as she furrowed her brow. James knew all about Raoul but was just as confused as Lucy as to why Matt had brought it up.

'He's Ian's father,' Lucy explained, sighing. 'Well, how can I put this… we enjoyed a brief affair, the result of which was Ian. I'm sure you must have heard of him yourself, Sergeant – he's *the* Raoul De'ath, the internationally renowned celebrity hypnotist and motivational speaker.'

Matt raised his eyebrows, looking impressed. 'So I guess he's worth a pretty penny, then?'

'Of course, but why are you asking about him?' Lucy queried. 'Other than the photographs I used to send him of Ian when he was growing up, he's never had anything to do with him – and believe me, I gave him plenty of opportunity.'

'Because he's the one who's been paying the other funds into Ian's account each month,' Matt explained, 'and it's a very health amount too.'

Lucy was agog, and she took a moment to exchange a look of utter bewilderment with James.

'But… I don't understand… why wouldn't he speak to me about that?'

Matt shook his head. 'I can't answer that right now but perhaps you might want to get in contact with Raoul yourself; it may well shed more light on the situation. Meanwhile, I'll get back to the station and see if our friends at Interpol have been in touch.' He stood up, hesitating for a moment before he left. 'I'll get to the bottom of this, Lucy,' he told her. 'I assure you.'

She nodded in response but her mind was already miles away.

James saw Matt out whilst she picked up the phone. *Perhaps he's more like his father than I'd realised.*

CHAPTER TWENTY-SEVEN

Lily Hambly-Jones felt somewhat brighter than she had earlier that day and was currently putting her heart and soul into her performance, excited at the prospect of the evening ahead. She was really looking forward to going out with just her mum and brother and she couldn't wait to give her mum an extra special cuddle too.

'That was much better,' Camilla chipped in. 'Let's take a five-minute break and then we'll concentrate on the chorus for the rest of this session.' She went over to check her phone whilst they helped themselves to cups of water, and seeing a missed call from Diana, she dialled through to her answerphone to pick up the message that had been left.

'Hello Camilla, it's Diana. I didn't see you at breakfast this morning and I meant to tell you that I won't be able to join you for rehearsals today. I'll be out late too, so don't wait up.'

Somewhat miffed, Camilla switched off the phone and tossed it into her handbag, wondering why Diana would be staying out late.

Her thoughts were suddenly interrupted by some sort of commotion developing behind her, and as she swung around she caught sight of Lily Hamby-Jones pushing Kerry Madison so hard it caused her to fall to the ground; Kerry was now sitting on the floor crying hysterically, but no one went rushing to her aid.

Already riled by Diana's message, Camilla released a tidal wave of rage at the girl in front of her. '*Lily Hambly-Jones*!' she screeched. 'Just what the hell do you think you're playing at?' Lily opened her mouth to explain but was cut off by Camilla. 'I don't want to hear it!' she shouted. 'My eyes saw everything I need to know, and believe me, I've seen enough. Despite the fact that you're only here because of who your precious mummy and daddy are,' she mocked, 'I won't have a bully in my group! Get your things together and get out; you're not welcome here anymore!'

The rest of the group gasped in horror at Camilla's outburst whilst Lily scurried off and grabbed her backpack, her bottom lip trembling almost as much as her legs.

Some of the elder children exchanged angry glances and Sara Palmer-Reid went to confront their teacher. 'Hang on a minute,' she started, though she got cut off too.

Camilla rounded on her. 'No, *you* hang on,' she retorted, placing her hands on her hips – a seemingly favoured position of hers. 'I'm sick and tired of having my decisions challenged. I know what I saw,

Sara,' she added as she helped Kerry to her feet whilst Sara glared at Sam, desperate for him to back her up.

'I'm sorry, miss, but that's my sister and you don't know what she...'

'*That's enough!*' Camilla shouted, stopping Sam in his tracks. 'I've dealt with the matter and that's all there is to it. Now, let's get on, shall we?'

She stomped to the front of the hall and switched the stereo on again. *Let's see what Miss Fortune makes of that.*

Lily stumbled out of Ashton Abbey hall quite unable to believe what had just happened. Tears were streaming down her face, and her top lip was dripping with mucus. She felt far too ashamed to go straight home and so she stumbled towards the Hampton Ash Road instead, thankful there wasn't anyone around to see her. *Mummy's going to be so angry with me.*

She thumped her leg in frustration, but that just made her cry even more. *What am I going to tell Mummy? I've never been thrown out of anything before; she's going to be so disappointed in me!*

Lily ambled along, not really thinking about where she was going.

The only thing on her mind right then was that she'd deserved to be punished for lashing out at Kerry Madison.

CHAPTER TWENTY-EIGHT

Francine Dubois was determined that, one way or another, Richard would be joining her for dinner that evening.

Despite her previous attempts at trying to lure him to dine with her and Emilia Weber some weeks ago, he'd managed to cancel at the last minute and she'd been blindsided by the sudden family emergency he claimed he'd had to rush off to deal with. *Not so tonight.*

Louise Carter was in town and it was well known that she was in high demand. She'd invited Francine to dine with her, following her visit several weeks ago, and she was keen to establish her brand within the Hambly-Jones empire.

'Any chance of catching a lift with you?' Francine asked, trying to appear casual. Richard glanced up from his computer, trying to disguise his displeasure. 'Seeing as how we're dining together and all,' she added.

'We're hardly dining *together*,' he shot back. 'It's a business dinner. Why can't you drive yourself, anyway?'

'Oh,' she rolled her eyes to express her frustration, 'my car's in the garage.'

He raised his eyebrows, this news surprising him. 'What? But it's practically brand new – what's gone wrong with it?'

She shrugged her shoulders, a blank look on her face. 'No idea. There's a loud banging noise coming from inside the engine, and when I took it into the local garage they said they'd need to keep it for a day or two to look at.'

'Hmmm, okay,' he replied, frowning now, 'well in that case I'd be happy to drive us both there, but you'll have to get a taxi home; Midford County is in the opposite direction to the Hamptons.'

Francine silently cheered as he got up and began getting ready to leave.

'I just need to go to the bathroom and then we can head off,' he said, walking out into the corridor.

He hadn't been gone two minutes when his mobile phone burst into life. Discreetly, she leaned forward to find out who the caller was and was enraged to see Poppy's name flashing up on the screen. *Oh no, not again!*

Francine picked it up and pressed the reject button – knowing it would send the call to voicemail – and then panicked for a brief moment, her heart thumping hard in her chest. Knowing he'd see there was a missed call, she decided to switch the phone off altogether. Then, after creeping around to the other side of his desk and carefully opening the bottom drawer, she hid his phone deep amongst the files inside. She closed the drawer again – her hands shaking slightly – and quickly returned to her position by the door.

By the time Richard returned, Francine had completely regained her cool composure and he had no reason to suspect a thing.

When he went to collect his keys she held her breath, desperately hoping that he wouldn't start looking for his phone. To her relief, however, he made his way towards the door and then closed and locked it behind them without a backward glance.

'Right, let's make this an evening to remember, shall we?' He was referring, of course, to the possibility of forming an exclusive relationship with Louise and her brand, and Francine followed him out smugly, thinking the same.

CHAPTER TWENTY-NINE

'Right, young man,' Poppy said, taking hold of Roderick's hand, 'let's go and collect your sister, shall we? Then we can go out for something to eat!' The enthusiasm in her voice made Roderick chuckle, and as they walked along the road leading towards Ashton Abbey they enjoyed the feel of the warm afternoon sunshine on their faces.

When they arrived and Poppy saw that the place was apparently empty, she became somewhat confused. 'That's odd,' she said, briefly letting go of her son's hand in an attempt to open the main door, only she couldn't – it appeared to be locked.

Together, they walked around to the side of the long rectangular building, enabling her to look through the windows of the Great Hall. This confirmed her first impression – it was deserted.

'Well, this is very odd indeed,' she said to Roderick. 'Maybe she's over at Anna-Maria's and has forgotten all about our date.'

As it wasn't at all unusual for Lily to head over to her best friend's house after rehearsals, Poppy wasn't in the least bit worried.

They retraced their steps and headed towards Hampton Lodge, which wasn't far off the village green. As they arrived Sara Palmer-Reid came out from next door and wandered towards them.

'Hello you,' she said, rustling Roderick's hair playfully before turning her attention towards Poppy. 'I was just wondering if Lily was alright now.'

Poppy gawped at her, somewhat perplexed. 'Why on earth wouldn't she be?' Then she realised: that's why the hall must be locked up. 'Ah,' she said, understanding now, 'is that why rehearsals seemed to have finished early today? I was just on my way to fetch her from Anna-Maria's.'

Sara suddenly looked uncomfortable, shifting her gaze from side to side.

Poppy frowned. 'What's wrong, Sara?' She tried and failed to make eye contact with her. 'What's going on? Did something happen?' Poppy was beginning to get a sense that something was terribly wrong.

'Look, I don't know how much Lily's told you,' Sara said, hesitating slightly as she didn't wish to cause Lily any more trouble, but also realising that it was about time the truth came out before something else happened, 'it's just that Kerry Madison has been bullying her for quite some time now.'

Poppy took a step back, aghast. She couldn't believe what she was hearing and she took a few moments to consider her words. 'What are you talking about, Sara? Lily's not mentioned anything at all to me!'

'Well, it's just that there was an incident at rehearsals earlier – between the two of them. I didn't see what went on exactly,' she tried to explain, 'but it seems Kerry did something to Lily and Lily lashed out – probably because she couldn't take any more of it.'

'Oh my good god, this is terrible,' Poppy replied, her mind reeling. 'Poor Lily – is she hurt? Oh, this explains now why she went back to Anna-Maria's.'

'I don't think she did – I mean, I don't really know,' Sara replied, pausing apprehensively. 'You see, Camilla threw her out of rehearsals.'

Poppy was stunned. 'She did *what*?'

'She went proper crazy,' Sara explained, gesturing with her hands. 'She began shouting at Lily – calling her a bully and stuff – and then she told her to get out. The rest of us did our best to stick up for Lily – to try and explain to Camilla what had really been going on with Kerry – but she shouted us all down and wouldn't let us speak. In the end, none of us wanted to carry on; that's why we left early.'

Poppy took a deep breath. She was finding it difficult to believe a word of what she was hearing, but she knew she had to think fast. 'Hang on to Roderick for a moment, would you?' she asked Sara. 'Just whilst I nip in to see if she's actually with Anna-Maria or not.'

Sara nodded, taking Roderick's hand whilst Poppy raced towards Hampton Lodge.

Consumed with dread and fear, she banged furiously on the front door, which was quickly opened by Anna-Maria's mother, Rachel – also a teacher at the Hamptons Primary School.

'Whoa! Where's the fire?' she joked with her friend, but when she saw the anguished look on Poppy's face she quickly became serious.

'Is Lily here, Rachel?' Poppy urged. 'I think there was some trouble at rehearsals earlier today – has Anna-Maria said anything to you?'

Rachel shook her head, appearing to be just as surprised at hearing this as Poppy had been. She hastily called out to her daughter, who was inside watching TV, 'Lily isn't here, is she?'

'No!' came the reply.

Rachel turned back to Poppy, shrugging. 'Lily's not here with us; are you sure she's not gone back home?'

Poppy shook her head, now more agitated than ever. 'No, I've just come from there. Sara's outside with Roderick; she said Lily had been thrown out of rehearsals earlier after there was some altercation with Kerry?'

'Thrown out? You've got to be kidding me!'

Anna-Maria appeared in the hallway then, stopping suddenly when she saw it was Poppy at the door.

'Anna-Maria, do you know where Lily is?' Rachel asked. She could tell her daughter was reticent to share what she knew and so she knelt down on the floor in front of her to be on her level. 'It's okay, you're not in any trouble – no one is. Her mummy's just a bit concerned because she's not at home. Did something happen at rehearsals today?'

Anna-Maria bit her lip nervously before answering; Lily was her best friend, after all. Eventually she let it all come out, Anna-Maria hardly taking a breath as she explained, 'It wasn't her fault what happened; it was Kerry Madison. She sort of kicked her in the back of the legs – I saw her – and it must have really hurt because Lily turned around and pushed her away, but I don't think she meant to do it quite so hard because Kerry fell over and then she started crying. It made Camilla very angry and she began shouting, telling Lily to leave – she was crying as well.'

Poppy was mortified. 'Do you know where she went?'

Anna-Maria shook her head. 'Sorry, no – she had to leave on her own, and when the rest of us came out I couldn't see her anywhere.'

Poppy placed a hand across her mouth whilst Rachel stepped towards her, placing her hands on her shoulders.

'Listen,' she told her friend, 'go home again, and check she's not there. I'll gather my three, and together with Sara and Roderick, we'll have a look around the village to see if we can find her. She's probably gone off somewhere to lick her wounds. I've seen it hundreds of times with the kids at school – she'll be fine.' Rachel smiled at her encouragingly but Poppy wasn't so convinced.

She went outside and quickly brought Sara up to speed before rushing back home. Once inside, she raced up the stairs and went quickly towards Lily's bedroom, looking around her along the way. There was no sign of her anywhere.

Really worried now, Poppy continued to check out the rest of the house, weaving in and out of one room after another and continually calling out her name, her voice becoming ever more urgent and anxious.

'Everything all right?' Billy Franklin shouted out. He'd been pottering about outside when he heard Poppy's frantic calls.

'Oh Billy, thank god. Have you seen Lily?' Poppy asked. 'She seems to have gone missing and I don't know where she is.'

Surprised, Billy hesitated as her words sank in. 'Er... I haven't seen her at all, no. I can go and check the gardens, though – and the sheds?'

'Yes! Yes please, that's a great idea.' Poppy replied, trying to remain calm.

Unsure what to do next she dithered in the hallway, trying to gather her thoughts together.

It occurred to her then that Lily might have gone to Anthony and Ianthe's house, knowing that she'd find comfort there, so she grabbed the telephone and quickly dialled their number. Anthony swiftly answered.

'I can't find Lily,' she blurted out, beginning to cry upon hearing his soothing voice. 'Is she with you?'

Anthony was also momentarily taken aback at Poppy's unexpected call and he floundered for a brief moment, causing Ianthe to glance up in concern.

'No, darling, she's not been here,' he replied, sitting up straight. 'Listen, we'll come straight over, Poppy. Just try and stay calm – we'll be there in a jiffy.' He put the phone down and looked across at his wife forlornly. 'She can't find Lily,' he told her in disbelief. 'I think we'd better get over there.'

CHAPTER THIRTY

Camilla Barrington-Smythe began humming merrily to herself. Having finished early for the day, she'd offered to cook dinner for Matt Hudson, seeing as how he'd had to rush off that morning and had therefore missed out on breakfast.

She was busy preparing the vegetables – which she was planning to serve with pan-fried salmon fillets – when Matt's mobile went off again. He was working in the lounge and had paperwork scattered everywhere. A moment later he came into the kitchen, shrugging on his jacket. She looked at him in disbelief. 'Not again!' she exclaimed.

'I'm afraid so – it's another mispers.'

'Another one?' she asked, incredulous. 'This village is getting rather careless, isn't it?'

Matt frowned, not in the slightest bit amused at her disparaging remark. 'I need to go,' he told her. 'It's a child and there's no time to waste.'

Camilla immediately regretted her outburst, looking concerned as she said, 'Oh my goodness, that's awful. Is it anyone I know?'

Matt hesitated. He didn't usually like to divulge any information until he was sure of the circumstances, but this one was rather close to his heart and he just couldn't help himself. 'It's Lily Hambly-Jones.'

Camilla rolled her eyes. 'Oh, that little madam,' she scoffed. 'Now, why doesn't that surprise me? I bet it's not the first time she's gone off like this either.'

Matt could hardly believe his ears and, unusually for him, he rounded on her. 'Just what on earth are you talking about?' he spat. He was confused as to why anyone would react in such a way to any child's disappearance, let alone Lily's.

'Well, she's nothing but a bully – clearly used to using bad behaviour to get her own way,' Camilla shot back. 'Do you know I had to send her away with a flea in her ear earlier today? I was sickened by her behaviour.'

'You did *what?*'

Camilla stopped what she was doing immediately, placing the knife she'd been using back down on the wooden chopping board. 'I sent her home,' she said tartly, 'for attacking another girl – Kerry Madison, it was – and for no good reason too. I dealt with the situation as I saw fit.' She shrugged. 'You have to nip this type of behaviour in the bud, Matt, before it escalates.'

Matt shook his head in disbelief. 'Apart from the fact that what you've just said doesn't sound in the slightest like the Lily Hambly-Jones I know, what do you mean when you said you sent her away?' he demanded.

Camilla suddenly felt uncomfortable. 'Well,' she replied, 'I told her to go home and that she wasn't welcome there anymore. I don't want someone like that in my majorette team.'

Matt was livid, but he knew he had to focus his attention on the case in hand. 'I don't have time to deal with you right now; I need to get over to her house urgently. In the meantime, I'll need you to detail exactly what happened earlier today, step by step. Okay?'

'Not a problem,' she said, sweeping her hair back off her shoulders. 'I'll fetch my bag and come along with you.'

'Oh no you won't,' he retorted. 'I want you to go straight back to The Boathouse and await one of my officers. They'll come and take a statement from you and then we'll take it from there. Now, grab your things – you won't be staying here tonight.'

Camilla was angry herself now. 'Hang on a minute, Matt – didn't you listen to a word I just said? I told you what I saw her do!' But her words fell on deaf ears.

He held open the door for her to step outside and then locked it behind them before rushing off to his car. A few seconds later he was heading towards Hampton Manor House.

* * *

Francine Dubois was smiling like the Cheshire cat; their meeting with Louise Carter had gone better than she could have anticipated. 'I think this calls for champagne,' she said, waving to grab the attention of a passing waiter who came over and took her order.

Richard, who was finishing up the last of his coffee, put his hand up in protest. 'Not for me, thanks – I'm about to leave too.'

Having needed to drive back to London, Louise had made her excuses straight after they'd finished the main course. Richard had only lingered because he wanted a drink to wash away the saltiness of the mushroom risotto he'd just enjoyed.

'Oh, come on!' Francine encouraged, smiling widely. 'It isn't every day I secure you such a prestigious deal with one of the world's leading lingerie designers.' Louise had offered Richard an exclusive contract on her latest designs, with more in the offing if sales went well.

'It's hardly all down to you; I think you'll find the Hambly-Jones brand played a large part in it,' Richard shot back.

The waiter reappeared then and began pouring out champagne, but Richard placed a hand over his glass and the waiter left them to it.

'Ah, yes – but you have to admit, if it wasn't for my initiative in the first place, we wouldn't be here now,' Francine pointed out.

'You mean when you were spending all that time swanning around the countryside?' he retaliated sarcastically.

Francine knew full well that the reason behind her avoiding the office during that time was purely tactical; she'd merely used it as an opportunity to divert attention away from having messed up when she'd gone over to Richard's house on the weekend of his dinner party. However, his comment irritated her and she became immediately defensive.

'I was doing my job, I'll have you know – and bloody well too, judging by tonight's events.'

'That's what I pay you to do, Francine,' he said. 'I expect you to do your job, just like anyone else. This is all that is.'

Francine groaned inwardly. Things weren't going at all as she'd planned and she knew Richard was on the brink of leaving. *I need to turn this around – and quick.*

Thinking fast, she cast her gaze downwards, looking quite forlorn. 'Honestly, Richard,' she muttered, 'I can't seem to do anything right.' She lifted her head up, looking directly into his eyes. 'I've actually brought a great deal of lucrative business to your company and you don't seem to be appreciative of my efforts at all.'

It was a performance worthy of earning her an Equity card, and Richard did feel somewhat sorry for her. He knew he'd been quite hard on her, but he couldn't shrug off the feeling he had – that there was something about her that just didn't sit right with him. However, the professional in him knew better.

He softened his voice, smiling as he said, 'I do appreciate you actually, Francine, and you're quite right – the additions you've brought to our brand have been significant.' He nodded. 'There'll be a bonus in your pay packet to reflect this too. We… we make a great team.'

Delighting in his praise she leant forward, placing her hand over his. 'We *do* make a great team.' She gazed dreamily into his eyes whilst he removed his hand, perplexed at her behaviour. 'In fact,' she breathed, 'the more I'm around you the more I want to get you know you further.'

Richard immediately leaned back. He was thoroughly disgusted to hear this and he didn't attempt to hide it either. 'What on earth are you talking about?' he snapped.

'Oh, come on, don't play games with me,' she flirted. 'You know perfectly well that I've developed feelings for you – and that's the real reason why you've been trying to push me away all these weeks, isn't it? I know you're as hungry for me as I am...'

'You have to be kidding!' he cut in, feeling sick to the stomach. 'Trust me, you must be living in some sort of dream world because I've never thought any such thing – or given you any reason to think I had!'

Francine smiled provocatively. She revelled in having triggered such a passionate response from him, knowing she was on the right track. 'Oh come on, Richard, don't play the innocent with me. What about all the late nights we've enjoyed back at the office?'

Incredulous, Richard threw his linen napkin on the table, narrowly missing unsettling a glass. 'What late nights?' he retorted, becoming quite agitated now.

'Well, what about the night I went through the designers I'd been visiting with you, when I returned to the office after my two weeks on the road?'

Richard certainly remembered the night in question but he didn't recall that anything out of the ordinary had happened. He frowned, confused.

Francine leaned in closer; she was really enjoying herself now. 'When you put your arm around me,' she whispered seductively.

'I did no such thing!' he exclaimed. He was feeling incredibly uncomfortable now, memories from that night racing through his mind until the penny finally dropped. 'Oh, for God's sake, do you mean when I accidently brushed up against you?' Her eyes widened and she laughed throatily. 'Get over yourself!' he continued. 'There's only one person in my life, and believe me, you'd never be able to come anywhere close to the wonderful person my wife is.'

'Ah, but I wonder what she'll think about you putting an arm around me whilst we were supposed to be working late? Or what about you slipping your hand inside my Hambly-Jones *Magnifique Madame* lacy bra and cupping my breast?'

Barely able to contain his anger, Richard began tapping his pockets, trying to locate his mobile phone. 'You must be fucking joking!' he exclaimed. 'I wouldn't touch you with a 10-foot pole! Let's see exactly what my wife thinks about this, shall we?' He was intent on calling her out but he couldn't find his phone, and as he started checking his pockets again, Francine fell about laughing.

'Oh, you won't find that, darling,' she mocked. 'I took care of it before we left.' She giggled again, heady from yet another glass of champagne. 'The silly bitch almost spoilt our evening by calling you, and I wasn't going to have her do that again.'

Richard glared at Francine, having to stop himself from reaching out and grabbing her throat. 'What do you mean?' he asked. He'd only lied about Poppy calling a few weeks before because, whilst he'd been keen to meet up with Emilia Weber that night, he also knew her very well; she was almost as irritating at Francine, so he'd made up a last minute emergency to avoid having to spend time with them both. Ironically, Poppy never called his mobile unless it was something urgent and it was this knowledge that now caused him immense concern.

'When you went to the bathroom back at the office, your phone went off,' Francine explained, 'and seeing it was your wife I switched it off and hid it in your desk.'

Richard's left eye twitched involuntarily. He couldn't recall a time when he'd ever felt so angry, yet so desperately concerned at the same time. *Except when Poppy took herself off that day.*

He was reminded of the time when they'd had a misunderstanding about his true identity – not helped by his mother's interference – and Poppy had taken off with Lily to clear her head. *I bloody hope it's nothing that serious.*

Instinct told him that he needed to get home – now – but he had to deal with Francine first.

Sighing, he stood up to leave. 'Your piss poor attempt at emotional blackmail is pathetic, as are you,' he told her, not even trying to keep his voice quiet. 'Don't bother coming back to the office – you can consider yourself fired after tonight's little display – and you can get out of my fucking house too!'

And with that he rushed out, eager to get back to the most important people in his life – his family – leaving Francine apoplectic with rage.

* * *

'Oh Camilla, what have you done!'

Diana Fortune was completely devastated to learn about the altercation involving Lily Hambly-Jones at rehearsals earlier that day; she'd returned back to the Hamptons having enjoyed meeting up with an old friend from London, and had been aghast to discover that a huge police presence had popped up in the meantime. She was even more aghast, however, when she learnt what – or rather *who* – was behind it.

'Honestly, Diana,' sighed Camilla, 'I don't know why you can't support me over this – perhaps you should have been there like you promised, instead of going out gallivanting about the place. Then you would have seen what happened.'

Diana arched an eyebrow. 'Be careful, Camilla – you're dancing on dodgy ground here. I don't need to explain myself to you, dear, and I think we should be honest: you've been sniping at the poor child since day one.'

Having been caught out, Camilla flushed. 'Now, hang on… it wasn't like that.'

'Well, from my perspective it was,' Diana insisted, 'and that's what I shall tell the police if I'm asked. You don't have to be Einstein to know that you don't send a 10-year-old child out on their own, in the middle of the afternoon, when no one else is around – goodness knows where she might be now.'

'Oh, for God's sake!' Camilla exclaimed. 'She's a bully; I saw it with my own eyes.'

'Well, that's absolutely no excuse,' Diana replied, 'and anyway, we now know otherwise, don't we?' She was referring to what the police had since learnt from the other students: the revelation that it was, in fact, Kerry who was the disgusting bully.

'Oh, here we go – can this child do no wrong?' Camilla spat. 'In fact, the whole family seem to be blessed saints the way everyone harks on about them – just because they're rich and famous!'

Diana was deeply dismayed, and she sat still as she waited for Camilla to stop ranting and raving. 'That might be your perception but there's a lot you don't know about the family, Camilla, or the enormous tragedy they've already suffered. They'll be absolutely mortified by Lily's disappearance.' She shook her head, hating to think what they must be going through. 'I suggest you keep your opinions to yourself,' she finished. 'I'm off to bed.'

With that Diana went upstairs, pausing to look out of the landing window that offered a view across the village green towards Hambly Manor House. A Police Incident Unit had arrived and there were several police cars parked nearby, all of them with their blue flashing lights on.

I'm beginning to think this house is cursed. First, her son Aster attempts to murder their next-door neighbour, and now her house guest was responsible for a missing child.

Diana shuddered as she made her way to her bedroom, silently praying that Lily would be found safe and well.

* * *

Charlotte Palmer-Reid was driving home. She felt brighter than she had in a long time and she reached out to put on the car radio, wanting to hear some upbeat music. Instead of the classical music that usually rang out on *Hampton FM* at that time of night, however, there was an extended news programme.

When she turned up the volume she almost crashed – *we can confirm our earlier reports of a missing schoolgirl from Hampton Waters. Police are appealing to the public for any information in...*

Sara!

* * *

Evie Coombes topped up her bath with a generous helping of hot water, using her foot to ease the tap back to the off position. She was in the depths of Agatha Christie's *The Murder at the Vicarage*, so when her mobile phone burst into life it took her a moment to drag her gaze to the flashing screen, which indicated a new message. Reaching over, she picked it up so she could read it.

On way – I'm bringing food – R xxx

'Oooh yummy,' she spoke out loud to herself. Having spent most of the day painting in her studio, she realised then that she hadn't actually eaten anything since breakfast.

The thought of food lured her out of the bath. She towelled herself dry and slipped into a black silk chemise before adding a few dabs of *Yves Saint Laurent's Black Opium eau de parfum.*

She went downstairs and floated into the kitchen, stopping to collect a chilled bottle of champagne along the way. Popping open the cork, she poured herself a glass before placing two white china plates in the oven to warm.

Smiling, she rubbed her hands together in anticipation of the feast ahead – *and not just the food.*

* * *

Jonathan Palmer-Reid mopped his brow. He'd stayed much longer than he'd intended to and was now racing along the Swinford St. George road, desperately trying to get home.

Charlotte will have my guts for garters if she finds out I've left Sara on her own for this long.

CHAPTER THIRTY-ONE

Quite a crowd had gathered outside Hampton Manor House. Having learnt about Lily's disappearance, they were all keen to help in the search, and Matt Hudson was currently talking through his proposed plan of action with Poppy. He could see that she was clearly struggling and was beside herself with worry.

He was thankful that Percy and Rosie had now arrived and, along with Anthony and Ianthe, they were able to support her – and each other. Rosie had taken Roderick off to the drawing room, although she was finding it quite a struggle to keep herself together, under the circumstances. Anthony continued trying to reach Richard but, much to his frustration, he just kept getting his answerphone.

'I know there are people outside desperate to help look for Lily,' Matt began, 'but it's too dark to see anything at this time of night. We've got police dogs on the way but I don't think we can do much more until first light.'

'But we can't just leave her out there!' Poppy cried, still distraught. 'What if someone's taken her?' Her words resounded uncomfortably with everyone else in the room; it was something that had already crossed their minds. 'She could be miles away by now!' Poppy added.

Matt did his best to reassure her, but as they had nothing to go on whatsoever, he felt frustrated too; no witnesses had come forward with any sightings, and without any clues of any kind, he knew they were struggling.

'There's no reason to suspect that,' he told her. 'We usually get the heads-up from other forces if a suspected kidnapper is heading towards our area.' *Or worse.* He kept that last thought to himself. 'All we can do at this stage is check again around all the places she might have possibly gone. If she was walking from Ashton Abbey she could have fallen somewhere and be lying injured right now – we don't know, but we *will* find her. I promise, I'm going to do everything I can.' He looked earnestly into Poppy's eyes, his heart going out to her as he took in her tear-stained face. He never believed he'd ever be in a position where he'd have to be searching for Lily. *But then no one was aware how much the poor little mite was suffering, keeping everything bravely to herself.*

After giving Poppy another smile, he turned to address the rest of them. 'Have you managed to locate Richard yet?'

Anthony shook his head. 'I can't reach him – his phone's switched off.'

'Maybe the battery's run out – these things can happen at the most inappropriate of times, he...' Matt stopped mid-sentence as his attention was drawn to the radio.

There's been an RTA on the Swinford St. George road, we require urgent assistance. Can anyone deal?'

Poppy gasped, horrified. 'An accident?' she asked, her voice wobbling with emotion. 'That's the road Richard uses – what if that's him?!'

'Hang on,' Matt said as he started heading outside, 'let me try and get some more info.'

He stepped into the hallway, but Poppy – having already made up her mind that it must be Richard – was now pacing the kitchen floor, completely distraught.

'No, no, no – not again!' She looked helplessly towards Percy, and Anthony stepped forward to catch her as she went to crumble onto her knees. 'Please God, no!'

As they looked at Poppy, it was hard for anyone in the room not to find themselves blinking back a tear.

'It's alright,' soothed Anthony, 'he doesn't know what's happened yet so he won't have been rushing; I'm certain it's not him.'

Another thought struck Poppy then and she lifted her head up off his shoulder as fresh tears sprung forth. 'What if it's Lily? What if someone's taken her and they were racing to get away – didn't Matt say they were trying to announce something on the news?'

Percy shook his head, unable to find any words to console her – the very same thought having already crossed his mind.

Also at a loss, Ianthe went and filled up the kettle, welcoming the brief distraction.

Outside, Matt was talking on the radio to Inspector Bill Wilson. 'I need more people over here, Bill; it's been almost eight hours since anyone's seen her and we've nothing to go on. You know every minute counts – can't you get someone to come across from Chipping Melbury?'

Matt was just wondering if there was a full moon that night, such was the frenzy of incidents they seemed to be facing that day, when Laura Benjamin radioed in.

'I'm just driving along the Swinford St. George road now, Sarge, on my way to join you; I can deal with the RTA until you can get someone else out here. Have the fire service and ambulance been notified?'

'Yes – and yes, please do, Laura. Can you assess the scene and report back? Firefighters are on the way but they've been delayed.'

'Agreed,' cut in Inspector Wilson. 'I'll come over too, Matt – at first dawn – and join in the search. Call me if anything changes; I'll be at the station for the rest of the night until then.'

Matt thanked him, then prepared himself for going back and speaking to Poppy.

It was going to be a long night for everyone.

CHAPTER THIRTY-TWO

Laura Benjamin didn't have to go too far along the Swinford St. George road before coming across the reported accident. She could see that traffic lights had been put in place due to roadworks, a large section of the road having been dug up, which could have been the cause of the crash.

She parked up, hopped out of the police car, and headed towards the carnage, shaking her head in dismay. *It's a head-on.* The car nearest to her was a blue Mercedes-Benz – or what was left of it, anyway – and she raced to the driver's door, wrenching it open and shining her torch inside. The driver was out cold, seemingly having been saved by the airbag.

'Hello, can you hear me?' Laura shouted, trying to rouse him. 'I'm a police officer and you've had an accident, but don't worry – we'll soon have you out of here.' She then raced across to the remains of the other car, a black BMW, radioing in along the way. 'This is PC Benjamin,' she said, loudly and clearly.

'I'm at the scene. We've got an IC1 male with a serious head injury, by the looks of it. He's going to have to be cut free – are the firefighters any closer?'

'They'll be with you in five, PC Benjamin,' came the reply.

'Thanks, I'm just making my way over to the other vehicle now,' she gasped, using her torch to assess the damage where the Mercedes had ploughed into it. There was a hissing sound and she could see that smoke was billowing out from the engine. She made for the driver's door, and when she peered inside it was obvious this man hadn't been so lucky.

She shone her torch across his face and froze.

Rupert!

* * *

Richard Hambly-Jones pulled up outside his home in disbelief – several police cars and a Police Incident Unit were parked outside. *I knew something was wrong.*

He practically flew out of the car and ran inside before anyone could stop him, and when he burst into the kitchen he found Matt Hudson comforting Poppy.

'What the hell's going on?' He rushed over to his wife as a mixture of Matt's, Percy's, and his father's voices all rallied to explain the situation.

Richard stared at them, open-mouthed, as he pulled his wife into his arms.

Could this day really get any worse!

* * *

Laura was facing one of the hardest battles of her life. Having recognised her boyfriend Rupert as being the driver of the black BMW, she was now attempting to report the fatality back to the station.

Moments later she heard the familiar wail of the fire engine, which quickly came into view. *Thank God.*

The fire crew shot out and began running around their vehicle, extracting the equipment that experience had taught them they would require before attending to the Mercedes driver.

Meanwhile, two other members of the crew came running towards Laura to assess the other vehicle, just as an ambulance arrived from Midford County. Everything was happening so fast.

The air was thick with smoke now and the sound of the pneumatic equipment the fire team were using to extract the other driver from the wreckage resounded around them. It was quickly established that Rupert would have to be cut free too and the paramedics, having confirmed his death, were on standby to remove his body.

As always, they'd extracted what information they could from him to enable identification; his wallet had been easy to retrieve from his pocket.

Fortunately, Sergeant Phil Harris – along with two of their colleagues – had now arrived, with Sergeant Harris immediately ordering them to the block off the road; although it was quiet – given the time of night – the emergency crew needed to get on without placing themselves in further danger. Sergeant Harris was also aware that the other driver had been found dead at the scene, and in the meantime he went to assist PC Benjamin.

'Is that the driver's wallet?' he asked.

Laura nodded her head slowly and Sergeant Harris eyed her with concern.

'Did you know him?'

She nodded again, clearly struggling to contain her distress.

Phil started looking through the driver's details, and pulling out his licence he said, 'We have a Mr Rupert Coombes, resides in Hampton Waters.'

Laura shook her head, brushing her tears away. 'No, Sarge, he lived in Chipping Melbury; that's the chap I've been seeing.' She swallowed hard, and feeling completely blindsided to learn this, Phil went to comfort her.

'Oh God, Laura, you should've said something; you must be in complete shock.' He put his arm protectively around her, even though it wasn't exactly professional to do so. 'Come on, let's get you back to the station – there's nothing more we can do here.'

He radioed to his colleagues and then drove Laura back to the station in the car she'd arrived in.

He didn't tell her about the photograph he'd found tucked further inside the wallet, along with a man's wedding ring.

* * *

Evie Coombes had been sleeping soundly on the sofa in the lounge when the police called at Hazel Lodge. *Judge Judy* was blaring out from the TV – she'd been watching *Dog The Bounty Hunter* on *CBS Reality* whilst she waited for Rupert to arrive home with their food, though the programme must have finished a while ago. Before falling asleep she'd also continued to drink the champagne she'd opened for them, and now her head was pounding.

She sat up slowly, groggy from the mixture of alcohol and deep sleep, taking a few moments to realise there was someone knocking on the door. Still dressed in her black silky chemise, she went to find out who on earth could be calling at this time.

The last thing she expected to see when she opened the door was two Midford County police officers standing on her doorstep.

CHAPTER THIRTY-THREE

It seemed that most of the village had turned out at first light the next morning, all champing at the bit to get on with the search; Lily had been missing for almost fourteen hours now and everyone was aware that time was of the essence.

Overnight, Matt and Inspector Bill Wilson had trawled over local maps of the area, allocating a section for each team to search, together with the use of police dogs. Ashdown Abbey had been reopened so that they could use the facilities as required, and a group of volunteers from the local WI had taken over the kitchens – they'd been handing out much-welcomed hot drinks and bacon rolls since the early hours.

Finally, they were ready to begin.

'Right,' Matt announced, 'let's get started.'

Everyone had been given a rundown of the clothes Lily had been wearing the previous day, together with her beloved pale pink rucksack and its contents. For those who weren't completely familiar with her, plenty of copies of a photograph had been handed out, depicting a smiling, blonde-haired, blue-eyed 10-year-old. She looked young and innocent in the picture, and so happy.

The groups went off in their individual search parties, all hopeful of finding her safe and sound.

*   *   *

'It's a terrible business, isn't it?' Rita asked, placing a fresh cup of coffee desolately in front of Ralph. Neither of them could stomach any food, given that Lily was still missing.

Despite the recent upset, they were nevertheless good friends with the family and had enjoyed many fun nights out partying with them whilst Lily, Roderick, and their other neighbours' children played happily alongside them. It was a close community here and they looked out for each other, no matter what.

Ralph nodded solemnly. 'Well, I did offer our services, but Matt said they've got all the volunteers they need for now.' He sighed. 'I just feel so useless sitting here.'

Just then their attention was drawn to the sound of the morning's paper being delivered, and Rita left the table to fetch it whilst Ralph took a sip from his drink.

'Well I never,' she exclaimed, coming back in and waving the front page of the Midford County Gazette at her husband, 'that's the bloke I saw in The Melbury Fox that night. You know, the one with the redhead.' She frowned as she read on. 'Oh no, it says he was killed in a car accident last night, along the Swinford St. George road.' She pulled the paper closer for a moment, then looked back at Ralph. 'It says he lived here, in Hampton Waters. I told you I'd seen him somewhere before.'

* * *

Poppy was beside herself. She'd wanted to go and join the search party but both Richard and Matt had insisted she stay at home in case Lily returned, knowing she'd need her mother when she was found.

Rachel Davies had taken Roderick to school, along with her daughter Anna-Maria, but she'd telephoned about an hour ago to tell them that Christine Fox – the head teacher of the Hamptons Primary School – had decided to close early as the children were too distressed with concern for their friend. Additionally, Kerry Madison had been on the receiving end of some most unpleasant behaviour, which Christine feared would escalate further, particularly if things didn't turn out well for Lily.

Ianthe had stayed behind to support Poppy, though she wasn't sure what she could do to help; she'd tried placing a ham salad sandwich in front of her earlier but she'd pushed it away.

'It's almost twenty-one hours now,' Poppy fretted. *'Oh Lily, where are you?'*

* * *

Harry and Tiggy kicked off their wellingtons in the boot room before heading into the kitchen and slumping down onto two kitchen chairs.

'How many fields do you think we've covered?' She looked over to her fiancé, who was leaning back in his chair with his eyes closed. Like everyone else, they'd had a sleepless night and had been up early to join in the search.

Harry rubbed at his eyes as if the gesture would rejuvenate them. 'I don't know, darling, but it feels like hundreds.' As neither of them were used to walking such a great distance, their feet were throbbing – their poor choice of footwear hadn't helped much either.

Suddenly, Tiggy jumped up. 'Tea and toast, I think. Then we'll get back out there.' When she went to fill the kettle her eye caught Mulbers' food bowl. 'Harry, have you see Mulbers? He's not touched his food.' She paused for a moment. 'Actually, that reminds me.' She turned to face Harry. 'When I was on the phone the other day, I heard a crash. I came in to find another glass smashed on the floor but I couldn't find the cat anywhere.'

Harry pointed towards the back door. 'It's the cat flap,' he explained. 'It's a great idea but you do get all the neighbours' cats coming in as well.'

'Oh, I hadn't thought of that,' she said, returning her focus to making the tea. As she placed some thick slices of white bread into the electric toaster, she said, 'Hang on, though… if that's the case, why haven't they eaten his food?'

'Because,' Harry said, going to stand behind her and snaking his arms around her waist, 'we've got the only cat in town with expensive taste – it's too rich for his other friends.'

Tiggy giggled, imagining Mulbers holding court with a host of local cats, whilst Harry's breath continued to tickle her ear.

'And besides,' he said as he pulled away – now it was his turn to laugh – 'I think another reason he's not eaten it yet is because he's probably full. I've been feeding him before I go to work and you feed him again when you get up, and that's without all the titbits he has during the day.'

'Cheeky old rascal,' she laughed. 'He's got us wrapped around his paw!'

* * *

Laura Benjamin was angry. More than angry.

I'm a police officer, for Christ's sake.

She was sitting on her bed in her flat, having been given a day's compassionate leave, and was berating herself for not having realised Rupert Coombes was a *supposedly* happily married man.

Her thoughts went out to his wife and how devastated she must be. Danny King and Amanda Baker – the PCs who'd been despatched to Hazel Lodge to deliver the grim news – said she was quite frantic and had quickly become completely hysterical. They'd had to call in Dr Anderson to give her something to calm her down whilst they tracked down someone who could come and stay with her.

Laura kept churning the events of the past few months over and over in her mind, and she had to admit, things were now beginning to look a lot clearer. He'd often cancelled dates at short notice – not something that was necessarily suspicious in itself, but then he'd also request to meet up at strange times of the day. If she was on the late shift, they'd have breakfast together. If she was on the early shift, they'd often met up in the afternoons, and then – of course – there were the times when he'd just turned up unannounced. She should have realised he was fitting their relationship around his normal life. *Whatever normal was.* She shook her head despondently.

I never seem to have much luck with men… well, it'll be a long time before I dip my toe in the water again.

* * *

Feeling suitably refreshed, Tiggy and Harry began getting ready to rejoin the search. This time, however, they decided walking boots would prove better attire than rubber wellingtons.

'I'm just going to go and get us a couple of those long sticks from the field at the back,' said Harry. 'You know, the ones we use to beat down the nettles when they get out of hand. They'll be a great help – some of the undergrowth around here hasn't been touched in years.'

Tiggy nodded. 'That's a great idea. I'll grab a load of water bottles to keep us all going.'

As Harry went out the back door and walked past the stables, he was reminded that they'd soon be filled with horses once LC's bar was up and running. Further along, there was roughly an acre of grassland that had yet to be converted into a training ground, and which would form part of their proposed riding school. At the very end of the garden was The Old Chapel, a place that Harry knew Tiggy often visited – she'd told him she felt safe and at peace inside the beautiful, quaint structure. It was thought that it dated back to the early nineteenth century, and it certainly would have been used as a place of worship at the time.

When Tiggy's parents had purchased Riverside Hall, Lydia had used it as a quiet space for meditation, and certainly in the later stages of her diagnosis, she spent many hours finding solace in the calming atmosphere contained within the chapel's stone walls. Her parents were now at peace together, having been buried underneath the beautiful oak tree there.

As Harry went to fetch the sticks he was after – he kept them tucked safely away just inside the chapel's entrance – something caught his attention. He stopped walking, listening hard. He was certain he'd heard the faintest of sounds. He stood very still then, straining to listen. *That sounds like a cat – Mulbers!*

The noise seemed to be coming from inside the chapel so he went to push open its heavy oak door; it seemed to have become quite stiff so he had to put all his weight behind it, pushing as hard as he could. It took several attempts before the door gave way, and when it did a burst of sunlight suddenly flooded the tiny stone room.

Two pairs of eyes blinked back at him.

A wave of relief engulfed Harry as he slowly crouched down, desperate not to startle anyone. 'Hello,' he spoke softly, 'I bet you must be hungry.'

CHAPTER THIRTY-FOUR

When Harry was spotted emerging from Riverside Hall carrying Lily Hambly-Jones, cries of disbelief could be heard for miles around.

Matt immediately rushed into Hampton Manor House to deliver the good news, quickly returning with a relieved set of parents and two sets of grandparents. Their reunion was so incredibly emotional, there was hardly a dry eye to be seen.

The gathered crowd – who'd given their time so selflessly to find Lily – were congratulating Poppy and Richard as well as each other, elated that she'd been found safe and well. Reverend Fisher offered up a prayer of thanks in joyful appreciation that one of his flock had been returned and had suffered no ill harm.

Matt called Dr Anderson – asking if he could come and check Lily over – whilst Poppy carried her back inside, showering her with kisses along the way.

Amongst the happy chaos, Richard quickly got everyone's attention. 'I can't thank all of you enough for what you've done in helping to find our daughter,' he announced. 'Putting her before your own lives… well, Poppy and I will be forever grateful. I am so proud to be part of this community.'

A huge cheer rang out at his words, followed by a loud round of applause, then Matt stepped up to debrief everyone before they wearily made their way back to their own homes, their hearts filled with the knowledge that their efforts hadn't gone to waste.

'For a minute there I feared we wouldn't find her alive,' Harry confessed to Tiggy. 'She must have been absolutely terrified in there too, bless her, although just how they both got in there in the first place is a mystery.'

Tiggy looked up, blinking guiltily. 'Oh dear,' she said sheepishly, 'I think I might have to hold my hand up to that. I seem to recall that I had some trouble closing the door last time I went down there; I hadn't realised that the hinge mechanism had deteriorated so badly. That must have been around March time at least – I meant to get it sorted but I completely forgot, and then with LC's bar and everything, it went straight out of my mind.'

Harry hugged her reassuringly. 'Don't beat yourself up about it, darling – these things just happen sometimes, unfortunately. In a way, at least Lily wound up there, which is a relatively safe sanctuary compared to what might have been. And anyway,' he kissed her briefly on the lips, 'at least we now know where Mulbers has been.'

* * *

Anthony embraced his son tenderly. 'I thought we'd lost her,' he gulped, 'and having already lost Oliver… I don't think Poppy would have coped.'

'My thoughts exactly; seeing her like that just tore me apart.' Richard shook his head, recalling how distressed she'd been when he'd finally arrived home the night before. 'If I'd had my phone on me, I would have been here so much sooner.'

'Don't worry about that now,' Anthony said, touching his shoulder reassuringly. 'I'm always forgetting mine; I completely understand.'

'But that's just it – I didn't forget it,' Richard replied. 'That bloody new buyer I took on has been playing stupid games at my expense.'

Anthony brought a hand to his mouth, rolling his eyes. 'Oh my goodness,' he said quietly, 'with everything that's been going on I'd forgotten all about her. The redhead, right? Francine Dubois?'

Richard nodded. 'Silly woman seemed to have got it into her head that I had a thing for her. She should be so lucky; you know I've only got eyes for Poppy.' He stared at his father, wanting to see his reaction. Francine's crazy behaviour had Richard momentarily doubting himself.

'Don't for one moment let that dreadful woman get to you – trust me.' Anthony sighed. 'I thought I recognised her when we arrived to help set up for the dinner that day, and if she hadn't darted off so quickly I probably wouldn't have given her another thought, but I did find it rather curious at the time. Of course, she looks somewhat different now, given that she's changed over the years, but then it all came back to me.' He shook his head, pausing for a moment before continuing. 'About eleven years ago, when I was working in the city, the rumour mill was rife about a possible fraud involving a senior investor – Dicon Lamont. It turned out that Francine had walked in on him having – shall we say – a 'moment' with his secretary, and she'd basically threatened to tell his wife if he didn't pay her a rather large sum of money. His wife – a high profile QC – was constantly in the papers at the time because she was fighting a similar case on behalf of her client, whose husband had enjoyed a cacophony of extramarital affairs. As you can imagine, it wasn't just Dicon's marriage that was at stake.' Anthony paused again. 'Francine got too greedy and she pushed the poor guy to breaking point – he ended up taking his own life.'

Completely flabbergasted, Richard briefly hesitated before saying, 'She tried to blackmail me too, Dad, claiming she'd tell Poppy I'd tried to feel her up.' He was incredulous, and he looked up to Anthony for support. 'Can you believe that?'

Anthony was furious, but also deeply concerned. 'Little vixen; I hope you've sent her packing?'

Richard nodded hurriedly in confirmation just as another thought struck Anthony.

'You know, she really shouldn't be allowed to get away with this,' he said. 'I shudder to think how many other victims have fallen foul to her games. I think a chat with Matt Hudson might be in order here, Richard, but let's forget about it for now and concentrate on Lily.'

He patted his son affectionately on the back. *Perhaps more good will come out of today than anyone could have anticipated.*

* * *

Having finished checking Lily over, Dr Anderson clicked his medical bag shut and smiled broadly at the family gathered in Poppy and Richard's drawing room. 'She's absolutely fine – a little dehydrated, but nothing a good meal won't cure.'

Everyone seemed to sigh with relief at the same moment, which trigged a succession of giggles – such was their euphoria – but whilst they were delighted by this happy ending in so much as Lily had been found safe and well, they still had to deal with the issue of why she'd gone off in the first place.

'I think this calls for a cup of tea,' jollied Rosie knowingly. 'Let's leave Lily with her mum and dad and I'll make us all a bite to eat too – come on, Roderick.' She held out her hand and he went to give his big sister another hug before accepting it.

As they left, Ianthe closed the door to the drawing room so that the three of them could have some privacy.

'First of all, darling, I want you to know that we're not angry with you and that you haven't done anything wrong,' Poppy said gently, kissing her daughter on the forehead. 'And, we know all about Kerry Madison and how she's been torturing you these past few months.'

Her words acting as a release, Lily began to cry; huge sobs wracked through her small body and Poppy held her tightly against her.

'Oh, Mummy,' she sobbed, 'she said some terrible things about you.' She glanced up at Richard, her lip trembling. 'And she said that Daddy wasn't my real daddy because my real daddy is dead.'

It was then that Poppy understood what she'd meant when she'd used Richard's name yesterday morning.

Richard crouched down in front of her, stroking her hair tenderly. 'We talked about this, didn't we?' he soothed. 'About your daddy. You know Oliver was my brother.' He gestured around the room. 'That's why we have photographs of him all around us, so that we won't ever forget him – and even though he's not here with us, he'll always be your daddy.'

'But I want *you* to be my daddy too,' she sobbed, holding out her arms towards him.

Richard scooped her up and hugged her tight, burying his face into her hair so she wouldn't notice his own tears. 'That's fine by me,' he gulped. 'Anyone would be proud to have a daughter like you.'

Having now settled down a little, Lily took the time to explain all about Kerry Madison and how she'd begun bullying her not just at school but at drama club too. 'When rehearsals for *The Fortunettes* began, it got worse because I was given lead position, and then, every time Camilla shouted at us, Kerry blamed me for it.'

'This Camilla has got an awful lot to answer for,' Richard commented, though he didn't take it any further.

'The day I got told off,' Lily continued, 'we were all having a drink when Kerry came up behind me and stood on the back of my plimsolls. Her shoes scraped the skin off the back of my ankles – look.' She pulled down her socks so they could see a very sore and bloodied patch on either foot. Richard bit his tongue. Lily sniffed and continued, 'It hurt so bad

I couldn't help myself and I went to push her off but it came out much harder than I'd meant it to and Camilla started screaming at me. I was so shocked, Mummy – she shouts louder than you do – and when I went outside my legs were shaking. I was scared you'd be angry with me – because she said I couldn't be in the majorettes anymore – so I went for a walk to calm down and think.'

'Oh, I'd never be angry at you for that,' Poppy said, trying to console her before asking, 'But how did you end up in the Old Chapel?' Poppy smoothed some hair from Lily's forehead and she smiled up at her brightly.

'Oh, that was the cat,' she beamed. 'He's lovely; he came and wound himself in and around my ankles, as though he knew I was feeling sad. I stroked him for ages, and when he started walking off I followed him.' She shrugged. 'I didn't really notice where I was going and when he went into that building, I followed him in there too. I couldn't quite fit through the gap in the door, though – I had to push it *really* hard to get inside – but then it suddenly slammed shut behind me. I couldn't see very well and I tried to open it again but it just wouldn't budge. So, I sat on the floor and the cat came over to me and I just cuddled it for a bit. When I got tired I lay down on the ground. I used my rucksack as a pillow and the cat slept right by me – can we get a cat?'

Poppy and Richard had been quite enthralled with her tale up to that point, and the two of them were caught completely off guard by her question.

'Absolutely,' Richard said as he ruffled her hair, 'but let's get something to eat first, shall we? My brave girl must be very hungry! Then we'll go over to that cat rescue home in Midford County.'

Lily squealed with delight before going off with him to share her exciting news with the others.

Poppy hung back to gather her thoughts, walking over to the occasional table and picking up one of her favourite pictures of Oliver. She liked to imagine that he was watching over them all, and that he'd guided the cat to Lily – knowing she wouldn't be able to resist it – leading her to a safe place where she could calm down. *She has your love of animals, my darling.* She stroked the glass frame before placing it back on the table to catch the last rays of sunlight, enjoying the illusion of rainbow light that filtered around it.

Somewhere over that rainbow, we'll all meet again.

CHAPTER THIRTY-FIVE

Rita and Ralph Denby boarded the luxury coach that was currently parked at the front of Georgina Fame's health and country club. They'd passed their luggage to the driver – who was now currently stowing it away, along with the others – and then Rita went to sit next to her friend Joy Brookes, whilst Ralph sat behind them next to Joy's husband, Alan. Rita welcomed the firm, rich, moquette seating as she settled her handbag by the side of her. They'd decided to join the weeks' retreat to Diskwithus Manor in Fowey, Cornwall and were looking forward to being *light and free* by the end of it.

They all looked towards the front as Georgina stepped on the coach, and accepting the microphone from the driver, she welcomed them with a glorious smile.

'Isn't she lovely?' whispered Rita, immediately getting shushed by Joy, who wanted to hear what she had to say.

'I telephoned the hotel this morning and they tell me they're currently experiencing beautiful sunshine and warm temperatures, so we're sure to have a great time!' Georgina announced. 'I'll be travelling to the hotel separately, but I'll be there to welcome you all at the other end – bon voyage!' She stepped off the coach and a buzz of excitement rang out as the driver started up the engine and closed the door.

'We're off!' giggled Rita, getting into the holiday spirit before taking a moment to have a good look around at her fellow travelling companions. 'I don't recognise many people on here, Joy. Do you?'

'Well, the trip was open to all members, so a lot of them will be from Swinford St. George,' she explained. 'Hopefully we'll make a few new friends this week!'

Rita smiled; *I like the sound of that.* 'It's good to be getting away after all the goings-on of late, isn't it?' she asked her friend.

Joy agreed. 'Terrible business. First Lily and then that poor chap near you – have you seen his wife yet?'

Rita shook her head solemnly. 'No, nothing – the place looks empty, although there's still a car parked on the drive. James Turvey said he'd heard that her mother had come and taken her back to the family home in Suffolk.'

Joy tutted. 'She must be frantic with grief, poor soul.' They bowed their heads together for a brief moment in an unconscious sign of respect. 'Now tell me,' Joy continued, what's afoot with the competition at the Midford County Showground – are we still entering or what?'

Rita shrugged her shoulders. 'I haven't got a clue, I'm afraid.'

Joy looked sideways at her. 'Oh, come on, you don't miss a thing,' she gently teased her friend, but Rita put her hand up, stopping her.

'No, I'm serious,' Rita told her. 'Anthony rang me up just after we got back from Greece and asked me how I was getting on – you know, with the 'task' he'd given me. I told him straight that I hadn't done anything and that I didn't intend to either.'

Joy sat back, looking quite surprised. 'You didn't! Whatever did he say?'

'I don't think he thought I was being serious for a moment, but when I said that I had to get on because Ralph and I were lunching out, I think he got the message. He hasn't called me since.'

'But you love being involved in all that – you know you do.' Joy grinned. 'I'm sure you'll soon be trying to wangle your way back in.'

Rita sneaked a glance behind her – which confirmed that Ralph and Alan were deep in conversation – and then leaned in closer to Joy. 'I bloody well won't,' she whispered. 'You've no idea what life's been like these past few months – I feel like a 30-year-old again! Ralph can't do enough for me, and there's plenty of life in the old dog yet, if you know what I mean.' She winked and nudged Joy, who began shrieking with laughter.

'Oh, Rita!' she chuckled. 'I've so missed this side of you – welcome back, my friend! I've got a feeling this is going to be a holiday to remember.'

Rita smiled. 'I have a feeling you're right about that.'

* * *

Diana Fortune answered the front door, warmly welcoming Poppy and Richard to her home before leading them through to the drawing room. Camilla greeted them politely – which earned her a hard glare from Richard – and Diana invited them all to take up a seat.

Fortunately, Diana had two sofas – which were situated opposite one another – and she hoped that the cool blue of their rich damask material would help to soak up any hot tempers. Diana went to join Camilla on one, whilst the Hambly-Joneses opted for the other.

As Diana began to speak, she brought her hands together as if the gesture would somehow help guide her words more clearly. 'I very much appreciate you giving me the opportunity to talk this dreadful situation through so that we can decide on what to do for the best.'

'It's not you who should be having to sort it out,' Richard cut in, '*she's* the one responsible!' He jabbed a finger towards Camilla. 'No one else.'

'Hang on a minute...' Camilla started, stopping when Diana threw her a stare that could have silenced Donald Trump.

'Enough!' Diana said before putting her attention back on their guests. 'Believe me, Richard, I completely understand your anger – I'm angry too – but I'm afraid it's not going to get us anywhere. Camilla is well aware of her shortcomings – and she knows she can consider herself most fortunate that things didn't turn out far, far worse – but there's still a competition to be won and I really think we can do it. And, I'd very much like Lily to be a part of it.'

'She's not going anywhere near my daughter!' Richard said, beginning to rant, this time being interrupted by his wife.

'Richard, please, let's hear Diana out,' Poppy said. She reached out for his hand and he returned her squeeze lovingly.

'You've been through hell because of her,' he replied pointedly, 'but fair enough – I'll certainly listen to what Diana has to say.'

Diana took a deep breath before starting to talk. 'I shouldn't have left Camilla alone that day; it was my fault, and for that I apologise. You can't expect her to know the children like I do in the short amount of time she's been here. I mean, yes, she can see what they're like during rehearsals but we all know what a little madam Kerry Madison can be at the best of times. I didn't communicate this sort of knowledge to Camilla, because I didn't think it was relevant. If I'd had the slightest feeling that Kerry had been targeting Lily in such a vociferous manner, she would have been asked to leave, I can assure you. I don't tolerate such behaviour.'

Poppy could see that Richard had become a bit more relaxed at hearing this, and she began to feel a little optimistic. She glanced across at Camilla, who was staring down at the floor. Her legs were crossed, as were her hands. 'What is it you're asking us exactly?' Poppy said.

'I'd like to begin rehearsals again,' Diana explained, 'and I'd like Lily to rejoin us – with your blessing. To be quite frank, I really don't think the other children will continue without her, but that's not what's behind my request.' She took another deep breath. 'It's no secret that I've endured bad behaviour myself, and the one thing I've learnt is, if you shut yourself away and hide from those responsible, that just empowers them even further. By continuing as we were, we're teaching not just the children a valuable life lesson, but we're teaching ourselves as well. Forgiveness is good for the soul.'

'What about Kerry Madison?' Richard challenged. 'Is she going to learn too? I don't see her rushing to ask forgiveness for the trauma she's put our daughter through.'

Diane chewed her lip, hesitating before continuing further. 'I think you'll find that Derek Madison had more than a few words to say to his daughter when he found out what had been going on. He rules their home with an iron rod and it's been noted that it's not the first time she's been given a good hiding.'

'But that's terrible!' Poppy cried.

'What does she expect if she's going to go around lashing out at people just because she feels like it?' Richard asked.

'*Monkey see monkey do*, Richard,' Diana stated wisely.

CHAPTER THIRTY-SIX

The quaint town of Diskwithus, which nestles on the bank of the river Fowey on the beguiling south coast of Cornwall, is home to thus Manor. Steeped in history – together with an impressive view over the estuary – this magnificent country house oozes appeal with its flagstone floors, swathes of rich velvet curtains, and eclectic soft chairs and furnishings. Having been previously owned by Sir Cecil Perrin, a world-renowned art collector, it became a hotel in the early 1980s and was subsequently expanded to include several outbuildings – these were joined by corridors, modelled on a horseshoe shape. The current proprietors – who own a spattering of similar properties throughout the South West – spend much of their time abroad and rely on the hired help to keep things afloat at all times. The Manor boasts a picturesque garden, a first-class restaurant, and an impressive range of facilities that include an indoor pool and steam room. It is where Georgina Fame's *light and free* retreat clients will spend the next seven days.

'They're here!' Georgina announced excitedly as she went out to greet her guests. She'd arrived just over an hour before and had taken the opportunity to freshen up before checking that everything was exactly as it should be.

Although weary, the coach party were nevertheless in good spirits and were soon enjoying the delicious cream tea that Georgina had arranged for them all upon arrival. The hotel porters, Frank and Douglas, were busy transferring the guests' luggage from the coach through to the reception area. The coach driver was currently enjoying a bit of sustenance too and was looking forward to a break himself, given that Georgina had also paid for him to stay the week.

'If I could just have everyone's attention, please!' Georgina announced. 'Do enjoy afternoon tea at your leisure, ladies and gentlemen, and when you are ready, go and introduce yourself to Penny, the receptionist. She will book you in and arrange for someone to show you to your rooms. The rest of the afternoon is yours so feel free to take advantage of a walk around the stunning hotel gardens, or maybe just take time to relax in your room. Whatever you decide I shall look forward to seeing you for dinner at 7 p.m.'

A rumble of acknowledgements – combined with thanks – followed her as she made her way to her own bedroom, but when something caught her eye she turned back and headed towards reception.

'Hello again, Penny, I've just seen one of your porters escorting an elderly couple to their room, and I have to say that I'm somewhat confused. I had understood that my party had the sole use of Diskwithus Manor this week?'

Judging by Penny's flushed face, this wasn't the case. 'Err, you really need to speak with Colin, the general manager, Ms Fame,' she said quietly.

Georgina stared at the receptionist for several moments before asking, 'Can you get him?'

'He's on a break...'

'*Now*, please.' Georgina tapped a perfectly manicured red fingernail against the polished wood surface of the desk, unamused.

You could cut the atmosphere with a knife.

It was several moments before the general manager appeared. He was trying to pull his trousers up but his protruding waistline proved it to be impossible; his striped burgundy shirt was straining at the buttons and he looked liked he'd just run 10 miles. 'Ms. Fame,' he breezed, shaking the tip of her hand as if she was carrying a contagious disease, 'I hear there's been a misunderstanding.'

She took a deep breath, and after suggesting that they discuss the matter away from the eyes and ears of her guests, they discreetly took themselves out to the garden.

'You took the booking yourself, Mr. Honeybone, and I have your confirmation in writing that we would be taking over the Manor for the whole week. Explain yourself.'

He began to flail and gesture, unable to find the right words. *Or trying to think up a suitable excuse.*

'The thing is,' he said eventually, 'that the rooms they're staying in are in the outbuildings, so I didn't think you'd mind. All of your guests are staying in the house, I promise, and it's only two other couples anyway.'

'I don't care how many people it is – we made a deal, Mr. Honeybone. Either you get rid of them of I'll have you for breach of contract.'

In response Colin began making strange noises and kept grabbing at a tuft of hair on the top of his head, causing Georgina to think he might suffer some sort of seizure at any moment. 'I can't!' he eventually gasped. 'We're in the middle of summer; we'll never be able to get them booked in anywhere else!'

'Well, I suggest you try,' she replied without any sympathy for the man whatsoever, 'my guests need complete peace and freedom to roam and express themselves as they see fit throughout this coming week – and it's essential they feel completely confident in being able to do so without being judged. Once I start my clients off on the *light and free* programme they need to know they're amongst like-minded souls – free to express themselves *at all times!* If *I* don't deliver, Mr. Honeybone, *I* don't get paid and *neither* will you.' She treated him to one of her trademark smiles. 'I'll leave that with you.'

Colin Honeybone stared after her, agog, suddenly wishing the ground would open up and swallow him whole.

CHAPTER THIRTY-SEVEN

'Hello, Kerry – come on inside and make yourself at home. Lily's really excited that you're joining us for tea today.'

Derek Madison gave his daughter a gentle shove through the doorway. She was somewhat quieter than usual, although Poppy didn't need to wonder why.

'Let's go and find her, shall we?' she asked as she reached for Kerry's hand, quickly sensing her unease.

Her thick brown hair had been styled into bunches – secured with silk yellow ribbons – and she was wearing a bright yellow sundress patterned with huge white daisies, together with the favoured clear jelly shoes all the girls seemed to be hankering for that summer.

'I love your hair; did your mummy style it for you?' Kerry nodded shyly. 'It's so pretty. Come on, let's go and show Lily; she loves the colour yellow.' Poppy took her inside, leaving Richard to deal with Kerry's father – a risk she considered worth taking.

'It's ever so good of you to invite our Kerry over,' Derek said, 'y'know, with everything that's happened an'all.' He was quite a stocky man, although not quite as tall as Richard, at 6 ft. His once dark hair was thinning and he was still wearing his butcher's apron over his dark linen trousers and a white shirt that had the sleeves rolled up to the elbows.

'Well, let's face it,' Richard jested, 'if it was up to me I'd have given her a good thrashing with a cat-o'-nine-tails – but that would just be cruel, right?' He forced out a laugh. 'Kids will be kids, Derek, and; it's our job to be a role model they can look up to. I mean, who wants a bully for a father, eh?'

Derek blinked several times, screwing up his face slightly as he tried to decipher Richard's point. When the penny finally dropped a look of shame crossed his face, causing him to dip his head.

'Listen, mate,' Richard continued, clearly on a roll, 'there's a fucking brand new gym just opened up at Swinford St. George, so get yourself over there and knock ten bells of shit out of their equipment instead – getting handy with your kids doesn't solve anything.' He wondered if he'd gone too far then, given the momentary glare in Derek's eyes, but it was quickly replaced by a look of guilt.

He nodded his head silently, allowing Richard's words to sink in. 'I hear you,' he eventually acknowledged, knowing full well he was going to have to mend his ways. 'I'm not proud, but I hear you.'

Poppy came breezing merrily along from the hallway then, instantly picking up on the charged air between the two men. 'Would you like to come in for a drink, Derek? You're more than welcome.'

He put up his hand, palm out. 'No thanks, love – I best get on – but I'll be back later to collect Kerry as arranged.' He glanced briefly at Richard before focussing back on Poppy. 'Thanks again.' He set off down the front pathway leading from Hampton Manor House and out towards the Church Green, and just before he got to the gate he paused to look back at Poppy. 'Do you know what?' he said. 'I didn't think you posh people swore like that.' And with that he went on his way.

CHAPTER THIRTY-EIGHT

Sergeant Matt Hudson was back on the doorstep of 34 King's Oak Road. This time he was joined by PC Laura Benjamin. 'Ready?' he asked. When she nodded, he rapped his knuckles hard against the solid wood door.

'Hello Matt,' said Lucy when she saw who it was, 'I wasn't expecting you tonight.' She led the way through to the lounge, where James was sitting on the sofa. Plates of half-eaten food were on the coffee table, alongside two glasses of red wine. He switched off the TV when he saw Matt and Laura.

'I'm sorry to disturb you both in the middle of your dinner,' Matt said.

Lucy made to take the plates through to the kitchen but James took over the task instead. 'It's only chicken salad,' she replied, 'it won't spoil. Would you like some tea?'

'No, we're fine, thank you.'

Lucy invited them to take a seat and then settled herself back onto the sofa. 'I presume this is about Ian?' she asked. 'I called Raoul, his father, and you won't believe what he told me. Ian had spun him a pack of lies, apparently – told him that I'd thrown him out to move in my toy boy lover and that I'd cut him off without a penny!' She tapped the arm of the sofa with the ends of her fingers, clearly trying to suppress how upset she was. 'I mean me, a *toy boy!* It's just so disrespectful. He hasn't even met James yet, and I'm only three years older than him. I mean, you'd think I was on the game the way he's...'

Matt stopped her mid-sentence, pausing for a moment before delivering the news. 'I'm so sorry to have to be the one to tell you this, Lucy, but Ian's been found dead.' He paused again, waiting for the shock to take hold.

'What?' she gasped, completely taken by surprise. Having heard this, James came rushing out of the kitchen to comfort her. 'No, no... he can't be!' Her hands and chin began to tremble as she looked back at Matt in complete disbelief. 'Not my Ian; he can't be dead!'

PC Benjamin went to make some hot, sweet tea whilst Matt gave Lucy time for his words to sink in.

Lucy began to sob hard into James' chest, clutching onto his shirt for support, desperate for it not to be true.

'It seems that the young lady he took up with was a heavy drug user,' Matt explained quietly but clearly. 'She'd been attracted to Ian – primarily, it seems, according to his ex-roommates, because he kept flashing his money about.' He paused for a moment. 'When I say she was a heavy drug user, she hid it very well. She was a popular student and no doubt Ian was flattered to receive her attention – though I'm just guessing somewhat here. What I do know is that it was she who came up with the idea of leaving the UK. They'd rented an apartment in the centre of Amsterdam, and they were both found dead yesterday afternoon from a suspected drug overdose.'

Lucy just stared at Matt, trying to comprehend the words she was hearing. This couldn't be happening… it just *couldn't*.

As James tried to comfort her, Lucy continued to sit there in silence, tears pouring down her face. There were simply no words to describe the sheer agony of losing a child.

'Again, I'm so sorry,' Matt said quietly.

'Do you know what the ironic thing is?' Lucy sobbed after a few moments. 'If Raoul hadn't given him so much money, he'd probably still be here.'

CHAPTER THIRTY-NINE

The next morning, another hot, sunny day greeted the guests of Diskwithus Manor as they made their way downstairs to the breakfast hall. They were given the choice of a traditional Cornish breakfast or a tempting array of succulent fresh fruits, cold meats, and cheeses – all locally sourced.

'It's a good job we're not on that *Nourish and Gain* plan, Ralph,' joked Rita brightly, 'else we'd never be able to eat all this.'

They tucked into their hearty breakfasts happily, washing it all down with cups of freshly brewed coffee.

Having used the hotel on several occasions now, Georgina had requested that during the retreat, all meals were to be taken in the breakfast hall. The traditional dining room had been transformed for them to use as a main meeting room, set out in

315

traditional boardroom style, with a screen and projector having been placed at the front, ready to use. A total of 47 people had signed up for the event, most of which were couples, and all of which were now patiently seated, awaiting Georgina's arrival.

'Good morning, ladies and gentlemen!' she exclaimed as she entered the room. 'I trust you all enjoyed a refreshing night's sleep and a fulfilling breakfast?' Everyone nodded enthusiastically in response. 'Great! Now, this morning I want to talk to you about the essence of becoming *light and free* – and I want to begin with my own journey.' She switched on the overhead projector, which displayed a photograph of her former self. A round of familiar gasps rang out, which was hardly surprising – not just because of her dramatic weight loss but also due to her complete transformation into the successful woman who stood before them now. 'For me, it wasn't just about losing weight – there was a lot more going on than that – and in order for me to be *light and free* I had to identify and heal what had caused me to overeat in the first place.'

Her audience were transfixed, and by the end of the day they would emerge with the knowledge that they had more power to bring about positive change in their own lives than they could ever have imagined.

* * *

'Good morning, love. Can you tell us where the dining room is, please?'

Penny the receptionist didn't bother to glance up; she was too busy browsing local B&Bs – given that it seemed every other hotel in Cornwall and Devon was currently booked solid. 'It's straight behind you, madam, and just to your right.'

'Thank you, love,' the customer replied before saying to her companion, 'come on, let's get ourselves some morning coffee seeing as how we missed breakfast.' She shuffled along, allowing her walking stick to bear most of her weight as her husband strode confidently behind. He was a tall man, not bad-looking for his age, and smartly dressed. His wrists and neck were shrouded in gold chains, proudly parading his wealth for all to see.

'Well, this doesn't look right, does it?' she said as she entered the room.

He followed her through the imposing wooden doors, taking a look for himself. 'This is a meeting room, love, not a dining room.'

'Well, this is where the receptionist sent us,' she said, looking back towards the door in confusion. 'Hang on – it is. Look, there's the sign: *dining room*, it says.'

There wasn't a waiter to be seen so they chanced their luck and went further inside.

'But this is clearly a meeting room,' she continued. 'Look – look at the wall. There's a presentation...'

He grabbed her arm before she fell, dragging the nearest chair out for her before taking the next one for himself.

'This can't be happening, Merv!' she cried. 'What's a picture of our Sadie doing up there?'

CHAPTER FORTY

D espite the end of the summer drawing ever near, the day of the Cotswolds County Majorette of the Year Competition was set to be one of the hottest on record.

The Midford County Showground – which was hosting this year's event – was already bursting with activity and the air was charged with anticipation of the day ahead. This annual event attracted visitors from miles around, and as well as hosting the competition that year, it offered a smorgasbord of attractions with an abundance of games, activities, and crafts celebrating the best the Cotswolds had to offer.

The arena had been separated into several zones, with the main event being held in zone 9, the central point. As the majorette teams arrived, they were guided towards zone 15, where a marquee had been erected for them to use as a training area.

Diana Fortune had organised a coach to transport *The Fortunettes* – along with Camilla and herself – and they were currently trundling along the Hampton Ash Road, heading towards their destination. The younger children were jiggling with excitement, eager to put their well-rehearsed show into practice.

Diana looked over at her travel companion. 'I'd like you to know, Camilla, that whatever happens today, I'm very grateful for all the time and effort you've put into this – especially these last few weeks.' She smiled. 'I'm really proud of you.'

Judging by the look on Camilla's face, her words were very much appreciated. 'Thank you, Diana,' she replied earnestly. 'I have to say that I've learnt a lot from this experience. In particular, not to judge a book by its cover.'

'Don't be too hard on yourself, my dear,' Diana replied kindly. 'None of us are perfect.' She paused for a moment before adding, 'I imagine you must be looking forward to getting back to your job after having had such a long break?'

Camilla snorted light-heartedly. 'Break? I've experienced more drama in the past six months than *Northern Rights* could shake a stick at – and you know it's renowned for its hard-hitting storylines. In fact, I thought about inviting the show's writers to come and stay at the Hamptons for a few weeks,' she joked. 'You really couldn't make some of this stuff up; they'd have a field day!'

They both laughed knowingly.

'And Matt?'

Camilla looked down at her hands, smiling melancholically. 'It was fun while it lasted, but I don't think I'll be seeing him again anytime soon.' She took a deep breath, trying to shift her focus. 'Right! That's enough of the gloom and doom – we've got a competition to win!'

* * *

Poppy and Richard were heading towards the central zone, closely followed by Anthony and Ianthe – who was holding tightly onto Roderick – and Percy and Rosie. Reverend Fisher and his wife Cathy had already settled themselves comfortably in the front row of seats that had been placed around zone 9, and Alexander and Skye Harvey had just taken up the seats next to them. By the time the others arrived, along with Charlotte and Jonathan Palmer-Reid and Don and Rachel Davies, they had quite the party going on – and there were still more people to come.

A succession of raucous laughter rang out as they exchanged gentle banter, helping to pass the time whilst they waited for the competition to begin.

'So, where's our stall exactly, Anthony?' called out Don Davies innocently. 'We couldn't find it when we were having a look round earlier.' This brought forth much mirth from the gathered friends and Anthony chuckled, accepting his comment in good spirits.

'We were let down at the last minute so had to abandon the idea,' he explained.

'I heard that she blew you out good and proper,' he chuckled. 'Rita Denby, of all people!'

'It's true, it's true,' Anthony said, holding up his hands in jest, 'and I hate to say it, but she caught me completely off guard.'

'What do you mean?' Charlotte interjected. 'We all know how she likes to stick her nose into everything, having a finger in every pie.'

'I agree, but I do have to say, I took her involvement for granted.' He shrugged. 'I mean, look at last year, when Alexander directed the Hampton Players.'

'Oh, don't remind me!' he groaned, playfully slapping himself on the forehead.

'Exactly. We've all said it – and we've all cringed when she's come flying out of her front door to interrogate us – but in actual fact, Rita's done a lot more for the Hamptons than any of us here, and let's not forget: she doesn't get paid for it either. I think we've all taken her a bit too much for granted, and I say good on her for going on Georgina Fame's retreat to Fowey – I jolly well hope she and Ralph are enjoying it.'

'I think you're right, Anthony,' Lizzie Anderson agreed. 'Most of us here have full-time jobs either working or looking after our families. Who can honestly give up more than a couple of hours a week to organise even one of the events our villages hold each year?'

'I think it's about time we showed Rita just how valuable she is,' Poppy added with enthusiasm, 'and I know just the right way to do it too.'

Their attention was drawn to the arena then as an announcement was made over the PA system, asking for all the competitors to make their way towards the central area.

'It's starting!' exclaimed Poppy excitedly. 'I can't wait to see the routine!'

* * *

'Right, everyone,' Camilla said loudly, capturing everyone's gaze, 'big smiles, okay? Once the music starts remember that you're meant to be feeling on top of the world – shake those pom-poms like you mean it!'

The group responded jubilantly, keen to get their routine underway. They looked every bit the professionals in their custom-made costumes – the girls in striped black and aqua pleated skirts with aqua-coloured tops, the boys in aqua shirts with black trousers. Their turn was just seconds away and they were all raring to go.

When the MC called them through they took up their positions, the sun reflecting off the silver plastic shards from the pom-poms and causing them to glisten like jewels.

The opening bars of Daz Rice's song, *Emily's Child* rang out and off they went – jumping and twisting and moving in time to the music whilst shaking their pom-poms like their lives depended on it.

The Fortunettes' supporters from the Hamptons were cheering them along – their parents proudly standing by, enthralled by their magical performance.

'I'm not sure I recognise this tune, but it's very catchy.'

'It's one of the songs from Daz Rice's debut album, Charlotte – *Precious Times*. I'll lend it to you if you like.'

The watching crowd were clearly enjoying the music as well as *The Fortunettes'* performance, everyone jigging along in time to the beat as they watched on, mesmerised.

As the routine came to an end the cheering culminated in loud applause, with many boisterous shouts and whistles of appreciation.

When Richard and Poppy gave Lily a big thumbs-up, she beamed back at them with pure happiness.

* * *

After the final majorette team had performed, they went to rejoin the other competitors who were currently ensconced in the marquee in zone 15. A small round of applause rang out encouragingly as they entered, but they weren't in the best of spirits. They'd secured second place last year but their hopes of being crowned winners had been dashed when their lead had lost his footing, taking out the second row with him.

A hum of chatter started up again, quickly turning to squeals as the MC's voice boomed out over the tannoy, declaring that the winners were about to be announced.

Diana and Camilla proudly led *The Fortunettes* over to zone 9, where they waited patiently for the results to be read out.

We want to congratulate everyone who took part today. You all gave such magnificent performances, which made our job as judges extremely difficult. And now, in third place...

Lily and her teammates huddled together, their fingers tightly crossed.

...it's The Melbury Foxes!

A huge cheer rang out as the group from Chipping Melbury went to accept their trophy.

Now, for second place. This is awarded to...

'Come on, come on, it's got to be us,' Millie Anderson pleaded.

...the Pethewick Ladies, from Upper Pethewick, of course!

'Oh, we're not going to get it,' Kerry grumbled anxiously whilst the second place winners accepted their award, taking time to lap up the crowd's applause.

Now, ladies and gentlemen, it's time for the big one. In first place, and commended for their use of an original song in addition to the cleverly crafted routine, it's... The Fortunettes from the Hamptons! Congratulations to you all!

Lily – together with Kerry and a few of the others – were so charged with emotion that they burst into tears of joy.

'I can't believe it!' cried Lily as her friends swooped her up and carried her along to the podium, where they proudly collected their award. Their supporters could be heard cheering loudly from the stands, the applause continuing to ring out for several minutes afterwards.

'Well done!' mouthed Camilla, straining to be heard above the noise.

Congratulations to The Fortunettes who – as the winning team – will take on the role of next year's competition hosts!

'Oh bugger!' exclaimed Richard, laughing. 'You'd better butter Rita up soon, Dad, or you and Mum are going to have your hands full for the next year!'

Anthony shook his head, laughing too.

CHAPTER FORTY-ONE

Georgina Fame was furious – but not noticeably so – having just seen a random couple sitting in what was supposed to be the *light and free* meeting room, she marched up the front steps from the garden into the reception area looking for Colin, the general manager.

As she approached the front desk, she became aware of a dreadful sound, realising it was coming from the dining room itself. After listening intently she realised it was the sound of a woman, crying hysterically, and while there was another voice in the background it was harder to decipher, such was the commotion.

Georgina hesitated, knowing that whilst the intruders were not part of her group, she couldn't walk away without at least trying to help in some way, and she certainly couldn't give them their marching orders right now.

As she made her way towards the source of the disturbance she came across an elderly couple towards the back of the room. The man was comforting the lady – who she presumed to be his wife, and who was terribly distressed.

Georgina walked right up to them. 'Hello there,' she spoke softly, 'is everything all right?'

The two of them looked up then, having not heard her approach, and Georgina's eyes flickered from one to the other until recognition set in.

'Mum!'

The next 20 minutes were akin to a comedy of errors. Penny, the receptionist – having picked up on the commotion from the dining room – had rushed off to fetch the general manager, who, by the time he'd arrived at the scene, had assumed Georgina was (in no uncertain terms) verbally assaulting two of his other guests. He was now standing in between them, shouting like a man possessed. '*If everyone could just calm down,*' he ordered, sweat pouring from his brow and running into the collar of his grey-white shirt, '*I* will deal with this, Ms. Fame, if you don't mind!'

'Oh, just shut up, will you, you supercilious imbecile!' she shot back. 'These are my parents!'

Upon realising his unfortunate mistake, Colin acted like a tramp on chips – fawning over them, desperate to rescind his outburst.

Rolling her eyes, Georgina shut the door behind him before going to sit with Jen and Merv, who she was pleased to see were a lot calmer now.

'I can't believe you're the same person,' Jen said, her eyes soaking up the unrecognisable woman in front of her that she now knew to be her daughter, 'if

I hadn't seen that photo up there I'd never have known it was you, Sadie.'

'I'm not Sadie anymore, Mum, I'm Georgina,' she explained. 'The Sadie you knew was a lost soul, disturbed by a devastating tragedy that she tried to overcome by overeating.'

As she sat there Jen began to get upset again, recalling the horrendous events of years ago, leading up to the night that Sadie's father had not only killed a teenage boy, but also himself.

'I did my best, love!' she cried. 'I got us away, didn't I? To Wales. We were safe there, in a place where no one knew us, and then I met Merv.' She looked up at her husband lovingly. 'He's been so good to us.'

'He was – you were – but it's not about that, Mum,' Georgina said, trying to explain. 'It's not about what you did or didn't do. It was *me*.' She pointed a finger towards her chest. '*I* had the problem, Mum, and being wrapped up in cotton wool by you was never going to solve it.'

'But what about the job you walked out on? Devastated, they were; thought the world of you too. They had nothing but praise for you when Merv contacted them.'

Georgina shook her head, smiling. 'Oh, Mum – that's what gave me the strength to take back control. I overheard a conversation between some of my friends – well, work colleagues, really. It wasn't something I was proud to hear at the time, but looking back, if I hadn't been at work that day – and much earlier than usual too – I wouldn't be where I am today.' She held their hands. 'I never meant to hurt you – I love you both more than you can know; I always have – but the reality is, Mum, I was slowly killing myself. My weight was unmanageable and my health was heading for a crisis. When I took back control of my life, I began to heal from the inside out – I rebalanced my mind, soul, and body and became the success I am today.'

'But why didn't you ever come back?' Jen asked, tears still in her eyes.

'Because, Mum, I was scared that as soon as I walked through the front door I would retrace the pattern that had become so ingrained in me for all those years – and I wasn't prepared to step into the darkness again.'

When Georgina Fame had arrived at Diskwithus Manor, she could never have anticipated that she would be finally *light and free* from a past that, despite her hard work and subsequent success, had continued to hover constantly on the periphery. Not only were the three of them now able to reconcile the traumatic events of years ago, as well as her subsequent disappearance, but it also afforded them an opportunity to rebuild their relationship – this time on an even keel.

'I can't believe you're *the* Georgina Fame,' Jen said, hugging her daughter proudly. 'We've even seen you on the TV and it never once occurred to us that it was you,' she chuckled. 'I mean, that it was our Sadie – our daughter.' She paused, another thought suddenly striking her. 'Merv, wait till we tell everyone back home – we'll be the talk of the valleys!'

Georgina shook her head and smiled. *Some things never change.*

'Come on, you two, let's go and get ourselves a drink – this deserves a celebration for sure.'

CHAPTER FORTY-TWO

Tiggy shimmied excitedly into LC's bar, contemplating the evening ahead. With everything that had been going on in the Hamptons that summer – combined with the fact that they'd struggled to source the right staff – they'd chosen to delay their opening night until the end of August, but now everything was in place and they were champing at the bit to get going, particularly following on from *The Fortunettes'* recent success.

'Oh wow, Winnie, this all smells amazing!' Tiggy exclaimed, unable to resist helping herself to one of the tempting hors d'oeuvres that had been prepared, ready to serve to their guests. The soft cream cheese and salty prosciutto lingered on her tongue and tantalised her taste buds. 'These are really yummy – I could eat them all day!'

'Well, I can't take the credit for all that; young Gavin over there did most of the work,' Winnie said, smiling. Her protégé – whom she'd rescued Poppy from on the night of the Hambly-Jones dinner party some months ago – smiled appreciatively. 'I knew the lad had prospects and he's certainly not let me down.'

'That's great to hear,' Tiggy said earnestly. After looking over the rest of the food she left them to it and went back through to the bar, checking and rechecking things along the way; she wanted the night to run as smoothly as possible.

Harry was upstairs with Sheldon – helping to stock the bar on the mezzanine floor above – and Mary, Sheldon's wife, was busy folding napkins that perfectly matched the bar's emerald green branding.

'What time's Barnaby getting here?' Mary asked, consulting her watch.

'He should be here by now but I think he said he was picking someone up along the way.' Tiggy smiled. *About time he got himself a girlfriend.*

* * *

'Have you lost weight?' Charlotte was attending to the collar of Jonathan's shirt, lovingly smoothing it into place.

'I was wondering when you'd notice,' he said, pulling her closer to him, 'I've not been able to fit into these trousers for years,' he confessed proudly.

'It's giving up the booze, darling – you look better for it too.'

'Actually, Charlotte,' he said, then hesitated.

She was just about to brush her hair when, catching his reflection in the dressing table mirror, she paused with concern. 'What's wrong, Jonathan?' She swung around. 'You're not ill, are you?'

He sat down on the edge of their bed and patted the spot next to him, indicating that he wanted her to sit down too. 'I wasn't totally honest about the health check I had earlier this year,' he admitted. 'It's nothing major, thank goodness, but some of my bloods gave cause for concern and Jon Anderson told me in no uncertain terms that I had to make some significant lifestyle changes – or face the possible consequences.'

'Why on earth didn't you tell me about this?' she asked, concern in her voice. 'You must have been so worried?'

'I was more concerned about your wellbeing,' he explained, 'and I certainly didn't want to burden you any further.'

As she met his gaze her heart swelled with love. 'You've been wonderful this past year, Jonathan, and so very patient. I hadn't really appreciated quite what a pickle I'd got myself into until I started seeing Pradeep Chandola. My psychotherapy sessions have made such a difference, and for the first time in a long time I feel more like my old self again.'

He picked up her hands, returning her gaze. 'I'm so very proud of you,' he told her, smiling. 'I know you've just embarked on this journey and I also want you to know that you're not alone – we're in this together.' He paused for a moment. 'I've been seeing Georgina Fame,' he confessed.

'Isn't she a bit young for you, darling?' she quipped, catching the twinkle of humour in his eye.

'I should be so lucky!' he chuckled. 'She's been fantastic, actually – no wonder her *Nourish and Gain* plan is so famous; it really works. I was surprised at how easy it was to follow.'

'Ah, so that's why you've been cutting out the carbs too. It all makes sense now.'

'And the late night munchies, although the lack of wine helps with that.' He shrugged. 'At the end of the day, this was just the wake-up call I needed, and one I was able to address before it escalated any further.' He lifted his hand, tenderly brushing his finger down the side of her cheek. 'And, instead of falling asleep on the sofa most evenings, it's afforded us an opportunity to rekindle our once vibrant love life,' he said, before adding artfully, 'wouldn't you agree, Mrs Palmer-Reid?'

She smirked, appreciating his sentiment. 'Amen to that – now let's get going before we get distracted again – we've got a party to go to!'

* * *

LC's bar was packed to the rafters. There was music booming out from every corner and the wine was flowing freely. The party atmosphere was in full swing and everyone seemed to be having a great time.

'Your Gabriel's an absolute angel, Peter.' Tiggy slipped onto a stool at the bar, next to Reverend Fisher. 'Who'd have thought a vicar's son would make such an excellent mixologist?'

'He takes after his mother, of course,' the Reverend teased, causing Cathy Fisher to roll her eyes playfully.

Barnaby Rose came over and joined them then, having brought Camilla Barrington-Smythe along as his guest.

'I thought she was dating Matt,' Tiggy whispered discreetly in his ear, causing Barnaby to smile and wink.

'I think you'll find he has other fish to fry – and besides, his loss in my gain.'

She laughed, raising her glass to him before their attention was drawn to Sheldon, who'd just stopped the music in order to make his opening speech.

'Thank you all for coming tonight; it's wonderful to see so many of you here to support our new venture!' The crowd applauded and he waited for the cheering to die down before continuing. 'As you know, Mary and I – along with Tiggy and Harry, and our son, Barnaby – invested in this venture together. We wanted to bring an establishment to the Hamptons that would not only complement the village's current offerings, but would also provide something different. Our vision was to create a place where people can come for a bite to eat, to enjoy a gourmet meal, or just to share a bottle of wine – or two,' he winked, 'but we also wanted to pay homage to a couple who literally put their life and soul into this community. Lydia and Charles Lawrence – Tiggy's parents and our dear friends – worked tirelessly for the benefit of others, and LC's bar will pay homage to their esteemed contribution to society.' He smiled widely. 'Now, please join me in a toast to its future success – LC's bar!'

The gathered crowd raised their glasses and joined in rowdily. When the music was fired up again everyone returned to their conversations, making the most of their patron's kind hospitality along the way.

* * *

'Hello, stranger.' Winnie looked up as Billy Franklin made his way into the kitchen.

'I thought I'd just pop in and say hello,' he said, pushing his hands nervously into his pockets. 'I wondered if you were settling in alright,' he added, referring to Winnie's new place – she'd moved into the apartment above the bistro.

'Oh, I love it, Billy.' She indicated for him to take a seat at the table, then offered up a plate of crispy bacon and avocado sandwiches she'd just made. 'Everything's brand new and Barnaby's already found a tenant for my house back over at Swinford St. George – he's offered to manage it for me too. It's a huge weight off my mind, I can tell you.'

'That sounds great, Winnie. I shall have to pop up and have a look some time.'

She smiled fondly back at Billy. 'Yes, you shall.'

* * *

'Matt's here at last!' Anthony announced.

Don nudged Richard's arm. 'And look who he's brought with him too.'

Richard laughed. 'Yes, I'd heard he was receiving more than weight loss advice,' he quipped with a wink, merely teasing as Matt walked in proudly with Georgina Fame on his arm. 'He looks well on it too,' Richard added, referring not just to Matt's weight loss but to how happy they both looked.

'Ay up!' Bill Wilson called out, also having noted Matt's arrival, 'Here comes the new Inspector!'

* * *

'So, come on,' Alexander Harvey encouraged his friend, Anthony. They'd managed to find themselves an empty table in the far corner opposite the bar. 'Tell me what happened with the floozy.' He was, of course, referring to Francine Dubois and her attempt to try and blackmail Anthony's son, Richard.

'A good result actually. Although there was insufficient evidence to charge her over Richard – as she didn't actually get around to asking him for money to stop her speaking to Poppy about him 'allegedly' sexually assaulting her – with Matt's help we did manage to convince the Metropolitan Police to re-open the Dicon Lamont case. Matt managed to track down Dicon's old secretary, and she was only too keen to step up when she heard that Francine had been up to her old tricks again. Apparently, it was his secretary who'd acted as the go between – she'd actually delivered the payments – and she's agreed to give evidence.'

'Oh, well done,' Alexander replied. 'She doesn't deserve to get away with it; we all know that Dicon would still be here – though not necessarily still married, given the affairs – if she hadn't blackmailed him and pushed him over the edge.' Alexander had a vested interest because Dicon had acted as his financial advisor at the time, which was how he'd first met Anthony. 'I meant to ask actually: how's Lily doing? Has she recovered from her ordeal?'

'She's doing surprisingly well,' Anthony smiled, 'although I think the new addition to the family's helped a lot.' Alexander looked perplexed. 'They took her and Roderick over to the Midford County Cattery and returned with not one but two kittens. They're actually quite cute, I have to say – tiny black fluffy things. I was worried Monty might try to eat them – he's getting quite big now, that dog – but it turns out it's him that needs protecting,' he laughed.

Alexander shook his head. 'It's been a crazy year, hasn't it? What with Lily and the Dubois woman...'

'...and that fatal accident on the Swinford St. George road.'

'Oh crikey, that was more of a mess than people realise.' Anthony leaned in closer. 'I have it on good authority,' he said, tapping the side of his nose, 'that our Rupert Coombes was a bit of a rascal.' Alexander raised his eyebrows, clearly intrigued and keen to hear more. 'I don't wish to speak ill of the dead, but despite him being married to the gorgeous Evie, he had an affair with Francine Dubois too.'

'Surely not! How do you know that?' Alexander scoffed, taking a drink from his glass.

'Phil Harris – one of the Sergeants from Midford County – saw them together at The Melbury Fox, and, what's even more shocking is that he'd been seeing Laura Benjamin too. She hadn't a clue he was married.'

'Good heavens, how on earth did he manage them all?'

'Well,' shrugged Anthony, 'one has to wonder if that's what caused the crash – he must have been completely exhausted, poor chap. Such a shame too, as they would have fitted in perfectly here. Let's hope whoever buys up Hazel Lodge will do too.'

'What about the other lad we lost this year – Lucy Whittaker's son?' Alexander sighed. 'Words fail me.'

'Oh, that poor woman. James says she's going through hell right now, continually torturing and blaming herself. It really is a sad affair.'

They were interrupted then by Jon Anderson pulling up a chair alongside them. 'What are you two old biddies gossiping about?' he teased. 'Or are we putting the world to rights?'

'Good to see you, Jon. How's that new doctor settling in? I thought he might be along tonight.'

'It's his wife's birthday so Pradeep's taken her somewhere quiet,' Jon explained. 'He's settled in very well, thanks – my list has been remarkably quieter of late so he's certainly popular.'

'We were just talking about all the drama that's gone on this year – it's been quite a rollercoaster, hasn't it?' Anthony asked.

'What do you expect?' he said, a twinkle in his eye. 'This is the Hamptons, after all.'

CHAPTER FORTY-THREE

Tiggy Lawrence came ambling slowly down the stairs. She was exhausted from the previous night's shenanigans when most of the Hamptons set had rolled up at LC's bar, keen to continue with their celebrations after winning the prestigious Cotswolds County Majorette of the Year competition.

As memories of the night flooded into her mind she smiled fondly to herself, recalling the look of complete shock on Rita Denby's face when she'd been presented with an enormous bouquet of colourful flowers – together with a voucher for a meal at the bistro for her and Ralph to enjoy – in recognition of her valuable contribution to the Hamptons. This then reminded Tiggy of Anthony's glee when he'd talked Rita into helping out at next year's competition, and she giggled to herself as that thought evoked images of him and Reverend Fisher singing *You'll Never Walk Alone*.

She went to fetch her laptop from the study with a spring in her step. Harry had left early that morning; he had several meetings lined up and he'd told her he wanted to get back as soon as possible to help out with the bar.

Suddenly, a loud crash rang out from the kitchen, resounding throughout the downstairs hallway. *Oh, here we go!*

Tiggy bounced on the balls of her feet, smiling to herself as she headed towards the kitchen. She swung open the door with ease – preparing to meet the feline villain responsible – but instead she felt her laptop slip and heard it crash to the floor, completely freezing to the spot as she took in the unexpected sight before her.

'Hello, darling.' Aster Maxwell brushed the remnants of glass from the sleeve of his bespoke navy blue jacket, smiling at her as he asked, 'I didn't startle you, did I?

ABOUT THE AUTHOR

I was born in the mid-60s to working class parents and grew up in a small village in the depths of the Oxfordshire countryside. My secondary school report details my social and sporting activity as 'Disco Dancing!' Whilst I might not be able to cut a groove on the dance floor these days, writing and music are very much in my soul.

I enjoyed a successful career working for a number of financial and pharmaceutical institutions based in London and the Home Counties before taking a break to bring up my children. Now that they are adults, I have the opportunity to write down all the stories that have been flowing through my mind all these years – and I so enjoy it!

My stories are filled with love, life, family and friendships. My books are also known for their surprising and unexpected twists!

These days, I have swapped the dance floor for the idyllic beaches of Cornwall where I now live. I can often be found somewhere along the coast, losing myself in a book or two or three...

You can discover more about me and my work at www.tinamariemiller.co.uk.

I love connecting with my readers, you can find me in the following social media platforms:

Twitter: @tinseymiller

Facebook: @tinseymiller

Instagram: @tinseymiller